MAID MARIAN & THE MISFORTUNES OF ELPHIN

Thomas Love Peacock (1785–1866) was an English novelist, poet, and satirist known for his witty, dialogue-driven novels that explore social, political and philosophical ideas. Born in Weymouth, Dorset, Peacock was largely self-educated and cultivated a broad literary knowledge, which shaped his sharp, satirical style. His best-known novels, such as *Headlong Hall* (1815), *Nightmare Abbey* (1818) and *Crotchet Castle* (1831), feature eccentric characters who debate contemporary issues, blending humour with critique. Peacock was a close friend of Percy Bysshe Shelley, whose Romantic ideals he gently mocked in his works.

L.A. Davenport, born in Cork, Ireland, in 1973, is a novelist and short story writer whose works include *The Nucleus of Reality, Escape,* and *No Way Home.* A graduate of Emmanuel College, Cambridge, he brings extensive experience in medical journalism to his insightful and engaging fiction.

P-WAVE CLASSICS

P-Wave Classics revives daring, distinctive works and neglected voices of the eighteenth and nineteenth centuries, alongside enduring literary favourites, for readers of today. With new introductions and detailed notes illuminating the historical and cultural context of the text, each edition blends accessibility and elegant design with rigorous scholarship, bringing works of wit, radical thought and lasting relevance back into the conversation.

Learn More

MAID MARIAN & THE MISFORTUNES OF ELPHIN

THOMAS LOVE PEACOCK

EDITED BY
L. A. DAVENPORT

INTRODUCTION BY
L. A. DAVENPORT

P-WAVE
PRESS

Maid Marian was first published in 1822.

The Misfortunes of Elphin was first published in 1829.

First published by P-Wave Press in 2025
under the P-Wave Classics imprint
Poole, United Kingdom
p-wavepress.co.uk/classics/

ISBN (paperback): 978-1-916937-10-9
ISBN (ebook): 978-1-916937-11-6

A catalogue record for this book is available from the British Library.

Printed and bound in the UK, USA and Europe.

CONTENTS

BIOGRAPHICAL INTRODUCTION

Thomas Love Peacock (1785–1866) was an English novelist, poet, essayist, and satirist best known for his sharp wit, distinctive style, and novels that critique the social and intellectual fashions of his day. Though he may be lesser known than some of his contemporaries, Peacock's works offer a unique blend of humour, satire, and philosophical insight, often set against the backdrop of lively discussions and memorable gatherings. His novels—among them *Headlong Hall* (1815), *Nightmare Abbey* (1818), and *Crotchet Castle* (1831)—continue to intrigue readers with their witty dialogue, colourful characters, and light-hearted yet incisive commentary on society.

Peacock was born on 18 October 1785 in Weymouth, Dorset, into a family of modest means. His father, Samuel Peacock, was a glass merchant who eventually left the family, leaving Thomas to be raised primarily by his mother, Sarah Love Peacock. Though his formal education was limited, he displayed a voracious appetite for learning. He was largely self-taught, immersing himself in classical and contemporary literature, philosophy and history.

His dedication to independent study shaped both his literary sensibilities and his sceptical approach to intellectual dogma.

By his teens, Peacock had begun writing poetry, and in 1804 he published his first collection, *The Monks of St Mark*, which, like much of his early work, was conventional in form and theme. Although his poetic aspirations continued, it was his distinctive satirical voice that eventually set him apart. His fascination with social and philosophical debates would later define his novels, which dispense with traditional narrative structures in favour of extended conversations that playfully skewer contemporary intellectual trends.

Peacock's early career was marked by a mix of literary ambition and financial instability. Moving to London in 1800, he worked in various positions while continuing his independent studies and writing. He spent time as secretary to the captain of HMS *Venerable*, an experience that led nowhere professionally but contributed to his lifelong interest in maritime affairs. His early literary efforts, including plays and verse, met with little success. At one point, he contemplated founding a school in the Lake District, which like many of his projects, never materialised.

His fortunes changed in 1812 when he befriended the poet Percy Bysshe Shelley. Introduced through the publisher Edward Hookham, Peacock and Shelley found common ground despite their contrasting outlooks—Peacock was sceptical of radical utopianism, whereas Shelley was an ardent reformer. Their friendship became pivotal for both writers. Peacock advised Shelley during his marital crisis, supporting him even as he maintained a personal loyalty to Shelley's first wife, Harriet. After her tragic suicide in 1816, Peacock urged Shelley to marry Mary Godwin without delay.

Shelley's influence, and the £120 annual pension he arranged for Peacock, allowed him to develop his signature literary style. He drew inspiration from the Shelleys' circle, which included Mary Shelley, Lord Byron, and other key figures of Romanticism, yet his novels often satirise their idealism. *Nightmare Abbey* (1818), his most famous work, caricatures Shelley as the brooding Scythrop Glowry, a young idealist plagued by philosophical angst. Byron appears as the melancholic poet Mr Cypress, while Mary Shelley is loosely represented in the character of Marionetta. The novel gently mocks the Romantic obsession with gloom and revolutionary fervour, offering a more detached, sceptical perspective.

Peacock's novels are distinctive in form, eschewing conventional plots in favour of conversational, episodic structures. Often set in country houses—such as *Headlong Hall, Nightmare Abbey*, and *Crotchet Castle*—they bring together diverse characters who debate aesthetics, philosophy, politics, and social reform. The novels are structured around these debates, allowing Peacock to satirise contemporary intellectual movements.

In *Headlong Hall* (1815), his first major success, Peacock introduces this format, presenting a gathering of guests who embody conflicting worldviews: Mr Foster is an enthusiastic reformer, Mr Escot a pessimist, and Mr Jenkison a pragmatic moderate. Through their exchanges, Peacock skewers both utopian optimism and reactionary conservatism. *Crotchet Castle* (1831) continues this tradition, targeting the dogmatism of social reformers, the pretensions of political economists, and the rise of utilitarian thought. The character Mr Mac Quedy, an amalgam of James Mill and John Ramsay McCulloch, epitomises the cold rationalism of early 19th-century economics.

Peacock was particularly critical of intellectual fads and blind faith in progress. His writing reveals a keen awareness of how ideas can be manipulated for personal or political gain. While he enjoyed satirising the excesses of the Romantic movement, he was equally sceptical of utilitarianism, phrenology, and the grandiose social engineering projects of his era.

Despite his literary success, Peacock sought financial stability through a career at the East India Company, securing a post in 1819 as an assistant examiner of Indian correspondence. He excelled in this role, eventually rising to become Chief Examiner in 1836, succeeding James Mill. He remained in this influential position until his retirement in 1856, when he was followed by John Stuart Mill.

At India House, Peacock was instrumental in modernising the company's approach to steam navigation, authoring the 1829 *Memorandum Respecting the Application of Steam Navigation to the Internal and External Communication of India*, which influenced imperial transport policies. Though initially optimistic about British governance in India, he later became increasingly disillusioned. In 1837, when testifying before a parliamentary committee on steam navigation, he remarked, "I am not sure that it would be any benefit to the people of India to send Europeans amongst them."

Notwithstanding his demanding administrative career, Peacock continued to write. His literary output slowed after Shelley's death in 1822, but he remained engaged in cultural and intellectual debates. He published essays and reviews, including critiques of British poetry and culture, demonstrating his erudition and sharp critical eye.

In his personal life, Peacock was known for his dry wit and reserved nature. His romantic history was chequered with failed courtships, but he eventually married Jane Griffith in 1820. Their daughter, Mary Ellen Peacock, later married the novelist George Meredith, whose *Modern Love* was inspired by the collapse of their marriage. Peacock's home became a gathering place for literary discussion, mirroring the salons depicted in his novels.

His final novel, *Gryll Grange* (1860), revisits many of the themes explored in his earlier works, reflecting on the clash of ideologies and the follies of dogmatism. It serves as a fitting conclusion to his literary career, reaffirming his belief in the value of wit, reason and intellectual scepticism.

Peacock died on 23 January 1866 at the age of 80. Though never as widely celebrated as his Romantic contemporaries, his novels remain valued for their wit, incisive dialogue and critical engagement with early 19th-century society. Today, he is recognised as a distinctive voice in English literature, his satires offering a uniquely sceptical perspective on human nature and intellectual fashions. His works continue to be read for their humour, insight and timeless commentary on the folly of ideological extremes.

L.A. Davenport

EDITORIAL NOTE

This edition of *Maid Marian* and *The Misfortunes of Elphin* has been prepared with reference to several previous editions in an effort to approximate a definitive text. Any corrections made are minor and intended solely to clarify the text and, where applicable, align it with the first edition.

All footnotes are by Thomas Love Peacock himself, except for those enclosed in square brackets, which have been newly added for this edition.

I must express my deepest gratitude to David Garnett for his excellent annotations in the 1948 edition of Peacock's collected novels.

L.A.D.

PREFACE

TO VOLUME LVII OF BENTLEY'S 'STANDARD NOVELS'
containing *Headlong Hall, Nightmare Abbey, Maid Marian,* and *Crotchet Castle.*

All these little publications appeared originally without prefaces. I left them to speak for themselves; and I thought I might very fitly reserve my own impersonality, having never intruded on the personality of others, nor taken any liberties but with public conduct and public opinions. But an old friend assures me, that to publish a book without a preface is like entering a drawing-room without making a bow. In deference to this opinion, though I am not quite clear of its soundness, I make my prefatory bow at this eleventh hour.

"Headlong Hall" was written in 1815; "Nightmare Abbey" in 1817; "Maid Marian," with the exception of the last three chapters, in 1818; "Crotchet Castle" in 1830. I am desirous to note the intervals, because, at each of those periods, things were true, in great matters and in small, which are true no longer.

"Headlong Hall" begins with the Holyhead Mail, and "Crotchet Castle" ends with a rotten borough. The Holyhead mail no longer keeps the same hours, nor stops at the Capel Cerig Inn, which the progress of improvement has thrown out of the road; and the rotten boroughs of 1830 have ceased to exist, though there are some very pretty pocket properties, which are their worthy successors. But the classes of tastes, feelings, and opinions, which were successively brought into play in these little tales, remain substantially the same. Perfectibilians, deteriorationists, statu-quo-ites, phrenologists, transcendentalists, political economists, theorists in all sciences, projectors in all arts, morbid visionaries, romantic enthusiasts, lovers of music, lovers of the picturesque, and lovers of good dinners, march, and will march for ever, *pari passu*[1] with the march of mechanics, which some facetiously call the march of the intellect. The fastidious in old wine are a race that does not decay. Literary violators of the confidences of private life still gain a disreputable livelihood and an unenviable notoriety. Match-makers from interest, and the disappointed in love and in friendship, are varieties of which specimens are extant. The great principle of the Right of Might is as flourishing now as in the days of Maid Marian: the array of false pretensions, moral, political, and literary, is as imposing as ever: the rulers of the world still feel things in their effects, and never foresee them in their causes: and political mountebanks continue, and will continue, to puff nostrums and practise legerdemain under the eyes of the multitude: following, like the "learned friend" of

---

1.   ["At the same pace" or "in parallel".]

Crotchet Castle, a course as tortuous as that of a river, but in a reverse process; beginning by being dark and deep, and ending by being transparent.

The Author of "Headlong Hall".
March 4, 1837.

MAID MARIAN

by

THE AUTHOR OF HEADLONG HALL.

Yet thanks I must you con, that you work not
In holier shapes: for there is boundless theft
In limited professions.

Timon of Athens.[1]

---

1. [Taken from Act 4, Scene 3:
    "Yet thanks I must you con
    That you are thieves profess'd, that you work not
    In holier shapes: for there is boundless theft
    In limited professions."]

CONTENTS

INTRODUCTION

Thomas Love Peacock's *Maid Marian* (1822) is a playful and subversive reimagining of the Robin Hood legend, blending historical romance, satire and comic wit. Set during the reign of Richard the Lionheart, the novella weaves a lively tale of adventure and love while gently mocking the romantic ideals of chivalry and heroism that characterised much of early 19th-century historical fiction. At its heart, Maid Marian challenges traditional notions of heroism and gender roles, presenting a heroine who is as cunning, brave, and resourceful as her famous outlaw lover.

The story of Robin Hood has long been a cornerstone of English folklore, with its themes of rebellion, social justice, and merry camaraderie resonating across centuries. By the time Peacock took up the tale, it had already undergone numerous retellings, each emphasising different aspects of the legend. Yet Peacock's version stands apart, not just for its wit but also for its modern sensibilities. His Marian is far from the passive damsel-in-distress or virtuous maiden of earlier renditions; she is, instead, an active participant in the band's exploits, a figure of agency and determination who readily dons disguises, devises strategies and stands shoulder-to-shoulder with Robin and his men.

Peacock's decision to focus on Marian—elevating her from the margins of the legend to its centre—was both innovative and reflective of his broader literary project. While many of his contemporaries, such as Sir Walter Scott, were romanticising the medieval past in sweeping epics like *Ivanhoe*, published in December 1819, Peacock approached the same subject with irreverence and scepticism. His tone is light-hearted and satirical, using the trappings of medieval romance to poke fun at both the period he depicts and the literary fashions of his own time.

When *Maid Marian* was first published, it was in the midst of a revival of interest in England's medieval past, driven by growing nationalism, antiquarian curiosity and the popularity of Scott's Waverley novels. This cultural milieu celebrated the chivalric virtues of loyalty, honour and fealty—qualities that Peacock cheerfully lampoons. He presents his medieval characters with all their pomp and pretensions, but he delights in exposing their foibles. The outlaws of Sherwood Forest may embody ideals of liberty and resistance to tyranny, but they are also cheerfully irreverent and far from solemn in their pursuit of justice. Similarly, the noblemen, clergy and other representatives of the establishment are portrayed with an eye for their absurdities, whether through their bluster, hypocrisy or self-importance.

The character of Marian herself epitomises Peacock's critique of societal norms. In many ways, she is a product of the Romantic era—spirited, independent and unapologetically passionate. But she is also a rejection of the clichéd heroines that populated much of the historical fiction of the time. Marian is not content to wait passively for rescue or to serve merely as a romantic prize; instead, she takes charge of her destiny, embracing life as an outlaw with gusto. She matches Robin Hood in wit and bravery, proving herself as capable with a bow and as sharp with a retort as any of the Merry Men. Peacock's portrayal of Marian as a partner and equal to Robin reflects a proto-feminist sensibility that was rare in the literature of his time.

Another hallmark of *Maid Marian* is Peacock's linguistic brilliance. The novella sparkles with clever dialogue, humorous asides and lyrical descriptions of the forested landscapes that serve as the outlaws' haven. Peacock's prose captures the exuberance and vitality of his characters, while his playful use of language adds a layer of sophistication that rewards attentive readers. The exchanges between Marian and Robin, in particular, are imbued with a spirited repartee that underscores their partnership, both romantic and strategic.

Although *Maid Marian* is primarily a comedic work, it is not without its serious undertones. The novella subtly interrogates the nature of authority, justice and morality, raising questions about the legitimacy of power and the responsibilities of those who wield it. The outlaws of Sherwood Forest, though idealised to some extent, are presented as an alternative to the oppressive structures of feudal society. Their communal way of life, bound by mutual loyalty rather than rigid hierarchies, offers a vision of social organisation that is both anarchic and egalitarian. In this sense, Peacock's novella resonates with the political currents of his own time, reflecting the radical ideas of liberty and reform that were gaining traction in the early 19th century.

The historical context of the novella's publication adds another layer of interest. Written during a period of intense political and social change in Britain, *Maid Marian* can be read as a commentary on contemporary issues, from the debates over parliamentary reform to the growing tensions between the landed gentry and the rising middle class. Peacock's own political leanings—he was a friend and contemporary of the radical poet Percy Bysshe Shelley—infuse the text with a subtle but pointed critique of conservatism and reactionary attitudes.

Despite its many virtues, *Maid Marian* has often been overshadowed by Peacock's other works, such as *Headlong Hall* and *Nightmare Abbey*. This relative neglect may be due in part to the novella's brevity and its departure from the more overtly philosophical discussions that characterise his best-known works. Yet it is precisely this lightness of touch that makes *Maid Marian* so enjoyable. It is a work of exuberant humour and charm, a novella that invites readers to revel in its mischief and merriment while still offering plenty of food for thought.

Today, *Maid Marian* stands as a testament to Peacock's versatility and originality as a writer. It is both a delightful romp through one of England's most beloved legends and a subtle critique of the societal and literary conventions of Peacock's time. For modern readers, it offers a fresh perspective on the Robin Hood myth, one that highlights the enduring appeal of the tale while challenging us to reconsider the roles of its characters and the values they embody.

Whether approached as a comic masterpiece, a proto-feminist text or a sly piece of social commentary, *Maid Marian* continues to enchant and entertain. Its combination of sharp wit, engaging characters, and timeless themes ensures that it remains as relevant today as it was when Peacock first penned it. As you delve into the merry world of Sherwood Forest, prepare to be charmed by Marian and her companions, and to discover why Peacock's reimagining of the legend is a treasure in its own right.

L.A.D.

MAID MARIAN

This little work, with the exception of the last three chapters, was written in the autumn of 1818. *March* 15, 1822.[1]

---

1.   [Almost certainly a pre-emptive defence against accusations of copying Sir Walter Scott's hugely popular historical novel *Ivanhoe*, published in 1819, which revived interest in medieval legends, including Robin Hood.]

CHAPTER 1

Now come ye for peace here, or come ye for war?

Scott.[1]

"The abbot, in his alb arrayed," stood at the altar in
the abbey-chapel of Rubygill, with all his plump,
sleek, rosy friars, in goodly lines disposed, to solem-
nize the nuptials of the beautiful Matilda Fitzwater,
daughter of the Baron of Arlingford, with the noble
Robert Fitz-Ooth, Earl of Locksley and Huntingdon.[2]

---

1. [From *Lochinvar*, a literary ballad from Canto 5 of the longer
poetic history of Scotland, *Marmion, a Tale of Flodden Field*, published in 1808.]

2. [The historical Earl of Huntingdon at the time *Maid Marian* is
set (the late 12th century during the reign of Richard I) was David
of Scotland, 8th Earl of Huntingdon (1152–1219). He was the
younger brother of Malcolm IV and William I, Kings of Scotland,
and his earldom stemmed from a grant by King Henry II of England. The idea that Robin Hood was descended from a noble
family such as the Fitz-Ooths is a romantic invention rather than a
historical fact. The Fitz-Ooth connection appears in later versions
of the Robin Hood legend, particularly those influenced by the desire to associate Robin with nobility and chivalric values. However,
there is no historical evidence to support the existence of a Robert

The abbey of Rubygill stood in a picturesque valley, at a little distance from the western boundary of Sherwood Forest, in a spot which seemed adapted by nature to be the retreat of monastic mortification, being on the banks of a fine trout-stream, and in the midst of woodland coverts, abounding with excellent game. The bride, with her father and attendant maidens, entered the chapel; but the earl had not arrived. The baron was amazed, and the bridemaidens were disconcerted. Matilda feared that some evil had befallen her lover, but felt no diminution of her confidence in his honour and love. Through the open gates of the chapel she looked down the narrow road that wound along the side of the hill, and her ear was the first that heard the distant trampling of horses, and her eye was the first that caught the glitter of snowy plumes and the light of polished spears. "It is strange," thought the baron, "that the earl should come in this martial array to his wedding;" but he had not long to meditate on the phænomenon, for the foaming steeds swept up to the gate like a whirlwind, and the earl, breathless with speed, and followed by a few of his yeomen, advanced to his smiling bride. It was then no time to ask questions, for the organ was in full peal and the choristers were in full voice.

The abbot began to intone the ceremony in a style of modulation impressively exalted, his voice issuing most canonically from the roof of his mouth, through

---

Fitz-Ooth or his connection to the real Earldom of Huntingdon. The Fitz-Ooth story seems to have originated in the late Middle Ages and became popularised in Elizabethan ballads, most notably through Anthony Munday's plays *The Downfall of Robert, Earl of Huntingdon* (1598) and *The Death of Robert, Earl of Huntingdon* (1598).]

the medium of a very musical nose newly tuned for the occasion. But he had not proceeded far enough to exhibit all the variety and compass of this melodious instrument, when a noise was heard at the gate, and a party of armed men entered the chapel. The song of the choristers died away in a shake of demisemiquavers, contrary to all the rules of psalmody. The organ-blower, who was working his musical air-pump with one hand, and with two fingers and a thumb of the other insinuating a peeping-place through the curtain of the organ-gallery, was struck motionless by the double operation of curiosity and fear; while the organist, intent only on his performance, and spreading all his fingers to strike a swell of magnificent chords, felt his harmonic spirit ready to desert his body on being answered by the ghastly rattle of empty keys, and in the consequent *agitato furioso*[3] of the internal movements of his feelings, was preparing to restore harmony by the *segue subito*[4] of an *appoggiatura con foco*[5] with the corner of a book of anthems on the head of his neglectful assistant, when his hand and his attention together were arrested by the scene below. The voice of the abbot subsided into silence through a descending scale of long-drawn melody, like the sound of the ebbing sea to the explorers of a cave. In a few moments all was silence, interrupted only by the iron tread of the armed intruders, as it rung on the marble floor and echoed from the vaulted aisles.

The leader strode up to the altar, and placing

---

3. [Agitated fury.]
4. [Immediate following.]
5. [A passionate embellishment.]

himself opposite to the abbot, and between the earl and Matilda in such a manner that the four together seemed to stand on the four points of a diamond, exclaimed: "In the name of King Henry, I forbid the ceremony, and attach Robert Earl of Huntingdon as a traitor!" and at the same time he held his drawn sword between the lovers, as if to emblem that royal authority which laid its temporal ban upon their contract. The earl drew his own sword instantly, and struck down the interposing weapon; then clasped his left arm round Matilda, who sprang into his embrace, and held his sword before her with his right hand. His yeomen ranged themselves at his side, and stood with their swords drawn, still and prepared, like men determined to die in his defence. The soldiers, confident in superiority of numbers, paused. The abbot took advantage of the pause to introduce a word of exhortation. "My children," said he, "if you are going to cut each other's throats, I entreat you, in the name of peace and charity, to do it out of the chapel."

"Sweet Matilda," said the earl, "did you give your love to the Earl of Huntingdon, whose lands touch the Ouse and the Trent, or to Robert Fitz-Ooth, the son of his mother?"

"Neither to the earl nor his earldom," answered Matilda firmly, "but to Robert Fitz-Ooth and his love."

"That I well knew," said the earl; "and though the ceremony be incomplete, we are not the less married in the eye of my only saint, our Lady, who will yet bring us together. Lord Fitzwater, to your care, for the present, I commit your daughter. Nay, sweet Matilda, part we must for a while; but we will soon meet under brighter skies, and be this the seal of our faith."

He kissed Matilda's lips and consigned her to the baron, who glowered about him with an expression of countenance that showed he was mortally wroth with somebody; but whatever he thought or felt he kept to himself. The earl, with a sign to his followers, made a sudden charge on the soldiers, with the intention of cutting his way through. The soldiers were prepared for such an occurrence, and a desperate skirmish succeeded. Some of the women screamed, but none of them fainted, for fainting was not so much the fashion in those days, when the ladies breakfasted on brawn and ale at sunrise, as in our more refined age of green tea and muffins at noon. Matilda seemed disposed to fly again to her lover, but the baron forced her from the chapel. The earl's bowmen at the door sent in among the assailants a volley of arrows, one of which whizzed past the ear of the abbot, who, in mortal fear of being suddenly translated from a ghostly friar into a friarly ghost, began to roll out of the chapel as fast as his bulk and his holy robes would permit, roaring "Sacrilege!" with all his monks at his heels, who were, like himself, more intent to go at once than to stand upon the order of their going.[6] The abbot, thus pressed from behind, and stumbling over his own drapery before, fell suddenly prostrate in the door-way that connected the chapel with the abbey, and was instantaneously buried under a pyramid of ghostly carcasses, that fell over him and each other, and lay a rolling

---

6. [Macbeth, Act III, Scene 4: "Stand not upon the order of your going, but go at once."]

chaos of animated rotundities, sprawling and bawling in unseemly disarray, and sending forth the names of all the saints in and out of heaven, amidst the clashing of swords, the ringing of bucklers, the clattering of helmets, the twanging of bow-strings, the whizzing of arrows, the screams of women, the shouts of the warriors, and the vociferations of the peasantry, who had been assembled to the intended nuptials, and who, seeing a fair set-to, contrived to pick a quarrel among themselves on the occasion, and proceeded, with staff and cudgel, to crack each other's skulls for the good of the king and the earl. One tall friar alone was untouched by the panic of his brethren, and stood steadfastly watching the combat with his arms a-kembo, the colossal emblem of an unarmed neutrality.

At length, through the midst of the internal confusion, the earl by the help of his good sword, the staunch valour of his men, and the blessing of the Virgin, fought his way to the chapel-gate: his bowmen closed him in: he vaulted into his saddle, clapped spurs to his horse, rallied his men on the first eminence, and exchanged his sword for a bow and arrow, with which he did old execution among the pursuers; who at last thought it most expedient to desist from offensive warfare, and to retreat into the abbey, where, in the king's name, they broached a pipe of the best wine and attached all the venison in the larder, having first carefully unpacked the tuft of friars, and set the fallen abbot on his legs.

The friars, it may be well supposed, and such of the king's men as escaped unhurt from the affray, found their spirits a cup too low, and kept the flask moving from noon till night. The peaceful brethren, unused to the tumult of war, had undergone, from fear and discomposure, an exhaustion of animal spirits that required extraordinary refection. During the repast they interrogated Sir Ralph Montfaucon, the leader of the soldiers, respecting the nature of the earl's offence.

"A complication of offences," replied Sir Ralph, "superinduced on the original basis of forest-treason. He began with hunting the king's deer, in despite of all remonstrance; followed it up by contempt of the king's mandates, and by armed resistance to his power, in defiance of all authority; and combined with it the resolute withholding of payment of certain monies to the abbot of Doncaster, in denial of all law; and has thus made himself the declared enemy of church and state, and all for being too fond of venison." And the knight helped himself to half a pasty.

"A heinous offender," said a little round oily friar, appropriating the portion of pasty which Sir Ralph had left.

"The earl is a worthy peer," said the tall friar whom we have already mentioned in the chapel scene, "and the best marksman in England."

"Why this is flat treason, Brother Michael," said the little round friar, "to call an attainted traitor a worthy peer."

"I pledge you," said Brother Michael. The little friar smiled and filled his cup. "He will draw the long bow," pursued Brother Michael, "with any bold yeoman among them all."

"Don't talk of the long bow," said the abbot, who had the sound of the arrow still whizzing in his ear: "what have we pillars of the faith to do with the long bow?"

"Be that as it may," said Sir Ralph, "he is an outlaw from this moment."

"So much the worse for the law then," said Brother Michael. "The law will have a heavier miss of him than he will have of the law. He will strike as much venison as ever, and more of other game. I know what I say: but *basta*[7]: Let us drink."

"What other game?" said the little friar. "I hope he won't poach among our partridges."

"Poach! not he," said Brother Michael: "if he wants your partridges, he will strike them under your nose (here's to you), and drag your trout-stream for you on a Thursday evening."

"Monstrous! and starve us on fast-day," said the little friar.

"But that is not the game I mean," said Brother Michael.

"Surely, son Michael," said the abbot, "you do not mean to insinuate that the noble earl will turn freebooter?"

"A man must live," said Brother Michael, "earl or no. If the law takes his rents and beeves without his consent, he must take beeves and rents where he can get them without the consent of the law. This is the *lex talionis*."[8]

"Truly," said Sir Ralph, "I am sorry for the damsel: she seems fond of this wild runagate."

---

7. [Enough.]

8. ["The law of retaliation". It refers to the principle of retributive justice, where punishment mirrors the crime, commonly summed up as "an eye for an eye, a tooth for a tooth". The concept is found in ancient legal codes, such as the Code of Hammurabi (Babylonian law, c. 1754 BCE), the Old Testament (Exodus 21:23–25) and Roman law, where it was formalised in legal discussions.]

"A mad girl, a mad girl," said the little friar.

"How a mad girl?" said Brother Michael. "Has she not beauty, grace, wit, sense, discretion, dexterity, learning, and valour?"

"Learning!" exclaimed the little friar; "what has a woman to do with learning? And valour! who ever heard a woman commended for valour? Meekness, and mildness, and softness, and gentleness, and tenderness, and humility, and obedience to her husband, and faith in her confessor, and domesticity, or, as learned doctors call it, the faculty of stayathomeitiveness, and embroidery, and music, and pickling, and preserving, and the whole complex and multiplex detail of the noble science of dinner, as well in preparation for the table, as in arrangement over it, and in distribution around it to knights and squires and ghostly friars, these are female virtues: but valour—why who ever heard—?"

"She is the all in all," said Brother Michael, "gentle as a ring-dove, yet high-soaring as a falcon: humble below her deserving, yet deserving beyond the estimate of panegyric: an exact economist in all superfluity, yet a most bountiful dispenser in all liberality: the chief regulator of her household, the fairest pillar of her hall, and the sweetest blossom of her bower: having, in all opposite proposings, sense to understand, judgment to weigh, discretion to choose, firmness to undertake, diligence to conduct, perseverance to accomplish, and resolution to maintain. For obedience to her husband, that is not to be tried till she has one: for faith in her confessor, she has as much as the law prescribes: for embroidery an Arachne: for music a Siren: and for pickling and preserving, did not one of her jars of sugared apricots give you your last surfeit at Arlingford Castle?"

"Call you that preserving?" said the little friar; "I call it destroying. Call you it pickling? Truly it pickled me. My life was saved by miracle."

"By canary,"[9] said Brother Michael. "Canary is the only life preserver, the true *aurum potabile*,[10] the universal panacea for all diseases, thirst, and short life. Your life was saved by canary."

"Indeed, reverend father," said Sir Ralph, "if the young lady be half what you describe, she must be a paragon: but your commending her for valour does somewhat amaze me."

"She can fence," said the little friar, "and draw the long bow, and play at single-stick, and quarter-staff."

"Yet mark you," said Brother Michael, "not like a virago or a hoyden, or one that would crack a serving-man's head for spilling gravy on her ruff, but with such womanly grace and temperate self-command, as if those manly exercises belonged to her only, and were become for her sake feminine."

---

9. [The reference to "canary" does not concern the bird, but rather Canary wine, a highly prized alcoholic drink produced in the Canary Islands. This type of wine, also known as Malmsey or sack, was popular in Europe during the medieval and Renaissance periods, including the time in which *Maid Marian* is set. So while actual canaries (the birds) were not widely known in Europe during the late 12th century, Canary wine was enjoyed by those who could afford it.]

10. [*Aurum potabile*, or "drinkable gold", was a term used by alchemists in medieval and Renaissance Europe to describe a mythical elixir that combined gold with other ingredients, supposedly granting health, longevity and even immortality to the drinker. Gold was believed to have medicinal properties, and the concept of a liquid form of gold was tied to alchemical pursuits of the philosopher's stone and universal panaceas.]

"You incite me," said Sir Ralph, "to view her more nearly. That madcap earl found me other employment than to remark her in the chapel."

"The earl is a worthy peer," said Brother Michael; "he is worth any fourteen earls on this side Trent, and any seven on the other." (The reader will please to remember, that Rubygill Abbey was *north* of Trent.)

"His mettle will be tried," said Sir Ralph. "There is many a courtier will swear to King Henry, to bring him in dead or alive."

"They must look to the brambles then," said Brother Michael.

"The bramble, the bramble, the bonny forest
bramble,
    Doth make a jest
    Of silken vest,
That will through greenwood scramble:
The bramble, the bramble, the bonny forest bramble."

"Plague on your lungs, son Michael," said the abbot; "this is your old coil: always roaring in your cups."

"I know what I say," said Brother Michael; "there is often more sense in an old song than in a new homily.

The courtly pad doth amble,
When his gay lord would ramble:
    But both may catch
    An awkward scratch,
If they ride among the bramble:
The bramble, the bramble, the bonny forest bramble."

"Tall friar," said Sir Ralph, "either you shoot the shafts of your merriment at random, or you know more of the earl's designs than beseems your frock."

"Let my frock," said Brother Michael, "answer for its own sins. It is worn past covering mine. It is too weak for a shield, too transparent for a screen, too thin for a shelter, too light for gravity, and too thread-bare for a jest. The wearer would be naught indeed, who should misbeseem such a wedding garment.

But wherefore does the sheep wear wool?
    That he in season sheared may be,
And the shepherd be warm though his flock be cool:
    So I'll have a new cloak about me."[11]

---

11. [This is a modified version of lines from the traditional Scottish folk song The Jolly Beggar. The original song dates back to at least the 17th century. It also shares similarities with the traditional ballad The Old Cloak, also known as Bell My Wife. This song features a dialogue between a husband and wife, where the wife urges the husband to buy her a new cloak, while he laments the cost and expresses his reluctance. A stanza from one version of the ballad reads:
    "Why should I cast my old cloak away,
      Yet go cold another day?"]

CHAPTER II

"Vray moyne si oncques en feut depuis que le monde
moynant moyna de moynerie."

RABELAIS.[1]

THE Earl of Huntingdon, living in the vicinity of a
royal forest, and passionately attached to the chase
from his infancy, had long made as free with the
king's deer as Lord Percy proposed to do with those of
Lord Douglas in the memorable hunting of Cheviot.[2]
It is sufficiently well known how severe were the forest-laws in those days, and with what jealousy the

---

1. ["A true monk, if ever there was one, since the world began
monkishly to monk its monkery." *Gargantua and Pantagruel*, Book
I, Chapter XXVII.]
2. [A reference to the Battle of Otterburn (1388), romanticised in
the famous ballad "The Battle of Otterburn" and closely associated with the older ballad "The Hunting of the Cheviot", better
known as "Chevy Chase". James Douglas, 2nd Earl of Douglas, led
a Scottish raiding force into Northumberland, where he clashed
with Sir Henry Percy (Hotspur) at Otterburn, south of the Cheviot
Hills. Douglas was killed during the battle, but the Scots won the
battle, taking Hotspur prisoner.]

Kings of England maintained this branch of their prerogative: but menaces and remonstrances were thrown away on the earl, who declared that he would not thank Saint Peter for admission into Paradise, if he were obliged to leave his bow and hounds at the gate. King Henry (the Second) swore by Saint Botolph to make him rue his sport, and, having caused him to be duly and formally accused, summoned him to London to answer the charge. The earl, deeming himself safer among his own vassals than among king Henry's courtiers, took no notice of the mandate. King Henry sent a force to bring him, *vi et armis*,[3] to court. The earl made a resolute resistance and put the king's force to flight under a shower of arrows: an act which the courtiers declared to be treason. At the same time, the abbot of Doncaster sued up the payment of certain monies, which the earl, whose revenue ran a losing race with his hospitality, had borrowed at sundry times of the said abbot: for the abbots and the bishops were the chief usurers of those days, and, as the end sanctifies the means, were not in the least scrupulous of employing what would have been extortion in the profane, to accomplish the pious purpose of bringing a blessing on the land by rescuing it from the frail hold of carnal and temporal into the firmer grasp of ghostly and spiritual possessors. But the earl, confident in the number and attachment of his retainers, stoutly refused either to repay the money, which he could not, or to yield the

---

3. ["By force and arms". The phrase was used in medieval and legal Latin to refer to the use of physical force or military intervention, while in common law, it was employed in legal writs to describe unlawful acts of violence or trespass.]

forfeiture, which he would not: a refusal, which in those days was an act of outlawry in a gentleman, as it is now of bankruptcy in a base mechanic; the gentleman having in our wiser times a more liberal privilege of gentility, which enables him to keep his land and laugh at his creditor. Thus the mutual resentments and interests of the king and the abbot concurred to subject the earl to the penalties of outlawry, by which the abbot would gain his due upon the lands of Locksley, and the rest would be confiscate to the king. Still the king did not think it advisable to assail the earl in his own strong-hold, but caused a diligent watch to be kept over his motions, till at length his rumoured marriage with the heiress of Arlingford seemed to point out an easy method of laying violent hands on the offender. Sir Ralph Montfaucon, a young man of good lineage and of an aspiring temper, who readily seized the first opportunity that offered of recommending himself to King Henry's favour by manifesting his zeal in his service, undertook the charge: and how he succeeded we have seen.

Sir Ralph's curiosity was strongly excited by the friar's description of the young lady of Arlingford; and he prepared in the morning to visit the castle, under the very plausible pretext of giving the baron an explanation of his intervention at the nuptials. Brother Michael and the little fat friar proposed to be his guides. The proposal was courteously accepted, and they set out together, leaving Sir Ralph's followers at the abbey. The knight was mounted on a spirited charger; Brother Michael on a large heavy-trotting horse; and the little fat friar on a plump soft-paced galloway, so correspondent with himself in size, rotundity, and sleekness, that if they had been amalgamated into a centaur, there would have been nothing to alter in their proportions.

"Do you know," said the little friar, as they wound along the banks of the stream, "the reason why lake-trout is better than river-trout, and shyer withal?"

"I was not aware of the fact," said Sir Ralph.

"A most heterodox remark," said Brother Michael: "know you not, that in all nice matters you should take the implication for absolute, and, without looking into the *fact whether*, seek only the *reason why*? But the fact is so, on the word of a friar; which what layman will venture to gainsay who prefers a down bed to a gridiron?"

"The fact being so," said the knight, "I am still at a loss for the reason; nor would I undertake to opine in a matter of that magnitude: since, in all that appertains to the good things either of this world or the next, my reverend spiritual guides are kind enough to take the trouble of thinking off my hands."

"Spoken," said Brother Michael, "with a sound Catholic conscience. My little brother here is most profound in the matter of trout. He has marked, learned, and inwardly digested the subject, twice a week at least for five-and-thirty years. I yield to him in this. My strong points are venison and canary."

"The good qualities of a trout," said the little friar, "are firmness and redness: the redness indeed being the visible sign of all other virtues."

"Whence," said Brother Michael, "we choose our abbot by his nose:

The rose on the nose doth all virtues disclose:
For the outward grace shows

That the inward overflows,
When it glows in the rose of a red, red nose."

"Now," said the little friar, "as is the firmness so is the redness, and as is the redness so is the shyness."

"Marry why?" said Brother Michael. "The solution is not physical-natural, but physical-historical, or natural-superinductive. And thereby hangs a tale, which may be either said or sung:

The damsel stood to watch the fight
   By the banks of Kingslea Mere,
And they brought to her feet her own true knight
   Sore-wounded on a bier.

She knelt by him his wounds to bind:
   She washed them with many a tear:
And shouts rose fast upon the wind,
   Which told that the foe was near.

'Oh! let not,' he said, 'while yet I live,
   The cruel foe me take:
But with thy sweet lips a last kiss give,
   And cast me in the lake.'

Around his neck she wound her arms,
   And she kissed his lips so pale:
And evermore the war's alarms
   Came louder up the vale.

She drew him to the lake's steep side,
   Where the red heath fringed the shore:
She plunged with him beneath the tide,
   And they were seen no more.

Their true blood mingled in Kingslea Mere,
  That to mingle on earth was fain:
And the trout that swims in that crystal clear
  Is tinged with the crimson stain.

"Thus you see how good comes of evil, and how a holy friar may fare better on fast-day for the violent death of two lovers two hundred years ago. The inference is most consecutive, that, wherever you catch a red-fleshed trout, love lies bleeding under the water: an occult quality, which can only act in the stationary waters of a lake, being neutralized by the rapid transition of those of a stream."

"And why is the trout shyer for that?" asked Sir Ralph.

"Do you not see?" said Brother Michael. "The virtues of both lovers diffuse themselves through the lake. The infusion of masculine valour makes the fish active and sanguineous: the infusion of maiden modesty makes him coy and hard to win: and you shall find through life, the fish which is most easily hooked is not the best worth dishing. But yonder are the towers of Arlingford."

The little friar stopped. He seemed suddenly struck with an awful thought, which caused a momentary pallescence in his rosy complexion: and after a brief hesitation, he turned his galloway, and told his companions he should give them good day.

"Why, what is in the wind now, Brother Peter?" said Friar Michael.

"The lady Matilda," said the little friar, "can draw the long-bow. She must bear no good will to Sir Ralph, and if she should espy him from her tower, she may testify her recognition with a cloth-yard shaft.

She is not so infallible a markswoman, but that she might shoot at a crow and kill a pigeon. She might peradventure miss the knight, and hit me, who never did her any harm."

"Tut, tut, man," said Brother Michael, "there is no such fear."

"Mass," said the little friar, "but there is such a fear, and very strong too. You who have it not may keep your way, and I who have it shall take mine. I am not just now in the vein for being picked off at a long shot." And saying these words he spurred up his four-footed better half, and galloped off as nimbly as if he had had an arrow singing behind him.

"Is this lady Matilda, then, so very terrible a damsel?" said Sir Ralph to Brother Michael.

"By no means," said the friar. "She has certainly a high spirit; but it is the wing of the eagle, without his beak or his claw. She is as gentle as magnanimous: but it is the gentleness of the summer wind, which, however lightly it wave the tuft of the pine, carries with it the intimation of a power, that, if roused to its extremity, could make it bend to the dust."

"From the warmth of your panegyric, ghostly father," said the knight, "I should almost suspect you were in love with the damsel."

"So I am," said the friar, "and I care not who knows it; but all in the way of honesty, master soldier. I am, as it were, her spiritual lover: and were she a damsel errant, I would be her ghostly esquire, her friar militant. I would buckle me in armour of proof, and the devil might thresh me black with an iron flail, before I would knock under in her cause. Though they be not yet one canonically, thanks to your soldiership, the earl is her liege lord, and she is his liege lady. I am her father confessor and ghostly director: I have taken on me to show her the way to the next world: and how can I do that if I lose sight of her in this? seeing that this is but the road to the other, and has so many circumvolutions and ramifications of bye-ways and beaten paths (all more thickly set than the true one with finger-posts and mile-stones, not one of which tells truth), that a traveller has need of some one who knows the way, or the odds go hard against him that he will ever see the face of Saint Peter."

"But there must surely be some reason," said Sir Ralph, "for Father Peter's apprehension."

"None," said Brother Michael, "but the apprehension itself; fear being its own father, and most prolific in self-propagation. The lady did, it is true, once signalize her displeasure against our little brother, for reprimanding her in that she would go hunting a-mornings instead of attending matins. She cut short the thread of his eloquence by sportively drawing her bow-string and loosing an arrow over his head: he waddled off with singular speed, and was in much awe of her for many months. I thought he had forgotten it: but let that pass. In truth, she would have had little of her lover's company, if she had liked the chaunt of the choristers better than the cry of the hounds: yet I know not: for they were companions from the cradle, and reciprocally fashioned each other to the love of the fern and the foxglove. Had either been less sylvan, the other might have been more saintly: but they will now never hear matins but those of the lark, nor reverence vaulted aisle but that of the greenwood canopy. They are twin plants of the forest, and are identified with its growth.

For the slender beech and the sapling oak,
    That grow by the shadowy rill,
You may cut down both at a single stroke,
    You may cut down which you will.

But this you must know, that as long as they grow,
    Whatever change may be,
You never can teach either oak or beech
    To be aught but a greenwood tree.

CHAPTER III

Inflamed wrath in glowing breast.

BUTLER.[1]

THE knight and the friar, arriving at Arlingford Castle, and leaving their horses in the care of lady Matilda's groom, with whom the friar was in great favour, were ushered into a stately apartment, where they found the baron alone, flourishing an enormous carving-knife over a brother baron—of beef—with as much vehemence of action as if he were cutting down an enemy. The baron was a gentleman of a fierce and choleric temperament: he was lineally descended from the redoubtable Fierabras of Normandy, who came over to England with the Conqueror, and who, in the battle of Hastings, killed with his own hand four-and-twenty Saxon cavaliers all on a row.[2] The

---

1.   [*Hudibras*, Part I, Canto 2.]
2.   [There were no Saxon cavaliers at the Battle of Hastings in 1066, as the Anglo-Saxons did not use cavalry in battle. The military forces of King Harold II's Anglo-Saxon army were primarily composed of infantry. These included housecarls, professional

very excess of the baron's internal rage on the preceding day had smothered its external manifestation: he was so equally angry with both parties, that he knew not on which to vent his wrath. He was enraged with the earl for having brought himself into such a dilemma without his privity; and he was no less enraged with the king's men for their very unseasonable intrusion. He could willingly have fallen upon both parties, but he must necessarily have begun with one: and he felt that on whichever side he should strike the first blow, his retainers would immediately join battle. He had therefore contented himself with forcing away his daughter from the scene of action. In the course of the evening he had received intelligence that the earl's castle was in possession of a party of the king's men, who had been detached by Sir Ralph Montfaucon to seize on it during the earl's absence. The baron inferred from this that the earl's case was desperate; and those who have had the opportunity of seeing a rich friend fall suddenly into poverty, may easily judge by their own feelings how quickly and completely the whole moral being of the earl was changed in the baron's estimation. The baron immediately proceeded to require in his daughter's mind the same summary revolution that had taken place in his own, and considered himself exceedingly ill-used by her non-compliance. The lady had retired to her chamber, and the baron had passed a supperless and sleepless night, stalking about his apartments till an advanced

---

well-trained soldiers of the king's retinue, and fyrd, the levied militia made up of common men, often less well-equipped and trained than the housecarls.]

hour of the morning, when hunger compelled him to summon into his presence the spoils of the buttery, which, being the intended array of an uneaten wedding feast, were more than usually abundant, and on which, when the knight and the friar entered, he was falling with desperate valour. He looked up at them fiercely, with his mouth full of beef and his eyes full of flame, and rising, as ceremony required, made an awful bow to the knight, inclining himself forward over the table and presenting his carving-knife *en militaire*, in a manner that seemed to leave it doubtful whether he meant to show respect to his visitor or to defend his provision: but the doubt was soon cleared up by his politely motioning the knight to be seated; on which the friar advanced to the table, saying, "For what we are going to receive," and commenced operations without further prelude by filling and drinking a goblet of wine. The baron at the same time offered one to Sir Ralph, with the look of a man in whom habitual hospitality and courtesy were struggling with the ebullitions of natural anger. They pledged each other in silence, and the baron, having completed a copious draught, continued working his lips and his throat, as if trying to swallow his wrath as he had done his wine. Sir Ralph, not knowing well what to make of these ambiguous signs, looked for instructions to the friar, who by significant looks and gestures seemed to advise him to follow his example and partake of the good cheer before him, without speaking till the baron should be more intelligible in his demeanour. The knight and the friar, accordingly, proceeded to refect themselves after their ride; the baron looking first at the one and then at the other, scrutinizing alternately the serious looks of the knight and the merry face of the friar, till at length, having calmed himself sufficiently to speak, he said, "Courteous knight and ghostly father, I presume you have some other business with me than to eat my beef and drink my canary: and if so, I patiently await your leisure to enter on the topic."

"Lord Fitzwater," said Sir Ralph, "in obedience to my royal master, King Henry, I have been the unwilling instrument of frustrating the intended nuptials of your fair daughter; yet will you, I trust, owe me no displeasure for my agency herein, seeing that the noble maiden might otherwise by this time have been the bride of an outlaw."

"I am very much obliged to you, sir," said the baron; "very exceedingly obliged. Your solicitude for my daughter is truly paternal, and for a young man and a stranger very singular and exemplary: and it is very kind withal to come to the relief of my insufficiency and inexperience, and concern yourself so much in that which concerns you not."

"You misconceive the knight, noble baron," said the friar. "He urges not his reason in the shape of a preconceived intent, but in that of a subsequent extenuation. True, he has done the lady Matilda great wrong——-"

"How great wrong?" said the baron. "What do you mean by great wrong? Would you have had her married to a wild fly-by-night, that accident made an earl and nature a deer-stealer? that has not wit enough to eat venison without picking a quarrel with monarchy? that flings away his own lands into the clutches of rascally friars, for the sake of hunting in other men's grounds, and feasting vagabonds that wear Lincoln green? and would have flung away mine into the bargain if he had had my daughter? What do you mean by great wrong?"

"True," said the friar: "great right, I meant."

"Right!" exclaimed the baron: "what right has any man to do my daughter right but myself? What right has any man to drive my daughter's bridegroom out of the chapel in the middle of the marriage ceremony, and turn all our merry faces into green wounds and bloody coxcombs,[3] and then come and tell me he has done us great right?"

"True," said the friar: "he has done neither right nor wrong."

"But he has," said the baron, "he has done both, and I will maintain it with my glove."

"It shall not need," said Sir Ralph; "I will concede any thing in honour."

"And I," said the baron, "will concede nothing in honour: I will concede nothing in honour to any man."

"Neither will I, Lord Fitzwater," said Sir Ralph, "in that sense: but hear me. I was commissioned by the king to apprehend the Earl of Huntingdon. I brought with me a party of soldiers, picked and tried men,

---

3. [Fresh untreated wounds were often described as "green" in older literary and medical contexts to signify their raw or un-healed state. The term "coxcomb" originally referred to the crest or comb of a rooster, which is often bright red, resembling the appearance of a head bleeding from cuts. In Elizabethan times, "coxcomb" was also used as a slang term for a fool or a dandy, owing to the jester's cap, which resembled a rooster's comb. Thus, "bloody coxcombs" suggests heads bloodied in combat, while also carrying a mocking undertone that likens the wounded to foolish jesters. Shakespeare often uses "coxcomb" metaphorically to ridicule pretentiousness or folly. For example, in *King Lear* (Act 1, Scene 4), the fool offers the king a coxcomb to signify his fool-ishness.]

knowing that he would not lightly yield. I sent my lieutenant with a detachment to surprise the earl's castle in his absence, and laid my measures for intercepting him on the way to his intended nuptials; but he seems to have had intimation of this part of my plan, for he brought with him a large armed retinue, and took a circuitous route, which made him, I believe, somewhat later than his appointed hour. When the lapse of time showed me that he had taken another track, I pursued him to the chapel; and I would have awaited the close of the ceremony, if I had thought that either yourself or your daughter would have felt desirous that she should have been the bride of an outlaw."

"Who said, sir," cried the baron, "that we were desirous of any such thing? But truly, sir, if I had a mind to the devil for a son-in-law, I would fain see the man that should venture to interfere."

"That would I," said the friar, "for I have undertaken to make her renounce the devil."

"She shall not renounce the devil," said the baron, "unless I please. You are very ready with your undertakings. Will you undertake to make her renounce the earl, who, I believe, is the devil incarnate? Will you undertake that?"

"Will I undertake," said the friar, "to make Trent run westward, or to make flame burn downward, or to make a tree grow with its head in the earth and its root in the air?"

"So then," said the baron, "a girl's mind is as hard to change as nature and the elements, and it is easier to make her renounce the devil than a lover. Are you a match for the devil, and no match for a man?"

"My warfare," said the friar, "is not of this world. I

am militant not against man, but the devil, who goes about seeking what he may devour."

"Oh! does he so?" said the baron: "then I take it that makes you look for him so often in my buttery. Will you cast out the devil whose name is Legion, when you cannot cast out the imp whose name is Love?"

"Marriages," said the friar, "are made in heaven. Love is God's work, and therewith I meddle not."

"God's work, indeed!" said the baron, "when the ceremony was cut short in the church. Could men have put them asunder, if God had joined them together? And the earl is now no earl, but plain Robert Fitz-Ooth: therefore, I'll none of him."

"He may atone," said the friar, "and the king may mollify. The earl is a worthy peer, and the king is a courteous king."

"He cannot atone," said Sir Ralph. "He has killed the king's men; and if the baron should aid and abet, he will lose his castle and land."

"Will I?" said the baron; "not while I have a drop of blood in my veins. He that comes to take them shall first serve me as the friar serves my flasks of canary: he shall drain me dry as hay. Am I not disparaged? Am I not outraged? Is not my daughter vilified, and made a mockery? A girl half-married? There was my butler brought home with a broken head. My butler, friar: there is that may move your sympathy. Friar, the earl-no-earl shall come no more to my daughter."

"Very good," said the friar.

"It is not very good," said the baron, "for I cannot get her to say so."

"I fear," said Sir Ralph, "the young lady must be much distressed and discomposed."

"Not a whit, sir," said the baron. "She is, as usual, in a most provoking imperturbability, and contradicts me so smilingly that it would enrage you to see her."

"I had hoped," said Sir Ralph, "that I might have seen her, to make my excuse in person for the hard necessity of my duty."

He had scarcely spoken, when the door opened, and the lady made her appearance.

CHAPTER IV

Are you mad, or what are you, that you squeak out
your catches without mitigation or remorse of voice?

Twelfth Night.[1]

MATILDA, not dreaming of visitors, tripped into the
apartment in a dress of forest-green, with a small
quiver by her side, and a bow and arrow in her hand.
Her hair, black and glossy as the raven's wing, curled
like wandering clusters of dark ripe grapes under the
edge of her round bonnet; and a plume of black
feathers fell back negligently above it, with an almost
horizontal inclination, that seemed the habitual effect of rapid motion against the wind. Her black eyes
sparkled like sunbeams on a river: a clear, deep, liquid
radiance, the reflection of ethereal fire, tempered not
subdued in the medium of its living and gentle mir-

---

1. [Act II, Scene 3: "My masters, are you mad? Or what are you?
Have you no wit, manners, nor honesty, but to gabble like tinkers
at this time of night? Do ye make an alehouse of my lady's house,
that ye squeak out your coziers' catches without any mitigation or
remorse of voice?"]

ror. Her lips were half-opened to speak as she entered the apartment, and with a smile of recognition to the friar, and a courtesy to the stranger knight, she approached the baron and said: "You are late at your breakfast, father."

"I am not at breakfast," said the baron. "I have been at supper: my last night's supper; for I had none."

"I am sorry," said Matilda, "you should have gone to bed supperless."

"I did not go to bed supperless," said the baron: "I did not go to bed at all: and what are you doing with that green dress and that bow and arrow?"

"I am going a-hunting," said Matilda.

"A-hunting!" said the baron. "What, I warrant you, to meet with the earl, and slip your neck into the same noose?"

"No," said Matilda: "I am not going out of our own woods to-day."

"How do I know that?" said the baron. "What surety have I of that?"

"Here is the friar," said Matilda. "He will be surety."

"Not he," said the baron: "he will undertake nothing but where the devil is a party concerned."

"Yes, I will," said the friar: "I will undertake any thing for the lady Matilda."

"No matter for that," said the baron: "she shall not go hunting to-day."

"Why, father," said Matilda, "if you coop me up here in this odious castle, I shall pine and die like a lonely swan on a pool."

"No," said the baron, "the lonely swan does not

die on the pool. If there be a river at hand, she flies to the river, and finds her a mate, and so shall not you."

"But," said Matilda, "you may send with me any, or as many, of your grooms as you will."

"My grooms," said the baron, "are all false knaves. There is not a rascal among them but loves you better than me. Villains that I feed and clothe."

"Surely," said Matilda, "it is not villainy to love me: if it be, I should be sorry my father were an honest man." The baron relaxed his muscles into a smile. "Or my lover either," added Matilda. The baron looked grim again.

"For your lover," said the baron, "you may give God thanks of him. He is as arrant a knave as ever poached."

"What, for hunting the king's deer?" said Matilda. "Have I not heard you rail at the forest-laws by the hour?"

"Did you ever hear me," said the baron, "rail myself out of house and land? If I had done that, then were I a knave."

"My lover," said Matilda, "is a brave man, and a true man, and a generous man, and a young man, and a handsome man; aye, and an honest man too."

"How can he be an honest man," said the baron, "when he has neither house nor land, which are the better part of a man?"

"They are but the husk of a man," said Matilda, "the worthless coat of the chesnut: the man himself is the kernel."

"The man is the grape-stone," said the baron, "and the pulp of the melon. The house and land are the true substantial fruit, and all that give him savour and value."

"He will never want house or land," said Matilda, "while the meeting boughs weave a green roof in the wood, and the free range of the hart marks out the bounds of the forest."

"Vert and venison! vert and venison!"[2] exclaimed the baron. "Treason and flat rebellion. Confound your smiling face! what makes you look so good-humoured? What! you think I can't look at you, and be in a passion? You think so, do you? We shall see. Have you no fear in talking thus, when here is the king's liegeman come to take us all into custody, and confiscate our goods and chattels?"

"Nay, Lord Fitzwater," said Sir Ralph, "you wrong me in your report. My visit is one of courtesy and excuse, not of menace and authority."

"There it is," said the baron: "every one takes a pleasure in contradicting me. Here is this courteous knight, who has not opened his mouth three times since he has been in my house, except to take in provision, cuts me short in my story with a flat denial."

"Oh! I cry you mercy, sir knight," said Matilda; "I did not mark you before. I am your debtor for no slight favour, and so is my liege lord."

"Her liege lord!" exclaimed the baron, taking large strides across the chamber.

"Pardon me, gentle lady," said Sir Ralph. "Had I known you before yesterday, I would have cut off my right hand ere it should have been raised to do you displeasure."

"Oh sir," said Matilda, "a good man may be forced on an ill office: but I can distinguish the man from his

____

2. [A reference to the two central concerns of medieval forest law: the protection of the forest (*vert*) and its game (*venison*).]

duty." She presented to him her hand, which he kissed respectfully, and simultaneously with the contact, thirty-two invisible arrows plunged at once into his heart, one from every point of the compass of his pericardia.

"Well, father," added Matilda, "I must go to the woods."

"Must you?" said the baron; "I say you must not."

"But I am going," said Matilda.

"But I will have up the drawbridge," said the baron.

"But I will swim the moat," said Matilda.

"But I will secure the gates," said the baron.

"But I will leap from the battlement," said Matilda.

"But I will lock you in an upper chamber," said the baron.

"But I will shred the tapestry," said Matilda, "and let myself down."

"But I will lock you in a turret," said the baron, "where you shall only see light through a loophole."

"But through that loophole," said Matilda, "will I take my flight, like a young eagle from its aery; and, father, while I go out freely, I will return willingly: but if once I slip out through a loop-hole——-" She paused a moment, and then added, singing:

The love that follows fain
    Will never its faith betray:
But the faith that is held in a chain
Will never be found again,
    If a single link give way.

The melody acted irresistibly on the harmonious

propensities of the friar, who accordingly sang in his turn:

> For hark! hark! hark!
> The dog doth bark,
>   That watches the wild deer's lair.
> The hunter awakes at the peep of the dawn,
> But the lair it is empty, the deer it is gone,
>   And the hunter knows not where.

Matilda and the friar then sang together:

Then follow, oh follow! the hounds do cry:
The red sun flames in the eastern sky:
    The stag bounds over the hollow.
He that lingers in spirit, or loiters in hall,
Shall see us no more till the evening fall,
And no voice but the echo shall answer his call:
    Then follow, oh follow, follow:
    Follow, oh follow, follow!

During the process of this harmony, the baron's eyes wandered from his daughter to the friar, and from the friar to his daughter again, with an alternate expression of anger differently modified: when he looked on the friar, it was anger without qualification; when he looked on his daughter, it was still anger, but tempered by an expression of involuntary admiration and pleasure. These rapid fluctuations of the baron's physiognomy—the habitual, reckless, resolute merriment in the jovial face of the friar,—and the cheerful, elastic spirits that played on the lips and sparkled in the eyes of Matilda,—would have presented a very amusing combination to Sir Ralph, if one of the three images in the group had not ab-sorbed his total attention with feelings of intense de-light very nearly allied to pain. The baron's wrath was somewhat counteracted by the reflection that his daughter's good spirits seemed to show that they would naturally rise triumphant over all disappoint-ments, and he had had sufficient experience of her humour, to know that she might sometimes be led but never could be driven. Then, too, he was always delighted to hear her sing, though he was not at all pleased in this instance with the subject of her song. Still he would have endured the subject for the sake of the melody of the treble, but his mind was not suf-ficiently attuned to unison to relish the harmony of the bass. The friar's accompaniment put him out of all patience, and "So," he exclaimed, "this is the way you teach my daughter to renounce the devil, is it? A hunting friar, truly! Who ever heard before of a hunting friar? A profane, roaring, bawling, bumper-bibbing, neck-breaking, catch-singing friar?"

"Under favour, bold baron," said the friar—but the friar was warm with canary, and in his singing vein; and he could not go on in plain unmusical prose. He therefore sang in a new tune:

Though I be now a grey, grey friar,
   Yet I was once a hale young knight:
The cry of my dogs was the only choir
   In which my spirit did take delight.

Little I recked of matin bell,
   But drowned its toll with my clanging horn:
And the only beads I loved to tell
   Were the beads of dew on the spangled thorn.

The baron was going to storm, but the friar paused, and Matilda sang in repetition:

Little I reck of matin bell,
　But drown its toll with my clanging horn:
And the only beads I love to tell
　Are the beads of dew on the spangled thorn.

And then she and the friar sang the four lines together, and rang the changes upon them alternately.

Little I reck of matin bell:

sang the friar.

"A precious friar," said the baron.

But drown its toll with my clanging horn:
sang Matilda.
"More shame for you," said the baron.

And the only beads I love to tell
　Are the beads of dew on the spangled
thorn:

sang Matilda and the friar together.
"Penitent and confessor," said the baron: "a hopeful pair truly."
The friar went on:

An archer keen I was withal,
　As ever did lean on greenwood tree;
And could make the fleetest roebuck fall,
　A good three hundred yards from me.

Though changeful time, with hand severe,
   Has made me now these joys forego,
Yet my heart bounds whene'er I hear
   Yoicks! hark away! and tally ho!

Matilda chimed in as before.

"Are you mad?" said the baron. "Are you insane? Are you possessed? What do you mean? What in the devil's name do you both mean?"

Yoicks! hark away! and tally ho!

roared the friar.

The baron's pent-up wrath had accumulated like the waters above the dam of an overshot mill. The pond-head of his passion being now filled to the utmost limit of its capacity, and beginning to overflow in the quivering of his lips and the flashing of his eyes, he pulled up all the flash-boards at once, and gave loose to the full torrent of his indignation, by seizing, like furious Ajax, not a massy stone more than two modern men could raise, but a vast dish of beef more than fifty ancient yeomen could eat, and whirled it like a coit,[3] *in terrorem*,[4] over the head of the friar, to the extremity of the apartment,

Where it on oaken floor did settle,

____

3. [Or "quoit". Refers to a ring-shaped object, similar to a metal or rope ring used in the game of quoits, a traditional British throwing game in which players tossed metal or rope rings at a target, similar to modern horseshoes.]
4. ["In terror" or "as a warning". In law, it is used to describe actions intended to intimidate or deter, such as an "in terrorem clause" in a will, meant to discourage legal disputes.]

With mighty din of ponderous metal.

"Nay father," said Matilda, taking the baron's hand, "do not harm the friar: he means not to offend you. My gaiety never before displeased you. Least of all should it do so now, when I have need of all my spirits to outweigh the severity of my fortune."

As she spoke the last words, tears started into her eyes, which, as if ashamed of the involuntary betraying of her feelings, she turned away to conceal. The baron was subdued at once. He kissed his daughter, held out his hand to the friar, and said: "Sing on, in God's name, and crack away the flasks till your voice swims in canary." Then turning to Sir Ralph, he said: "You see how it is, sir knight. Matilda is my daughter; but she has me in leading-strings, that is the truth of it."

CHAPTER V

'Tis true, no lover has that power
To enforce a desperate amour
As he that has two strings to his bow
And burns for love and money too.

BUTLER.[1]

THE friar had often had experience of the baron's testy humour; but it had always before confined itself to words, in which the habit of testiness often mingled more expression of displeasure than the internal feeling prompted. He knew the baron to be hot and choleric, but at the same time hospitable and generous, passionately fond of his daughter, often thwarting her in seeming, but always yielding to her in fact. The early attachment between Matilda and the Earl of Huntingdon, had given the baron no serious reason to interfere with her habits and pursuits, which were so congenial to those of her lover; and not being over-burdened with orthodoxy, that is to say,

---

1. [*Hudibras*, Part III, Canto I.]

not being seasoned with more of the salt of the spirit than was necessary to preserve him from excommunication, confiscation, and philotheoparoptesism,[2] he was not sorry to encourage his daughter's choice of her confessor in Brother Michael, who had more jollity and less hypocrisy than any of his fraternity, and was very little anxious to disguise his love of the good things of this world under the semblance of a sanctified exterior. The friar and Matilda had often sung duets together, and had been accustomed to the baron's chiming in with a stormy *capriccio*,[3] which was usually charmed into silence by some sudden turn in the witching melodies of Matilda. They had therefore naturally calculated, as far as their wild spirits calculated at all, on the same effects from the same causes. But the circumstances of the preceding day had made an essential alteration in the case. The baron knew well, from the intelligence he had received, that the earl's offence was past remission: which would have been of less moment but for the awful fact of his castle being in the possession of the king's forces, and in those days possession was considerably more than eleven points of the law. The baron was therefore convinced that the earl's outlawry was infallible, and that Matilda must either renounce her lover or become with him an outlaw and a fugitive. In proportion, therefore, to the baron's knowledge of the strength and duration of her attachment, was his fear of the difficulty of its ever

------

2. Roasting by a slow fire for the love of god.
3. [In music, a capriccio (from the Italian, meaning "whim" or "fancy") refers to a lively, unpredictable and often improvisatory composition.]

being overcome: her love of the forest and the chase, which he had never before discouraged, now presented itself to him as matter of serious alarm; and if her cheerfulness gave him hope on the one hand by indicating a spirit superior to all disappointments, it was suspicious to him on the other as arising from some latent certainty of being soon re-united to the earl. All these circumstances concurred to render their songs of the vanished deer, and greenwood archery, and Yoicks and Harkaway, extremely *mal-a-propos*, and to make his anger boil and bubble in the cauldron of his spirit, till its more than ordinary excitement burst forth with sudden impulse into active manifestation.

> But as it sometimes happens, from the might
>   Of *rage* in minds that can no farther go,
> As high as they have mounted in *despite*
>   In their *remission* do they sink as low,
> To *our bold baron* did it happen so.[4]

For his discobolic exploit proved the climax of his rage, and was succeeded by an immediate sense that he had passed the bounds of legitimate passion; and he sunk immediately from the very pinnacle of opposition to the level of implicit acquiescence. The friar's spirits were not to be marred by such a little incident.

---

4. Of these lines all that is not in italics belongs to Mr. Wordsworth: *Resolution and Independence*. [The original lines read:
  But, as it sometimes chanceth, from the might
  Of joys in minds that can no further go,
  As high as we have mounted in delight
  In our dejection do we sink as low;
  To me that morning did it happen so;]

He was half-inclined, at first, to return the baron's compliment; but his love of Matilda checked him; and when the baron held out his hand, the friar seized it cordially, and they drowned all recollection of the affair by pledging each other in a cup of canary.

The friar, having stayed long enough to see every thing replaced on a friendly footing, rose, and moved to take his leave. Matilda told him, he must come again on the morrow, for she had a very long confession to make to him. This the friar promised to do, and departed with the knight.

Sir Ralph, on reaching the abbey, drew his followers together, and led them to Locksley Castle, which he found in the possession of his lieutenant; whom he again left there with a sufficient force to hold it in safe keeping in the king's name; and proceeded to London to report the results of his enterprise.

Now Henry our royal king was very wroth at the earl's evasion, and swore by Saint Thomas-a-Becket (whom he had himself translated into a saint by having him knocked on the head), that he would give the castle and lands of Locksley to the man who should bring in the earl. Hereupon ensued a process of thought in the mind of the knight. The eyes of the fair huntress of Arlingford had left a wound in his heart which only she who gave could heal. He had seen, that the baron was no longer very partial to the outlawed earl, but that he still retained his old affection for the lands and castle of Locksley. Now the lands and castle were very fair things in themselves, and would be pretty appurtenances to an adventurous knight; but they would be doubly valuable as certain passports to the father's favour, which was one step towards that of the daughter, or at least towards obtaining possession of her either quietly or perforce: for the knight was not so nice in his love as to consider the lady's free grace a *sine qua non*: and to think of being, by any means whatever, the lord of Locksley and Arlingford, and the husband of the bewitching Matilda, was to cut in the shades of futurity a vista very tempting to a soldier of fortune. He set out in high spirits with a chosen band of followers, and beat up all the country far and wide around both the Ouse and the Trent, but fortune did not seem disposed to second his diligence, for no vestige whatever could he trace of the earl. His followers, who were only paid with the wages of hope, began to murmur and fall off; for, as those unenlightened days were ignorant of the happy invention of paper machinery, by which one promise to pay is satisfactorily paid with another promise to pay, and that again with another in infinite series, they would not, as their wiser posterity has done, take those tenders for true pay which were not sterling; so that, one fine morning, the knight found himself sitting on a pleasant bank of the Trent, with only a solitary squire, who still clung to the shadow of preferment, because he did not see at the moment any better chance of the substance.

The knight did not despair because of the desertion of his followers: he was well aware that he could easily raise recruits if he could once find trace of his game; he therefore rode about indefatigably over hill and dale, to the great sharpening of his own appetite and that of his squire, living gallantly from inn to inn when his purse was full, and quartering himself in the king's name on the nearest ghostly brotherhood when it happened to be empty. An autumn and a winter had passed away, when the course of his per-lustrations brought him one evening into a beautiful sylvan valley, where he found a number of young women, weaving garlands of flowers, and singing over their pleasant occupation. He approached them, and courteously inquired the way to the nearest town.

"There is no town within several miles," was the answer.

"A village, then, if it be but large enough to furnish an inn?"

"There is Gamwell just by, but there is no inn nearer than the nearest town."

"An abbey, then?"

"There is no abbey nearer than the nearest inn."

"A house, then, or a cottage, where I may obtain hospitality for the night?"

"Hospitality!" said one of the young women; "you have not far to seek for that. Do you not know that you are in the neighbourhood of Gamwell-Hall?"

"So far from it," said the knight, "that I never heard the name of Gamwell-Hall before."

"Never heard of Gamwell-Hall?" exclaimed all the young women together, who could as soon have dreamed of his never having heard of the sky.

"Indeed, no," said Sir Ralph; "but I shall be very happy to get rid of my ignorance."

"And so shall I," said his squire; "for it seems that in this case knowledge will for once be a cure for hunger, wherewith I am grievously afflicted."

"And why are you so busy, my pretty damsels, weaving these garlands?" said the knight.

"Why, do you not know, sir," said one of the young women, "that to-morrow is Gamwell feast?"

The knight was again obliged, with all humility, to confess his ignorance.

"Oh! sir," said his informant, "then you will have something to see, that I can tell you: for we shall choose a Queen of the May, and we shall crown her with flowers, and place her in a chariot of flowers, and draw it with lines of flowers, and we shall hang all the trees with flowers, and we shall strew all the ground with flowers, and we shall dance with flowers, and in flowers, and on flowers, and we shall be all flowers."

"That you will," said the knight, "and the sweetest and brightest of all the flowers of the May, my pretty damsels." On which all the pretty damsels smiled at him and each other.

"And there will be all sorts of May-games, and there will be prizes for archery, and there will be the knight's ale, and the foresters' venison, and there will be Kit Scrapesqueak with his fiddle, and little Tom Whistlerap with his fife and tabor, and Sam Trumtwang with his harp, and Peter Muggledrone with his bagpipe, and how I shall dance with Will Whitethorn!" added the girl, clapping her hands as she spoke, and bounding from the ground with the pleasure of the anticipation.

A tall athletic young man approached, to whom the rustic maidens courtesied with great respect; and one of them informed Sir Ralph that it was young Master William Gamwell. The young gentleman invited and conducted the knight to the hall, where he introduced him to the old knight his father, and to the old lady his mother, and to the young lady his sister, and to a number of bold yeomen, who were laying siege to beef, brawn, and plum pie around a ponderous table, and taking copious draughts of old October.[5] A motto was inscribed over the interior door,—

Eat, Drink, and Be Merry:

an injunction which Sir Ralph and his squire showed remarkable alacrity in obeying. Old Sir Guy of Gamwell gave Sir Ralph a very cordial welcome, and entertained him during supper with several of his best stories, enforced with an occasional slap on the back, and pointed with a peg in the ribs; a species of vivacious eloquence in which the old gentleman excelled; and which is supposed by many of that pleasant variety of the human species, known by the name of choice fellows and comical dogs, to be the genuine tangible shape of the cream of a good joke.

---

5. [Old October refers to a type of ale brewed in October, which was considered an ideal time for brewing because of the cooler weather and favourable conditions for fermentation. This ale would be stored and aged over the winter months, developing a richer flavour and higher alcohol content. Such ale was often prized for its depth of taste and warming qualities, making it especially popular during the colder seasons. Old October ale would have been seen as a symbol of tradition and robust English life, commonly associated with rural settings and festivities.]

CHAPTER VI

What! shall we have incision? shall we embrew?

Henry IV.[1]

OLD Sir Guy of Gamwell, and young William Gamwell, and fair Alice Gamwell, and Sir Ralph Montfaucon and his squire, rode together the next morning to the scene of the feast. They arrived on a village-green, surrounded with cottages peeping from among the trees by which the green was completely encircled. The whole circle was hung round with one continuous garland of flowers, depending in irregular festoons from the branches. In the centre of the green was a may-pole hidden in boughs and garlands; and a multitude of round-faced bumpkins and cherry-cheeked lasses were dancing around it, to the quadruple melody of Scrapesqueak, Whistlerap, Trumtwang, and Muggledrone; harmony we must

---

1. [Part II, Act II, Scene 4:
   "What! shall we have incision? Shall we imbrue?
   Then death rock me asleep, abridge my doleful days!"]

not call it: for though they had agreed to a partner-ship in point of tune, each, like a true painstaking man, seemed determined to have his time to himself: Muggledrone played *allegretto*, Trumtwang *allegro*, Whistlerap *presto*, and Scrapesqueak *prestissimo*. There was a kind of mathematical proportion in their discrepancy: while Muggledrone played the tune four times, Trumtwang played it five, Whistlerap six, and Scrapesqueak eight; for the latter completely dis-tanced all his competitors, and indeed worked his elbow so nimbly, that its outline was scarcely distin-guishable through the mistiness of its rapid vibration.

While the knight was delighting his eyes and ears with these pleasant sights and sounds, all eyes were turned in one direction, and Sir Ralph, looking round, saw a fair lady in green and gold come riding through the trees, accompanied by a portly friar in grey, and several fair damsels and gallant grooms. On their nearer approach, he recognised the lady Matilda and her ghostly adviser Brother Michael. A party of foresters arrived from another direction, and then en-sued cordial interchanges of greeting, and collisions of hands and lips, among the Gamwells and the new-comers. "How does my fair coz, Mawd?" and "How does my sweet coz, Mawd?" and "How does my wild coz, Mawd?" And "Eh! jolly friar, your hand, old boy:" and "Here, honest friar:" and "To me, merry friar:" and "By your favour, mistress Alice:" and "Hey! cousin Robin:" and "Hey! cousin Will:" and "Od's life! merry Sir Guy, you grow younger every year," as the old knight shook them all in turn with one hand, and slapped them on the back with the other, in token of his affection. A number of young men and women advanced, some drawing, and others dancing round, a floral car; and having placed a crown of flowers on Matilda's head, they saluted her Queen of the May, and drew her to the place appointed for the rural sports.

A hogshead of ale was abroach under an oak, and a fire was blazing in an open space before the trees, to roast the fat deer which the foresters brought. The sports commenced: and after an agreeable series of bowling, coiting, pitching, hurling, racing, leaping, grinning, wrestling or friendly dislocation of joints, and cudgel-playing or amicable cracking of skulls, the trial of archery ensued. The conqueror was to be rewarded with a golden arrow from the hand of the Queen of the May, who was to be his partner in the dance till the close of the feast. This stimulated the knight's emulation: young Gamwell supplied him with a bow and arrow, and he took his station among the foresters, but had the mortification to be out-shot by them all, and to see one of them lodge the point of his arrow in the golden ring of the centre, and receive the prize from the hand of the beautiful Matilda, who smiled on him with particular grace. The jealous knight scrutinized the successful champion with great attention, and surely thought he had seen that face before. In the mean time the forester led the lady to the station. The luckless Sir Ralph drank deep draughts of love from the matchless grace of her attitudes, as, taking the bow in her left hand, and adjusting the arrow with her right, advancing her left foot, and gently curving her beautiful figure with a slight motion of her head that waved her black feathers and her ringleted hair, she drew the arrow to its head, and loosed it from her open fingers. The arrow struck within the ring of gold, so close to that of the victorious forester that the points were in contact and the feathers were intermingled. Great acclamations succeeded, and the forester led Matilda to the dance. Sir Ralph gazed on her fascinating motions till the torments of baffled love and jealous rage became unendurable, and approaching young Gamwell, he asked him if he knew the name of that forester who was leading the dance with the Queen of the May?

"Robin, I believe," said young Gamwell carelessly, "I think they call him Robin."

"Is that all you know of him?" said Sir Ralph.

"What more should I know of him?" said young Gamwell.

"Then I can tell you," said Sir Ralph, "he is the outlawed Earl of Huntingdon, on whose head is set so large a price."

"Ay, is he?" said young Gamwell, in the same careless manner.

"He were a prize worth the taking," said Sir Ralph.

"No doubt," said young Gamwell.

"How think you?" said Sir Ralph, "are the foresters his adherents?"

"I cannot say," said young Gamwell.

"Is your peasantry loyal and well-disposed?" said Sir Ralph.

"Passing loyal," said young Gamwell.

"If I should call on them in the king's name," said Sir Ralph, "think you they would aid and assist?"

"Most likely they would," said young Gamwell, "one side or the other."

"Ay, but which side?" said the knight.

"That remains to be tried," said young Gamwell.

"I have King Henry's commission," said the

knight, "to apprehend this earl that was. How would you advise me to act, being, as you see, without attendant force?"

"I would advise you," said young Gamwell, "to take yourself off without delay, unless you would relish the taste of a volley of arrows, a shower of stones, and a hailstorm of cudgel-blows, which would not be turned aside by a God save King Henry."

Sir Ralph's squire no sooner heard this, and saw by the looks of the speaker that he was not likely to prove a false prophet, than he clapped spurs to his horse and galloped off with might and main. This gave the knight a good excuse to pursue him, which he did with great celerity, calling, "Stop, you rascal." When the squire fancied himself safe out of the reach of pursuit, he checked his speed, and allowed the knight to come up with him. They rode on several miles in silence, till they discovered the towers and spires of Nottingham, where the knight introduced himself to the sheriff, and demanded an armed force to assist in the apprehension of the outlawed Earl of Huntingdon. The sheriff, who was willing to have his share of the prize, determined to accompany the knight in person, and regaled him and his man with good store of the best: after which, they, with a stout retinue of fifty men, took the way to Gamwell feast.

"God's my life," said the sheriff, as they rode along, "I had as lief you would tell me of a service of plate. I much doubt if this outlawed earl, this forester Robin, be not the man they call Robin Hood, who has quartered himself in Sherwood Forest, and whom in endeavouring to apprehend I have fallen divers times into disasters. He has gotten together a band of disinherited prodigals, outlawed debtors, excommunicated heretics, elder sons that have spent all they had, and younger sons that never had any thing to spend; and with these he kills the king's deer, and plunders wealthy travellers of five sixths of their money; but if they be abbots or bishops, them he despoils utterly."

The sheriff then proceeded to relate to his companion the adventure of the abbot of Doubleflask (which some grave historians have related of the abbot of Saint Mary's, and others of the bishop of Hereford): how the abbot, returning to his abbey in company with his high selerer, who carried in his portmanteau the rents of the abbey-lands, and with a numerous train of attendants, came upon four seeming peasants, who were roasting the king's venison by the king's highway: how, in just indignation at this flagrant infringement of the forest laws, he asked them what they meant, and they answered that they meant to dine: how he ordered them to be seized and bound, and led captive to Nottingham, that they might know wild-flesh to have been destined by Providence for licensed and privileged appetites, and not for the base hunger of unqualified knaves: how they prayed for mercy, and how the abbot swore by Saint Charity that he would show them none: how one of them thereupon drew a bugle-horn from under his smock-frock and blew three blasts, on which the abbot and his train were instantly surrounded by sixty bowmen in green: how they tied him to a tree, and made him say mass for their sins: how they unbound him, and sate him down with them to dinner, and gave him venison and wild-fowl and wine, and made him pay for his fare all the money in his high selerer's portmanteau, and enforced him to sleep all night under a tree in his cloak, and to leave the cloak behind him in the morning: how the abbot, light in pocket and heavy in heart, raised the country upon Robin Hood, for so he had heard the chief forester called by his men, and hunted him into an old woman's cottage: how Robin changed dresses with the old woman, and how the abbot rode in great triumph to Nottingham, having in custody an old woman in a green doublet and breeches: how the old woman discovered herself, how the merrymen of Nottingham laughed at the abbot, how the abbot railed at the old woman, and how the old woman out-railed the abbot, telling him that Robin had given her food and fire through the winter, which no abbot would ever do, but would rather take it from her for what he called the good of the church, by which he meant his own laziness and gluttony, and that she knew a true man from a false thief, and a free forester from a greedy abbot.

"Thus you see," added the sheriff, "how this villain perverts the deluded people by making them believe that those who tithe and toll upon them for their spiritual and temporal benefit are not their best friends and fatherly guardians; for he holds that in giving to boors and old women what he takes from priests and peers, he does but restore to the former what the latter had taken from them; and this the impudent varlet calls distributive justice. Judge now if any loyal subject can be safe in such neighbourhood."

While the sheriff was thus enlightening his companion concerning the offenders, and whetting his own indignation against them, the sun was fast sinking to the west. They rode on till they came in view of a bridge, which they saw a party approaching from the opposite side, and the knight presently discovered that the party consisted of the lady Matilda and friar Michael, young Gamwell, cousin Robin, and about half-a-dozen foresters. The knight pointed out the earl to the sheriff, who exclaimed, "Here, then, we have him an easy prey;" and they rode on manfully towards the bridge, on which the other party made halt.

"Who be these," said the friar, "that come riding so fast this way? Now, as God shall judge me, it is that false knight Sir Ralph Montfaucon, and the sheriff of Nottingham, with a posse of men. We must make good our post, and let them dislodge us if they may."

The two parties were now near enough to parley; and the sheriff and the knight, advancing in the front of the cavalcade, called on the lady, the friar, young Gamwell, and the foresters, to deliver up that false traitor, Robert, formerly Earl of Huntingdon. Robert himself made answer by letting fly an arrow that struck the ground between the fore feet of the sheriff's horse. The horse reared up from the whizzing, and lodged the sheriff in the dust: and at the same time the fair Matilda favoured the knight with an arrow in his right arm, that compelled him to withdraw from the affray. His men lifted the sheriff carefully up, and replaced him on his horse, whom he immediately with great rage and zeal urged on to the assault with his fifty men at his heels, some of whom were intercepted in their advance by the arrows of the foresters and Matilda, while the friar, with an eight-foot staff, dislodged the sheriff a second time, and laid on him with all the vigour of the church militant on earth, in spite of his ejaculations of "Hey, friar Michael! What means this, honest friar? Hold, ghostly friar! Hold, holy friar!" till Matilda interposed, and delivered the battered sheriff to the care of the foresters. The friar continued flourishing his staff among the sheriff's men, knocking down one, breaking the ribs of another, dislocating the shoulder of a third, flattening the nose of a fourth, cracking the skull of a fifth, and pitching a sixth into the river,[2] till the few, who were lucky enough to escape with whole bones, clapped spurs to their horses and fled for their lives, under a farewell volley of arrows.

Sir Ralph's squire, meanwhile, was glad of the excuse of attending his master's wound to absent himself from the battle; and put the poor knight to a great deal of unnecessary pain by making as long a business as possible of extracting the arrow, which he had not accomplished when Matilda, approaching, extracted it with great facility, and bound up the wound with her scarf, saying, "I reclaim my arrow, sir knight, which struck where I aimed it, to admonish you to desist from your enterprise. I could as easily have lodged it in your heart."

"It did not need," said the knight, with rueful gallantry; "you have lodged one there already."

"If you mean to say that you love me," said Matilda, "it is more than I ever shall you: but if you will show your love by no further interfering with mine, you will at least merit my gratitude."

The knight made a wry face under the double pain of heart and body caused at the same moment by the material or martial, and the metaphorical or erotic arrow, of which the latter was thus barbed by a declaration more candid than flattering; but he did not choose to put in any such claim to the lady's grat-

---

2. Mimicking the style of Rabelais in *Gargantua and Pantagruel.*

itude as would bar all hopes of her love: he therefore remained silent; and the lady and her escort, leaving him and the sheriff to the care of the squire, rode on till they came in sight of Arlingford Castle, when they parted in several directions. The friar rode off alone, and after the foresters had lost sight of him they heard his voice through the twilight, singing:,

> A staff, a staff, of a young oak graff,
>   That is both stoure and stiff,
> Is all a good friar can needs desire
>   To shrive a proud sheriffe.
> And thou, fine fellowe, who hast tasted so
>   Of the forester's greenwood game,
> Wilt be in no haste thy time to waste
>   In seeking more taste of the same:
> Or this can I read thee, and riddle thee well,
> Thou hadst better by far be the devil in hell
>   Than the sheriff of Nottinghame.

CHAPTER VII

Now, master sheriff, what's your will with me?

Henry IV.[1]

Matilda had carried her point with the baron of
ranging at liberty whithersoever she would, under
her positive promise to return home; she was a sort of
prisoner on parole: she had obtained this indulgence
by means of an obsolete habit of always telling the
truth and keeping her word, which our enlightened
age has discarded with other barbarisms, but which
had the effect of giving her father so much confidence
in her, that he could not help considering her word a
better security than locks and bars.

The baron had been one of the last to hear of the
rumours of the new outlaws of Sherwood, as Matilda
had taken all possible precautions to keep those rumours from his knowledge, fearing that they might
cause the interruption of her greenwood liberty; and
it was only during her absence at Gamwell feast, that

______

1.   [Part I, Act II, Scene IV.]

the butler, being thrown off his guard by liquor, forgot her injunctions, and regaled the baron with a long story of the right merry adventure of Robin Hood and the abbot of Doubleflask.

The baron was one morning, as usual, cutting his way valorously through a rampart of cold provision, when his ears were suddenly assailed by a tremendous alarum, and sallying forth, and looking from his castle wall, he perceived a large party of armed men on the other side of the moat, who were calling on the warder, in the king's name, to lower the drawbridge and raise the portcullis, which had both been secured by Matilda's order. The baron walked along the battlement till he came opposite to these unexpected visitors, who, as soon as they saw him, called out, "Lower the drawbridge, in the king's name."

"For what, in the devil's name?" said the baron.

"The sheriff of Nottingham," said one, "lies in bed grievously bruised: and many of his men are wounded, and several of them slain: and Sir Ralph Montfaucon knight is sore wounded in the arm: and we are charged to apprehend William Gamwell the younger, of Gamwell-Hall, and Father Michael of Rubygill Abbey, and Matilda Fitzwater of Arlingford Castle, as agents and accomplices in the said breach of the king's peace."

"Breach of the king's fiddle-stick!" answered the baron. "What do you mean by coming here with your cock and bull stories of my daughter grievously bruising the sheriff of Nottingham? You are a set of vagabond rascals in disguise: and I hear, by the bye, there is a gang of thieves that has just set up business in Sherwood Forest: a pretty presence, indeed, to get into my castle with force and arms, and make a famine in my buttery, and a drought in my cellar, and a void in my strong box, and a vacuum in my silver scullery."

"Lord Fitzwater," cried one, "take heed how you resist lawful authority: we will prove ourselves——-"

"You will prove yourselves arrant knaves, I doubt not," answered the baron; "but, villains, you shall be more grievously bruised by me than ever was the sheriff by my daughter, (a pretty tale truly!) if you do not forthwith avoid my territory."

By this time the baron's men had flocked to the battlements, with long-bows and cross-bows, slings and stones, and Matilda with her bow and quiver at their head. The assailants, finding the castle so well defended, deemed it expedient to withdraw till they could return in greater force, and rode off to Rubygill Abbey, where they made known their errand to the father abbot, who having satisfied himself of their legitimacy, and conned over the allegations, said that doubtless Brother Michael had heinously offended, but it was not for the civil law to take cognizance of the misdoings of a holy friar: that he would summon a chapter of monks, and pass on the offender a sentence proportionate to his offence. The ministers of civil justice said that would not do. The abbot said it would do and should; and bade them not provoke the meekness of his Catholic charity to lay them under the curse of Rome. This threat had its effect, and the party rode off to Gamwell-Hall, where they found the Gamwells and their men just sitting down to dinner, which they saved them the trouble of eating by consuming it in the king's name themselves, having first seized and bound young Gamwell; all which they accomplished by dint of superior numbers, in despite of a most vigorous stand made by the Gamwellites in defence of their young master and their provisions.

The baron, meanwhile, after the ministers of justice had departed, interrogated Matilda concerning the alleged fact of the grievous bruising of the sheriff of Nottingham. Matilda told him the whole history of Gamwell feast, and of their battle on the bridge, which had its origin in a design of the sheriff of Nottingham to take one of the foresters into custody.

"Ay! ay!" said the baron, "and I guess who that forester was: but truly this friar is a desperate fellow. I did not think there could have been so much valour under a grey frock. And so you wounded the knight in the arm. You are a wild girl, Mawd: a chip of the old block, Mawd. A wild girl, and a wild friar, and three or four foresters, wild lads all, to keep a bridge against a tame knight, and a tame sheriff and fifty tame varlets: by this light, the like was never heard: but do you know, Mawd, you must not go about so any more, sweet Mawd: you must stay at home: you must ensconce: for there is your tame sheriff on the one hand, that will take you per force; and there is your wild forester on the other hand, that will take you without any force at all, Mawd: your wild forester, Robin, cousin Robin, Robin Hood of Sherwood Forest, that beats and binds bishops, spreads nets for archbishops, and hunts a fat abbot as if he were a buck: excellent game, no doubt: but you must hunt no more in such company. I see it now: truly I might have guessed before that the bold outlaw Robin, the most courteous Robin, the new thief of Sherwood Forest, was your lover, the earl that has been: I might have guessed it before, and what led you so much to the woods; but you hunt no more in such company. No more May games and Gamwell feasts. My lands and castle would be the forfeit of a few more such pranks: and I think they are as well in my hands as the king's, quite as well."

"You know, father," said Matilda, "the condition of keeping me at home: I get out if I can, and not on parole."

"Ay! ay!" said the baron, "if you can: very true: watch and ward, Mawd, watch and ward is my word: if you can is yours. The mark is set, and so start fair."

The baron would have gone on in this way for an hour: but the friar made his appearance with a long oak staff in his hand, singing,

> Drink, and sing, and eat, and laugh,
>   And so go forth to battle:
> For the top of a skull and the end of a staff
>   Do make a ghostly rattle.

"Ho! ho! friar!" said the baron, "singing friar, laughing friar, roaring friar, fighting friar, hacking friar, thwacking friar, cracking, cracking, cracking friar, joke-cracking, bottle-cracking, skull-cracking friar!"

"And ho! ho!" said the friar, "bold baron, old baron, sturdy baron, wordy baron, long baron, strong baron, mighty baron, flighty baron, mazed baron, crazed baron, hacked baron, thwacked baron, cracked, cracked, cracked baron, bone-cracked, sconce-cracked, brain-cracked baron!"

"What do you mean," said the baron, "bully friar, by calling me hacked and thwacked?"

"Were you not in the wars?" said the friar, "where he who escapes unhacked does more credit to his heels than his arms? I pay tribute to your valour in calling you hacked and thwacked."

"I never was thwacked in my life," said the baron; "I stood my ground manfully, and covered my body with my sword. If I had had the luck to meet with a fighting friar indeed, I might have been thwacked, and soundly too: but I hold myself a match for any two laymen: it takes nine fighting laymen to make a fighting friar."

"Whence come you now, holy father?" asked Matilda.

"From Rubygill Abbey," said the friar, "whither I never return:

For I must seek some hermit cell,
Where I alone my beads may tell,
And on the wight who that way fares
Levy a toll for my ghostly pray'rs,
  Levy a toll, levy a toll,
  Levy a toll for my ghostly pray'rs."

"What is the matter then, father?" said Matilda.

"This is the matter," said the friar: "my holy brethren have held a chapter on me, and sentenced me to seven years' privation of wine. I therefore deemed it fitting to take my departure, which they would fain have prohibited. I was enforced to clear the way with my staff; I have grievously beaten my dearly beloved brethren: I grieve thereat: but they enforced me thereto. I have beaten them much; I mowed them down to the right and to the left, and left them like an ill-reaped field of wheat, ear and straw, pointing all ways, scattered in singleness and jumbled in masses; and so bade them farewell, saying,

Peace be with you. But I must not tarry, lest danger be in my rear: therefore, farewell, sweet Matilda; and farewell, noble baron; and farewell, sweet Matilda again; the alpha and omega of Father Michael, the first and the last."

"Farewell, father," said the baron, a little softened, "and God send you be never assailed by more than fifty men at a time."

"Amen," said the friar, "to that good wish."

"And we shall meet again, father, I trust," said Matilda.

"When the storm is blown over," said the baron.

"Doubt it not," said the friar, "though flooded Trent were between us, and fifty devils guarded the bridge."

He kissed Matilda's forehead, and walked away without a song.

CHAPTER VIII

Let gallows gape for dog: let man go free.

Henry V.[1]

A PAGE had been brought up in Gamwell-Hall, who while he was little had been called Little John, and continued to be so called after he had grown to be a foot taller than any other man in the house. He was full seven feet high. His latitude was worthy of his longitude, and his strength was worthy of both: and though an honest man by profession, he had practised archery on the king's deer for the benefit of his master's household and for the improvement of his own eye and hand, till his aim had become infallible within the range of two miles.[2] He had fought man-

----

1. [Act III, Scene 6:
   "Let gallows gape for dog; let man go free
   And let not hemp his wind-pipe suffocate:
   But Exeter hath given the doom of death
   For pax of little price."]
2. [The English longbow, famously used during the Hundred Years' War (e.g., at Agincourt in 1415), had an effective combat

fully in defence of his young master, took his captivity exceedingly to heart, and fell into bitter grief and boundless rage when he heard that he had been tried in Nottingham and sentenced to die. Alice Gamwell, at Little John's request, wrote three letters of one tenour; and Little John, having attached them to three blunt arrows, saddled the fleetest steed in old Sir Guy of Gamwell's stables, mounted, and rode first to Arlingford Castle, where he shot one of the three arrows over the battlements, then to Rubygill Abbey, where he shot the second into the abbey-garden, then back past Gamwell-Hall to the borders of Sherwood Forest, where he shot the third into the wood. Now the first of these arrows lighted in the nape of the neck of Lord Fitzwater, and lodged itself firmly between his skin and his collar; the second rebounded with the hollow vibration of a drumstick from the

---

range of about 150 to 200 yards (137–183 metres). Skilled archers could deliver a deadly volley within this range, but precise aiming at individual targets was limited to closer distances. The maximum range of a longbow, with a skilled archer using a heavy war bow (draw weights often exceeding 100 pounds), was around 300–400 yards (275–365 metres), although the accuracy was negligible. The Ottomans were renowned for their expertise in "flight archery"—a form of archery focused on achieving maximum distance. In the 16th and 17th centuries, Turkish archers using composite bows set astonishing records. Mahmoud Effendi reportedly shot an arrow a remarkable distance of 482 yards (441 metres) in 1670. This feat was achieved using a highly specialised Turkish composite bow designed for flight archery, along with light flight arrows crafted for maximum range. The greatest known historical distance was achieved by Sultan Selim III's archery master, Tozkoparan Iskender, who reportedly shot an arrow over 972 yards (889 metres) in 1798. In modern archery, with advanced materials and equipment, the farthest recorded arrow shot is by Matt Stutzman, who shot a distance of 310 yards (283 metres) with a compound bow in 2015.]

shaven sconce of the abbot of Rubygill; and the third pitched perpendicularly into the centre of a venison pasty in which Robin Hood was making incision.

Matilda ran up to her father in the court of Arlingford Castle, seized the arrow, drew off the letter, and concealed it in her bosom before the baron had time to look round, which he did with many expressions of rage against the impudent villain who had shot a blunt arrow into the nape of his neck.

"But you know, father," said Matilda, "a sharp arrow in the same place would have killed you; therefore the sending a blunt one was very considerate."

"Considerate, with a vengeance," said the baron. "Where was the consideration of sending it at all? This is some of your forester's pranks. He has missed you in the forest, since I have kept watch and ward over you, and by way of a love-token and a remembrance to you takes a random shot at me."

The abbot of Rubygill picked up the missile-missive or messenger arrow, which had rebounded from his shaven crown, with a very unghostly malediction on the sender, which he suddenly checked with a pious and consolatory reflection on the goodness of Providence in having blessed him with such a thickness of skull, to which he was now indebted for temporal preservation as he had before been for spiritual promotion. He opened the letter, which was addressed to Father Michael; and found it to contain an intimation that William Gamwell was to be hanged on Monday at Nottingham.

"And I wish," said the abbot, "Father Michael were to be hanged with him: an ungrateful monster, after I had rescued him from the fangs of civil justice, to reward my lenity by not leaving a bone unbruised among the holy brotherhood of Rubygill."

Robin Hood extracted from his venison pasty a similar intimation of the evil destiny of his cousin, whom he determined, if possible, to rescue from the jaws of Cerberus.

The sheriff of Nottingham, though still sore with his bruises, was so intent on revenge, that he raised himself from his bed to attend the execution of William Gamwell. He rode to the august structure of retributive Themis, as the French call a gallows, in all the pride and pomp of shrievalty, and with a splendid retinue of well-equipped knaves and varlets, as our ancestors called honest serving-men.

Young Gamwell was brought forth with his arms pinioned behind him; his sister Alice and his father, Sir Guy, attending him in disconsolate mood. He had rejected the confessor provided by the sheriff, and had insisted on the privilege of choosing his own, whom Little John had promised to bring. Little John, however, had not made his appearance when the fatal procession began its march; but when they reached the place of execution, Little John appeared, accompanied by a ghostly friar.

"Sheriff," said young Gamwell, "let me not die with my hands pinioned: give me a sword, and set any odds of your men against me, and let me die the death of a man, like the descendant of a noble house, which has never yet been stained with ignominy."

"No, no," said the sheriff; "I have had enough of setting odds against you. I have sworn you shall be hanged, and hanged you shall be."

"Then God have mercy on me," said young Gamwell, "and now, holy friar, shrive my sinful soul."

The friar approached.

"Let me see this friar," said the sheriff: "if he be the friar of the bridge, I had as lief have the devil in Nottingham; but he shall find me too much for him here."

"The friar of the bridge," said Little John, "as you very well know, sheriff, was father Michael of Rubygill Abbey, and you may easily see that this is not the man."

"I see it," said the sheriff; "and God be thanked for his absence."

Young Gamwell stood at the foot of the ladder. The friar approached him, opened his book, groaned, turned up the whites of his eyes, tossed up his arms in the air, and said, "*Dominus vobiscum.*"[3] He then crossed both his hands on his breast under the folds of his holy robes, and stood a few moments as if in inward prayer. A deep silence among the attendant crowd accompanied this action of the friar; interrupted only by the hollow tone of the death-bell, at long and dreary intervals. Suddenly, the friar threw off his holy robes, and appeared a forester clothed in green, with a sword in his right hand and a horn in his left. With the sword he cut the bonds of William Gamwell, who instantly snatched a sword from one of the sheriff's men, and with the horn he blew a loud blast, which was answered at once by four bugles from the quarters of the four winds, and from each quarter came five-and-twenty bowmen running all on a row.

---

3. ["The Lord be with you," to which is typically responded *Et cum spiritu tuo* ("And with your spirit"). There are parallels with the password *Pax vobiscum* ("Peace be with you") used in *Ivanhoe*.]

"Treason! treason!" cried the sheriff. Old Sir Guy sprang to his son's side, and so did Little John; and the four setting back to back, kept the sheriff and his men at bay till the bowmen came within shot and let fly their arrows among the sheriff's men, who, after a brief resistance, fled in all directions. The forester, who had personated the friar, sent an arrow after the flying sheriff, calling with a strong voice: "To the sheriff's left arm, as a keepsake from Robin Hood." The arrow reached its destiny: the sheriff redoubled his speed; and with the one arrow in his arm, did not stop to breathe till he was out of reach of another.

The foresters did not waste time in Nottingham, but were soon at a distance from its walls. Sir Guy returned with Alice to Gamwell-Hall; but thinking he should not be safe there, from the share he had had in his son's rescue, they only remained long enough to supply themselves with clothes and money, and departed, under the escort of Little John, to another seat of the Gamwells in Yorkshire. Young Gamwell, taking it for granted that his offence was past remission, determined on joining Robin Hood, and accompanied him to the forest, where it was deemed expedient that he should change his name, and he was rechristened without a priest, and with wine instead of water, by the immortal name of Scarlet.

CHAPTER IX

Who set my man i' the stocks?—
I set him there, Sir: but his own disorders
Deserved much less advancement.

Lear.[1]

THE baron was inflexible in his resolution not to let
Matilda leave the castle. The letter, which announced
to her the approaching fate of young Gamwell, filled
her with grief, and increased the irksomeness of a privation which already preyed sufficiently on her spirits, and began to undermine her health. She had no
longer the consolation of the society of her old friend
Father Michael: the little fat friar of Rubygill was substituted as the castle confessor; not without some
misgivings in his ghostly bosom: but he was more al-
lured by the sweet savour of the good things of this

---

1. [Act II, Scene 4:
   "*Lear.* O sides, you are too tough!
   Will you yet hold? How came my man i' th' stocks?
   Duke of Cornwall. I set him there, sir; but his own disorders
   Deserv'd much less advancement."]

world at Arlingford Castle, than deterred by his awe of the lady Matilda, which nevertheless was so excessive, from his recollection of the twang of the bow-string, that he never ventured to find her in the wrong, much less to enjoin any thing in the shape of penance, as was the occasional practice of holy confessors, with or without cause, for the sake of pious discipline, and what was in those days called social order, namely, the preservation of the privileges of the few, who happened to have any, at the expense of the swinish multitude, who happened to have none, except that of working and being shot at for the benefit of their betters: which is obviously not the meaning of social order in our more enlightened times: let us therefore be grateful to Providence, and sing *Te Deum laudamus* in chorus with the Holy Alliance.[2]

The little friar, however, though he found the lady spotless, found the butler a great sinner: at least so it was conjectured from the length of time he always took to confess him in the buttery.

Matilda became every day more pale and dejected: her spirit, which could have contended against any strenuous affliction, pined in the monotonous

---

2.   [*Te Deum laudamus* translates to "Thee, O God, we praise." It is the opening line of the Te Deum, an ancient Christian hymn of praise traditionally sung in thanksgiving or celebration. The hymn is part of the liturgical tradition of both the Catholic and Anglican Churches and is often used for solemn or festive occasions. The Holy Alliance refers to the 1815 treaty between Austria, Russia, and Prussia, aimed at preserving the conservative order in Europe after the Napoleonic Wars. The solemnity of singing the Te Deum contrasts with the political reality of the alliance, which was criticised for its repressive measures to maintain monarchical and religious authority.]

inaction to which she was condemned. While she could freely range the forest with her lover in the morning, she had been content to return to her father's castle in the evening, thus preserving underanged the balance of her duties, habits, and affections; not without a hope that the repeal of her lover's outlawry might be eventually obtained, by a judicious distribution of some of his forest-spoils among the holy fathers and saints-that-were-to-be, pious proficients in the ecclesiastic art equestrian, who rode the conscience of King Henry with double-curb bridles, and kept it well in hand, when it showed mettle and seemed inclined to rear and plunge. But the affair at Gamwell feast threw many additional difficulties in the way of the accomplishment of this hope; and very shortly afterwards King Henry the Second went to make up in the next world his quarrel with Thomas a Becket; and Richard Cœur de Lion made all England resound with preparations for the crusade; to the great delight of many zealous adventurers, who eagerly flocked under his banner in the hope of enriching themselves with Saracen spoil; which they called fighting the battles of God. Richard, who was not remarkably scrupulous in his financial operations, was not likely to overlook the lands and castle of Locksley, which he appropriated immediately to his own purposes, and sold to the highest bidder. Now, as the repeal of the outlawry would involve the restitution of the estates to the rightful owner, it was obvious that it could never be expected from that most legitimate and most Christian king, Richard the First of England, the arch-crusader and anti-jacobin by excellence, the very type, flower, cream, pink, symbol, and mirror of all the Holy Alliances that have ever existed on earth, excepting that he seasoned his superstition and love of conquest with a certain condiment of romantic generosity and chivalrous self-devotion, with which his imitators in all other points have found it convenient to dispense. To give freely to one man what he had taken forcibly from another, was generosity of which he was very capable; but to restore what he had taken to the man from whom he had taken it, was something that wore too much of the cool physiognomy of justice to be easily reconcilable to his kingly feelings. He had besides not only sent all King Henry's saints about their business, or rather about their no-business—their *fainéantise*[3]—but he had laid them under rigorous contribution for the purposes of his holy war, and having made them refund to the piety of the successor what they had extracted from the piety of the precursor, he compelled them, in addition, to give him their blessing for nothing. Matilda, therefore, from all these circumstances, felt little hope that her lover would be anything but an outlaw for life.

The departure of King Richard from England was succeeded by the episcopal regency of the bishops of Ely and Durham. Longchamp, bishop of Ely, proceeded to show his sense of Christian fellowship by arresting his brother bishop, and despoiling him of

---

3. [*Fainéantise* is derived from the French term "fainéant", meaning "do-nothing" or "idle", and translates to "laziness", "idleness", or "slothfulness" in English. Peacock may also be subtly referring to the historical use of the word "fainéant" to describe ineffectual monarchs, such as the "rois fainéants" (do-nothing kings) of early medieval France. These were the later Merovingian kings, who held nominal power while their mayors of the palace ruled in practice.]

his share in the government; and to set forth his humility and loving-kindness, in a retinue of nobles and knights who consumed in one night's entertainment some five years' revenue of their entertainer, and in a guard of fifteen hundred foreign soldiers whom he considered indispensable to the exercise of a vigour beyond the law in maintaining wholesome discipline over the refractory English. The ignorant impatience of the swinish multitude with these fruits of good living brought forth by one of the meek who had inherited the earth, displayed itself in a general ferment, of which Prince John took advantage to make the experiment of getting possession of his brother's crown in his absence. He began by calling at Reading a council of barons, whose aspect induced the holy bishop to disguise himself (some say as an old woman, which in the twelfth century perhaps might have been a disguise for a bishop), and make his escape beyond sea. Prince John followed up his advantage by obtaining possession of several strong posts, and among others of the castle of Nottingham.

While John was conducting his operations at Nottingham, he rode at times past the castle of Arlingford. He stopped on one occasion to claim Lord Fitzwater's hospitality, and made most princely havoc among his venison and brawn. Now it is a matter of record among divers great historians and learned clerks, that he was then and there grievously smitten by the charms of the lovely Matilda, and that a few days after he despatched his travelling minstrel, or laureate, Harpiton[4] (whom he retained at moderate wages to keep a journal of his proceedings and

---

4. Harp-it-on: or, a corruption of "Erpeton", a creeping thing.

prove them all just and legitimate), to the castle of Arlingford, to make proposals to the lady. This Harpiton was a very useful person. He was always ready, not only to maintain the cause of his master with his pen, and to sing his eulogies to his harp, but to undertake at a moment's notice any kind of courtly employment, called dirty work by the profane, which the blessings of civil government, namely his master's pleasure, and the interests of social order, namely his own emolument, might require. In short

> Il eût l'emploi qui certes n'est pas mince,
> Et qu'à la cour, où tout se peint en beau,
> On appelloit être l'ami du prince;
> Mais qu'à la ville, et surtout en province,
> Les gens grossiers ont nommé maquereau.[5]

Prince John was of opinion, that the love of a prince actual and king expectant, was in itself a sufficient honour to the daughter of a simple baron, and that the right divine of royalty would make it sufficiently holy without the rite divine of the church. He was, therefore, graciously pleased to fall into an exceeding passion when his confidential messenger returned from his embassy in piteous plight, having been, by the baron's order, first tossed in a blanket and set in the stocks to cool, and afterwards ducked

---

5. [Votaire. *La Pucelle d'Orléans* (*The Maid of Orleans*), Chant I:
    "He held a position which, to be sure, is not small,
    And which, at court, where everything is painted in a flattering light,
    We call being the prince's friend;
    But in the city, and especially in the provinces,
    The coarse folk have called it pimp."]

in the moat and set again in the stocks to dry. John swore to revenge horribly this flagrant outrage on royal prerogative, and to obtain possession of the lady by force of arms; and accordingly collected a body of troops, and marched upon Arlingford castle. A letter, conveyed as before on the point of a blunt arrow, announced his approach to Matilda: and Lord Fitzwater had just time to assemble his retainers, collect a hasty supply of provision, raise the draw-bridge, and drop the portcullis, when the castle was surrounded by the enemy. The little fat friar, who during the confusion was asleep in the buttery, found himself, on awaking, inclosed in the besieged castle, and dolefully bewailed his evil chance.

CHAPTER X

A noble girl, i' faith. Heart! I think I fight with a familiar, or the ghost of a fencer. Call you this an amorous visage? Here's blood that would have served me these seven years, in broken heads and cut fingers, and now it runs out all together.

MIDDLETON, Roaring Girl.[1]

PRINCE JOHN sate down impatiently before Arlingford castle in the hope of starving out the besieged; but finding the duration of their supplies extend itself in an equal ratio with the prolongation of his hope, he made vigorous preparations for carrying the place by storm. He constructed an immense machine on wheels, which, being advanced to the edge of the moat, would lower a temporary bridge, of which one end would rest on the bank and the other on the battlements, and which, being well furnished with stepping boards, would enable his men to ascend the inclined plane with speed and facility. Matilda re-

---

1. [Act III, Scene 1.]

ceived intimation of this design by the usual friendly channel of a blunt arrow, which must either have been sent from some secret friend in the prince's camp, or from some vigorous archer beyond it: the latter will not appear improbable, when we consider that Robin Hood and Little John could shoot two English miles and an inch point-blank,

Come scrive Turpino, che non erra.[2]

The machine was completed, and the ensuing morning fixed for the assault. Six men, relieved at intervals, kept watch over it during the night. Prince John retired to sleep, congratulating himself in the expectation that another day would place the fair culprit at his princely mercy. His anticipations mingled with the visions of his slumber, and he dreamed of wounds and drums, and sacking and firing the castle, and bearing off in his arms the beautiful prize through the midst of fire and smoke. In the height of this imaginary turmoil, he awoke, and conceived for a few moments that certain sounds which rang in his

---

2. ["As Turpin writes, who does not err." This refers to the legendary Archbishop Turpin, a fictional character who appears in medieval French and Italian literature, particularly in the *chansons de geste* (songs of heroic deeds) such as the *Matter of France*. Turpin is traditionally depicted as a warrior-bishop and a close companion of Charlemagne. The reference to Turpin likely points to the Pseudo-Turpin Chronicle (*Historia Caroli Magni et Rotholandi*), a medieval Latin text falsely attributed to Archbishop Turpin. This chronicle served as a source for many legendary tales about Charlemagne and his knights, especially Roland (or Orlando). In Renaissance Italian literature, such as Ariosto's *Orlando Furioso* or Boiardo's *Orlando Innamorato*, Turpin is humorously referenced as an "authoritative" source for fantastical tales, even though the stories are pure fiction.]

ears were the continuation of those of his dream, in that sort of half-consciousness between sleeping and waking, when reality and phantasy meet and mingle in dim and confused resemblance. He was, however, very soon fully awake to the fact of his guards calling on him to arm, which he did in haste, and beheld the machine in flames, and a furious conflict raging around it. He hurried to the spot, and found that his camp had been suddenly assailed from one side by a party of foresters, and that the baron's people had made a sortie on the other, and that they had killed the guards, and set fire to the machine, before the rest of the camp could come to the assistance of their fellows.

The night was in itself intensely dark, and the fire-light shed around it a vivid and unnatural radiance. On one side, the crimson light quivered by its own agitation on the waveless moat, and on the bastions and buttresses of the castle, and their shadows lay in massy blackness on the illuminated walls: on the other, it shone upon the woods, streaming far within among the open trunks, or resting on the closer foliage. The circumference of darkness bounded the scene on all sides: and in the centre raged the war; shields, helmets, and bucklers gleaming and glittering as they rang and clashed against each other; plumes confusedly tossing in the crimson light, and the massy light and shade that fell on the faces of the combatants giving additional energy to their ferocious expression.

John, drawing nearer to the scene of action, observed two young warriors fighting side by side, one of whom wore the habit of a forester, the other that of a retainer of Arlingford. He looked intently on them both: their position towards the fire favoured the scrutiny; and the hawk's eye of love very speedily discovered that the latter was the fair Matilda. The forester he did not know: but he had sufficient tact to discern that his success would be very much facilitated by separating her from this companion, above all others. He therefore formed a party of men into a wedge, only taking especial care not to be the point of it himself, and drove it between them with so much precision, that they were in a moment far asunder.

"Lady Matilda," said John, "yield yourself my prisoner."

"If you would wear me, prince," said Matilda, "you must win me:" and without giving him time to deliberate on the courtesy of fighting with the lady of his love, she raised her sword in the air, and lowered it on his head with an impetus that would have gone nigh to fathom even that extraordinary depth of brain which always by divine grace furnishes the interior of a head-royal, if he had not very dexterously parried the blow. Prince John wished to disarm and take captive, not in any way to wound or injure, least of all to kill, his fair opponent. Matilda was only intent to get rid of her antagonist at any rate: the edge of her weapon painted his complexion with streaks of very unlovelike crimson, and she would probably have marred John's hand for ever signing Magna Charta, but that he was backed by the advantage of numbers, and that her sword broke short on the boss of his buckler. John was following up his advantage to make a captive of the lady, when he was suddenly felled to the earth by an unseen antagonist. Some of his men picked him carefully up, and conveyed him to his tent, stunned and stupified.

When he recovered, he found Harpiton diligently assisting in his recovery, more in the fear of losing his place than in that of losing his master: the prince's first inquiry was for the prisoner he had been on the point of taking at the moment when his *habeas corpus* was so unseasonably suspended. He was told that his people had been on the point of securing the said prisoner, when the devil suddenly appeared among them in the likeness of a tall friar, having his grey frock cinctured with a sword-belt, and his crown, which whether it were shaven or no they could not see, surmounted with a helmet, and flourishing an eight-foot staff, with which he laid about him to the right and to the left, knocking down the prince and his men as if they had been so many nine-pins; in fine, he had rescued the prisoner, and made a clear passage through friend and foe, and in conjunction with a chosen party of archers, had covered the retreat of the baron's men and the foresters, who had all gone off in a body towards Sherwood forest.

Harpiton suggested that it would be desirable to sack the castle, and volunteered to lead the van on the occasion, as the defenders were withdrawn, and the exploit seemed to promise much profit and little danger: John considered that the castle would in itself be a great acquisition to him, as a strong hold in furtherance of his design on his brother's throne; and was determining to take possession with the first light of morning, when he had the mortification to see the castle burst into flames in several places at once. A piteous cry was heard from within, and while the prince was proclaiming a reward to any one who would enter into the burning pile and elucidate the mystery of the doleful voice, forth waddled the little fat friar in an agony of fear, out of the fire into the frying-pan; for he was instantly taken into custody and carried before Prince John, wringing his hands and tearing his hair.

"Are you the friar," said Prince John in a terrible voice, "that laid me prostrate in battle, mowed down my men like grass, rescued my captive, and covered the retreat of my enemies? and not content with this, have you now set fire to the castle in which I intended to take up my royal quarters?"

The little friar quaked like a jelly: he fell on his knees, and attempted to speak: but in his eagerness to vindicate himself from this accumulation of alarming charges, he knew not where to begin; his ideas rolled round upon each other like the radii of a wheel; the words he desired to utter, instead of issuing, as it were, in a right line from his lips, seemed to conglobate themselves into a sphere turning on its own axis in his throat: after several ineffectual efforts his utterance totally failed him, and he remained gasping, with his mouth open, his lips quivering, his hands clasped together, and the whites of his eyes turned up towards the prince with an expression most ruefully imploring.

"Are you that friar?" repeated the prince.

Several of the by-standers declared that he was not that friar. The little friar, encouraged by this patronage, found his voice and pleaded for mercy. The prince questioned him closely concerning the burning of the castle. The little friar declared, that he had been in too great fear during the siege to know much of what was going forward, except that he had been conscious during the last few days of a lamentable deficiency of provisions, and had been present that very morning at the broaching of the last butt of sack. Harpiton groaned in sympathy. The little friar added, that he knew nothing of what had passed since, till he heard the flames roaring at his elbow.

"Take him away, Harpiton," said the prince, "fill him with sack, and turn him out."

"Never mind the sack," said the little friar, "turn me out at once."

"A sad chance," said Harpiton, "to be turned out without sack."

But what Harpiton thought a sad chance the little friar thought a merry one, and went bounding like a fat buck towards the abbey of Rubygill.

An arrow, with a letter attached to it, was shot into the camp, and carried to the prince. The contents were these:

"PRINCE JOHN—I do not consider myself to have resisted lawful authority in defending my castle against you, seeing that you are at present in a state of active rebellion against your liege sovereign Richard; and if my provisions had not failed me, I would have maintained it till doomsday. As it is, I have so well disposed my combustibles that it shall not serve you as a strong hold in your rebellion. If you hunt in the chases of Nottinghamshire, you may catch other game than my daughter. Both she and I are content to be houseless for a time, in the reflection that we have deserved your enmity and the friendship of Cœur-de-Lion.

"FITZWATER."

CHAPTER XI

—Tuck, the merry friar, who many a sermon made
In praise of Robin Hood, his outlaws, and their trade.

DRAYTON.[1]

THE baron, with some of his retainers and all the foresters, halted at daybreak in Sherwood forest. The foresters quickly erected tents, and prepared an abundant breakfast of venison and ale.

"Now, Lord Fitzwater," said the chief forester, "recognise your son-in-law that was to have been, in the outlaw Robin Hood."

"Ay, ay," said the baron, "I have recognised you long ago."

"And recognise your young friend Gamwell," said the second, "in the outlaw Scarlet."

---

1. [*Poly-Olbion*, Song 26. These lines are cited in Joseph Ritson's *Robin Hood. A Collection of all the Ancient Poems, Songs and Ballads, now extant, Relative to that Celebrated English Outlaw*, published in 1795.]

"And Little John, the page," said the third, "in Little John the outlaw."

"And Father Michael, of Rubygill Abbey," said the friar, "in Friar Tuck of Sherwood forest. Truly, I have a chapel here hard by, in the shape of a hollow tree, where I put up my prayers for travellers, and Little John holds the plate at the door, for good praying deserves good paying."

"I am in fine company," said the baron.

"In the very best of company," said the friar, "in the high court of Nature, and in the midst of her own nobility. Is it not so? This goodly grove is our palace: the oak and the beech are its colonnade and its canopy: the sun and the moon and the stars are its everlasting lamps: the grass, and the daisy, and the primrose, and the violet, are its many-coloured floor of green, white, yellow, and blue; the may-flower, and the woodbine, and the eglantine, and the ivy, are its decorations, its curtains, and its tapestry: the lark, and the thrush, and the linnet, and the nightingale, are its unhired minstrels and musicians. Robin Hood is king of the forest both by dignity of birth and by virtue of his standing army: to say nothing of the free choice of his people, which he has indeed, but I pass it by as an illegitimate basis of power. He holds his dominion over the forest, and its horned multitude of citizen-deer, and its swinish multitude or peasantry of wild boars, by right of conquest and force of arms. He levies contributions among them by the free consent of his archers, their virtual representatives. If they should find a voice to complain that we are 'tyrants and usurpers to kill and cook them up in their assigned and native dwelling-place,' we should most convincingly admonish them, with point of arrow, that they have nothing to do with our laws but to obey them. Is it not written that the fat ribs of the herd shall be fed upon by the mighty in the land? And have not they withal my blessing? my orthodox, canonical, and archiepiscopal blessing? Do I not give thanks for them when they are well roasted and smoking under my nose? What title had William of Normandy to England, that Robin of Locksley has not to merry Sherwood? William fought for his claim. So does Robin. With whom, both? With any that would or will dispute it. William raised contributions. So does Robin. From whom, both? From all that they could or can make pay them. Why did any pay them to William? Why do any pay them to Robin? For the same reason to both: because they could not or cannot help it. They differ, indeed, in this, that William took from the poor and gave to the rich, and Robin takes from the rich and gives to the poor: and therein is Robin illegitimate; though in all else he is true prince. Scarlet and John, are they not peers of the forest? lords temporal of Sherwood? And am not I lord spiritual? Am I not archbishop? Am I not pope? Do I not consecrate their banner and absolve their sins? Are not they state, and am not I church? Are not they state monarchical, and am not I church militant? Do I not excommunicate our enemies from venison and brawn, and by 'r Lady, when need calls, beat them down under my feet? The state levies tax, and the church levies tithe. Even so do we. Mass, we take all at once. What then? It is tax by redemption and tithe by commutation. Your William and Richard can cut and come again, but our Robin deals with slippery subjects that come not twice to his exchequer. What need we then to constitute a court, except a fool and a laureate? For the fool, his only use is to make false knaves merry by art, and we are true men and are merry by nature. For the laureate, his only office is to find virtues in those who have none, and to drink sack for his pains. We have quite virtue enough to need him not, and can drink our sack for ourselves."

"Well preached, friar," said Robin Hood: "yet there is one thing wanting to constitute a court, and that is a queen. And now, lovely Matilda, look round upon these sylvan shades where we have so often roused the stag from his ferny covert. The rising sun smiles upon us through the stems of that beechen knoll. Shall I take your hand, Matilda, in the presence of this my court? Shall I crown you with our wild-wood coronal, and hail you queen of the forest? Will you be the queen Matilda of your own true king Robin?"

Matilda smiled assent.

"Not Matilda," said the friar: "the rules of our holy alliance require new birth. We have excepted in favour of Little John, because he is great John, and his name is a misnomer. I sprinkle, not thy forehead with water, but thy lips with wine, and baptize thee MARIAN."

"Here is a pretty conspiracy," exclaimed the baron. "Why, you villanous friar, think you to nick-name and marry my daughter before my face with impunity?"

"Even so, bold baron," said the friar; "we are strongest here. Say you, might overcomes right? I say no. There is no right but might: and to say that might overcomes right is to say that right overcomes itself: an absurdity most palpable. Your right was the stronger in Arlingford, and ours is the stronger in

Sherwood. Your right was right as long as you could maintain it; so is ours. So is King Richard's, with all deference be it spoken; and so is King Saladin's: and their two mights are now committed in bloody fray, and that which overcomes will be right, just as long as it lasts, and as far as it reaches. And now if any of you know any just impediment——"

"Fire and fury!" exclaimed the baron.

"Fire and fury," said the friar, "are modes of that might which constitutes right, and are just impediments to any thing against which they can be brought to bear. They are our good allies upon occasion, and would declare for us now if you should put them to the test."

"Father," said Matilda, "you know the terms of our compact: from the moment you restrained my liberty, you renounced your claim to all but compulsory obedience. The friar argues well. Right ends with might. Thick walls, dreary galleries, and tapestried chambers, were indifferent to me while I could leave them at pleasure, but have ever been hateful to me since they held me by force. May I never again have roof but the blue sky, nor canopy but the green leaves, nor barrier but the forest-bounds: with the foresters to my train, Little John to my page, Friar Tuck to my ghostly adviser, and Robin Hood to my liege lord. I am no longer lady Matilda Fitzwater, of Arlingford Castle, but plain Maid Marian of Sherwood Forest."

"Long live Maid Marian!" re-echoed the foresters.

"Oh false girl!" said the baron, "do you renounce your name and parentage?"

"Not my parentage," said Marian, "but my name indeed: do not all maids renounce it at the altar?"

"The altar!" said the baron: "grant me patience! what do you mean by the altar?"

"Pile green turf," said the friar, "wreathe it with flowers, and crown it with fruit, and we will show the noble baron what we mean by the altar."

The foresters did as the friar directed.

"Now, Little John," said the friar, "on with the cloak of the abbot of Doubleflask. I appoint thee my clerk: thou art here duly elected in full mote."

"I wish you were all in full moat together," said the baron, "and smooth wall on both sides."

"Punnest thou?" said the friar. "A heinous antichristian offence. Why anti-christian? Because anti-catholic? Why anti-catholic? Because anti-roman. Why anti-roman? Because Carthaginian. Is not pun from Punic? *Punica fides*: the very quint-essential quiddity of bad faith: double-visaged: double-tongued. He that will make a pun will—- I say no more. Fie on it. Stand forth, clerk. Who is the bride's father?"

"There is no bride's father," said the baron. "I am the father of Matilda Fitzwater."

"There is none such," said the friar. "This is the fair Maid Marian. Will you make a virtue of necessity, or will you give laws to the flowing tide? Will you give her, or shall Robin take her? Will you be her true natural father, or shall I commute paternity? Stand forth, Scarlet."

"Stand back, sirrah Scarlet," said the baron. "My daughter shall have no father but me. Needs must when the devil drives."

"No matter who drives," said the friar, "so that, like a well-disposed subject, you yield cheerful obedience to those who can enforce it."

"Mawd, sweet Mawd," said the baron, "will you then forsake your poor old father in his distress, with his castle in ashes, and his enemy in power?"

"Not so, father," said Marian; "I will always be your true daughter: I will always love, and serve, and watch, and defend you: but neither will I forsake my plighted love, and my own liege lord, who was your choice before he was mine, for you made him my associate in infancy; and that he continued to be mine when he ceased to be yours, does not in any way show remissness in my duties or falling off in my affections. And though I here plight my troth at the altar to Robin, in the presence of this holy priest and pious clerk, yet...... Father, when Richard returns from Palestine, he will restore you to your barony, and perhaps, for your sake, your daughter's husband to the earldom of Huntingdon: should that never be, should it be the will of fate that we must live and die in the greenwood, I will live and die MAID MARIAN."[2]

"A pretty resolution," said the baron, "if Robin will let you keep it."

"I have sworn it," said Robin. "Should I expose her tenderness to the perils of maternity, when life and death may hang on shifting at a moment's notice from Sherwood to Barnsdale, and from Barnsdale to the sea-shore? And why should I banquet when my merry men starve? Chastity is our forest law, and even the friar has kept it since he has been here."

---

2.   And therefore is she called Maid Marian
     Because she leads a spotless maiden life,
     And shall till Robin's outlaw life have end.
     Old Play [Garnett cites this as taken from *The Downfall of Robert, Earl of Huntingdon* (1598), Act III, Scene 2, by Antony Munday.]

"Truly so," said the friar: "for temptation dwells with ease and luxury: but the hunter is Hippolytus, and the huntress is Dian. And now, dearly beloved——-"

The friar went through the ceremony with great unction, and Little John was most clerical in the intonation of his responses. After which, the friar sang, and Little John fiddled, and the foresters danced, Robin with Marian, and Scarlet with the baron, and the venison smoked, and the ale frothed, and the wine sparkled, and the sun went down on their unwearied festivity: which they wound up with the following song, the friar leading, and the foresters joining chorus:

Oh! bold Robin Hood is a forester good,
As ever drew bow in the merry greenwood:
At his bugle's shrill singing the echoes are ringing,
The wild deer are springing for many a rood:
Its summons we follow, through brake, over hollow,
The thrice-blown shrill summons of bold Robin
Hood.

And what eye hath e'er seen such a sweet Maiden
Queen,
As Marian, the pride of the forester's green?
A sweet garden-flower, she blooms in the bower,
Where alone to this hour the wild rose has been:
We hail her in duty the queen of all beauty:
We will live, we will die, by our sweet Maiden queen.

And here's a grey friar, good as heart can desire,
To absolve all our sins as the case may require:
Who with courage so stout, lays his oak-plant about,

And puts to the rout all the foes of his choir:
For we are his choristers, we merry foresters,
Chorussing thus with our militant friar.

And Scarlet doth bring his good yew-bough and
string,
Prime minister is he of Robin our king:
No mark is too narrow for little John's arrow,
That hits a cock sparrow a mile on the wing:
Robin and Mariòn, Scarlet, and Little John,
Long with their glory old Sherwood shall ring.

Each a good liver, for well-feathered quiver
Doth furnish brawn, venison, and fowl of the river:
But the best game we dish up, it is a fat bishop:
When his angels we fish up, he proves a free giver:
For a prelate so lowly has angels more holy,
And should this world's false angels to sinners
deliver.

Robin and Mariòn, Scarlet and Little John,
Drink to them one by one, drink as ye sing:
Robin and Mariòn, Scarlet and Little John,
Echo to echo through Sherwood shall fling:
Robin and Mariòn, Scarlet and Little John,
Long with their glory old Sherwood shall ring.

CHAPTER XII

A single volume paramount: a code:
A master spirit: a determined road.

WORDSWORTH.[1]

THE next morning Robin Hood convened his foresters, and desired Little John, for the baron's edification, to read over the laws of their forest society. Little John read aloud with a stentorophonic voice.

"At a high court of foresters, held under the greenwood tree, an hour after sun-rise, Robin Hood President, William Scarlet Vice-President, Little John Secretary: the following articles, moved by Friar Tuck

---

1. [A misquote and inversion of lines from Great Men Have Been Among Us by William Wordsworth, published in 1807 as part of the collection *Poems, in Two Volumes*. The poem is one of his Sonnets Dedicated to Liberty, in which he reflects on England's historical figures and its national spirit in the face of the Napoleonic Wars. The correct lines:
   "No single Volume paramount, no code,
   No master spirit, no determined road;
   But equally a want of Books and Men!"]

in his capacity of Peer Spiritual, and seconded by Much the Miller, were unanimously agreed to.

"The principles of our society are six: Legitimacy, Equity, Hospitality, Chivalry, Chastity, and Courtesy.

"The articles of Legitimacy are four:[2]

"I. Our government is legitimate, and our society is founded on the one golden rule of right, consecrated by the universal consent of mankind, and by the practice of all ages, individuals, and nations: namely, To keep what we have, and to catch what we can.

"II. Our government being legitimate, all our proceedings shall be legitimate: wherefore we declare war against the whole world, and every forester is by this legitimate declaration legitimately invested with a roving commission, to make lawful prize of every thing that comes in his way.

"III. All forest laws but our own we declare to be null and void.

"IV. All such of the old laws of England as do not in any way interfere with, or militate against, the

---

2. [Peacock is mocking the Holy Alliance, a treaty signed in 1815 by Russia, Austria and Prussia, with the stated aim of upholding Christian principles in European politics. It was spearheaded by Tsar Alexander I of Russia and ostensibly sought to ensure peace and cooperation among Christian monarchs. However, in practice, it was widely seen as a reactionary tool used to suppress revolutionary movements and maintain monarchical rule. The Alliance promoted legitimacy (hereditary right to rule), while claiming to uphold moral and religious values. Peacock's list of six "principles"—Legitimacy, Equity, Hospitality, Chivalry, Chastity, and Courtesy—sounds lofty and noble, much like the stated ideals of the Holy Alliance. However, the way he structures it (with numbered "articles") and the absurdity of mixing political legitimacy with chivalric and moral virtues suggest he is lampooning the self-righteousness and hypocrisy of the Alliance.]

views of this honourable assembly, we will loyally adhere to and maintain. The rest we declare null and void as far as relates to ourselves, in all cases wherein a vigour beyond the law may be conducive to our own interest and preservation."

"The articles of Equity are three:

"I. The balance of power among the people being very much deranged, by one having too much and another nothing, we hereby resolve ourselves into a congress or court of equity, to restore as far as in us lies the said natural balance of power, by taking from all who have too much as much of the said too much as we can lay our hands on; and giving to those who have nothing such a portion thereof as it may seem to us expedient to part with.

"II. In all cases a quorum of foresters shall constitute a court of equity, and as many as may be strong enough to manage the matter in hand shall constitute a quorum.

"III. All usurers, monks, courtiers, and other drones of the great hive of society, who shall be found laden with any portion of the honey whereof they have wrongfully despoiled the industrious bee, shall be rightfully despoiled thereof in turn; and all bishops and abbots shall be bound and beaten,[3]

3.　"These byshoppes and these archbyshoppes
　　Ye shall them bete and bynde,"

says Robin Hood, in an old ballad. Perhaps, however, thus is to be taken not in a literal, but in a figurative sense, from the binding and beating of wheat: for as all rich men were Robin's harvest, the bishops and archbishops must have been the finest and fattest ears among them, from which Robin merely proposes to thresh the grain when he directs them to be bound and beaten: and as Pharaoh's fat kine were typical of fat ears of wheat, so may fat ears of wheat, *mutatis mutandis*, be typical of fat kine. [In Peacock's ref-

especially the abbot of Doncaster, as shall also all sheriffs, especially the sheriff of Nottingham.

"The articles of Hospitality are two:

"I. Postmen, carriers and market-folk, peasants and mechanics, farmers and millers, shall pass through our forest-dominions without let or molestation.

"II. All other travellers through the forest shall be graciously invited to partake of Robin's hospitality; and if they come not willingly they shall be compelled; and the rich man shall pay well for his fare; and the poor man shall feast scot free, and peradventure receive bounty in proportion to his desert and necessity.

"The article of Chivalry is one:

"I. Every forester shall, to the extent of his power, aid and protect maids, widows, and orphans, and all weak and distressed persons whomsoever: and no woman shall be impeded or molested in any way; nor shall any company receive harm which any woman is in.

"The article of Chastity is one:

"I. Every forester, being Diana's forester and minion of the moon, shall commend himself to the

---

erence to "an old ballad", he most likely means *A Lytell Geste of Robyn Hode*, one of the most famous early Robin Hood ballads and which contains strong anti-clerical themes. The phrase "Pharaoh's fat kine" is a biblical reference to the Book of Genesis, specifically Pharaoh's dream in Genesis 41:1–7. In this dream, Pharaoh sees seven fat, or well-fed, cows ("kine") emerge from the Nile, followed by seven lean, or gaunt, cows, which then devour the fat ones. The "fat kine" (fat cows) symbolise seven years of abundance, while the lean kine represent seven years of famine. The dream is interpreted by Joseph, who advises Pharaoh to prepare for the coming scarcity by storing grain during the plentiful years.]

grace of the Virgin, and shall have the gift of continency on pain of expulsion: that the article of chivalry may be secure from infringement, and maids, wives, and widows pass without fear through the forest.

"The article of Courtesy is one:

"I. No one shall miscall a forester. He who calls Robin Robert of Huntingdon, or salutes him by any other title or designation whatsoever except plain Robin Hood; or who calls Marian Matilda Fitzwater, or salutes her by any other title or designation whatsoever except plain Maid Marian; and so of all others; shall for every such offence forfeit a mark to be paid to the friar.

"And these articles we swear to keep as we are good men and true. Carried by acclamation. God save King Richard.

"Little John, Secretary."

"Excellent laws," said the baron: "excellent, by the holy rood. William of Normandy, with my great great grandfather Fierabras at his elbow, could not have made better. And now, sweet Mawd—"

"A fine, a fine," cried the friar, "a fine, by the article of courtesy."

"Od's life," said the baron, "shall I not call my own daughter Mawd? Methinks there should be a special exception in my favour."

"It must not be," said Robin Hood; "our constitution admits no privilege."

"But I will commute," said the friar: "for twenty marks a year duly paid into my ghostly pocket you shall call your daughter Mawd two hundred times a day."

"Gramercy," said the baron, "and I agree, honest friar, when I can get twenty marks to pay: for till Prince John be beaten from Nottingham, my rents are like to prove but scanty."

"I will trust," said the friar, "and thus let us ratify the stipulation; so shall our laws and your infringement run together in an amicable parallel."

"But," said Little John, "this is a bad precedent, master friar. It is turning discipline into profit, penalty into perquisite, public justice into private revenue. It is rank corruption, master friar."

"Why are laws made?" said the friar. "For the profit of somebody. Of whom? Of him who makes them first, and of others as it may happen. Was not I legislator in the last article, and shall I not thrive by my own law?"

"Well then, sweet Mawd," said the baron, "I must leave you, Mawd: your life is very well for the young and the hearty, but it squares not with my age or my humour. I must house, Mawd. I must find refuge: but where? That is the question."

"Where Sir Guy of Gamwell has found it," said Robin Hood, "near the borders of Barnsdale. There you may dwell in safety with him and fair Alice till King Richard return, and Little John shall give you safe conduct. You will have need to travel with caution, in disguise and without attendants, for Prince John commands all this vicinity, and will doubtless lay the country for you and Marian. Now it is first expedient to dismiss your retainers. If there be any among them who like our life, they may stay with us in the greenwood: the rest may return to their homes."

Some of the baron's men resolved to remain with

Robin and Marian, and were furnished accordingly with suits of green, of which Robin always kept good store.

Marian now declared that as there was danger in the way to Barnsdale, she would accompany Little John and the baron, as she should not be happy unless she herself saw her father placed in security. Robin was very unwilling to consent to this, and assured her that there was more danger for her than the baron: but Marian was absolute.

"If so, then," said Robin, "I shall be your guide instead of Little John, and I shall leave him and Scarlet joint-regents of Sherwood during my absence, and the voice of Friar Tuck shall be decisive between them if they differ in nice questions of state policy." Marian objected to this, that there was more danger for Robin than either herself or the baron: but Robin was absolute in his turn.

"Talk not of my voice," said the friar; "for if Marian be a damsel errant, I will be her ghostly esquire."

Robin insisted that this should not be, for number would only expose them to greater risk of detection. The friar, after some debate, reluctantly acquiesced.

While they were discussing these matters, they heard the distant sound of horses' feet.

"Go," said Robin to Little John, "and invite yonder horseman to dinner."

Little John bounded away, and soon came before a young man, who was riding in a melancholy manner, with the bridle hanging loose on the horse's neck, and his eyes drooping towards the ground.

"Whither go you?" said Little John.

"Whithersoever my horse pleases," said the young man.

"And that shall be," said Little John, "whither I please to lead him. I am commissioned to invite you to dine with my master."

"Who is your master?" said the young man.

"Robin Hood," said Little John.

"The bold outlaw?" said the stranger. "Neither he nor you should have made me turn an inch aside yesterday; but to-day I care not."

"Then it is better for you," said Little John, "that you came to-day than yesterday, if you love dining in a whole skin: for my master is the pink of courtesy: but if his guests prove stubborn, he bastes them and his venison together, while the friar says mass before meat."

The young man made no answer, and scarcely seemed to hear what Little John was saying, who therefore took the horse's bridle and led him to where Robin and his foresters were setting forth their dinner. Robin seated the young man next to Marian. Recovering a little from his stupor, he looked with much amazement at her, and the baron, and Robin, and the friar; listened to their conversation, and seemed much astonished to find himself in such holy and courtly company. Robin helped him largely to numble-pie and cygnet and pheasant and the other dainties of his table, and the friar pledged him in ale and wine, and exhorted him to make good cheer. But the young man drank little, ate less, spake nothing, and every now and then sighed heavily.

When the repast was ended, "Now," said Robin, "you are at liberty to pursue your journey: but first be pleased to pay for your dinner."

"That would I gladly do, Robin," said the young man, "but all I have about me are five shillings and a ring. To the five shillings you shall be welcome: but for the ring I will fight while there is a drop of blood in my veins."

"Gallantly spoken," said Robin Hood. "A love-token, without doubt: but you must submit to our forest laws. Little John must search; and if he find no more than you say, not a penny will I touch: but if you have spoken false, the whole is forfeit to our fraternity."

"And with reason," said the friar; "for thereby is the truth maintained. The abbot of Doubleflask swore there was no money in his valise, and Little John forthwith emptied it of four hundred pounds. Thus was the abbot's perjury but of one minute's duration: for though his speech was false in the utterance, yet was it no sooner uttered than it became true, and we should have been *participes criminis* to have suffered the holy abbot to depart in falsehood: whereas he came to us a false priest, and we sent him away a true man. Marry, we turned his cloak to further account: and thereby hangs a tale that may be either said or sung: for in truth I am minstrel here as well as chaplain: I pray for good success to our just and necessary warfare, and sing thanksgiving odes when our foresters bring in booty:

Bold Robin has robed him in ghostly attire,
And forth he is gone like a holy friar,
   Singing, hey down, ho down, down, derry down:
And of two grey friars he soon was aware,
Regaling themselves with dainty fare,
   All on the fallen leaves so brown.

"Good morrow, good brothers," said bold Robin
Hood,
"And what make you in the good greenwood,
    Singing hey down, ho down, down, derry down?
Now give me, I pray you, wine and food;
For none can I find in the good greenwood,
    All on the fallen leaves so brown."

"Good brother," they said, "we would give you full
fain,
But we have no more than enough for twain,
    Singing, hey down, ho down, down, derry down."
"Then give me some money," said bold Robin Hood,
"For none can I find in the good greenwood,
    All on the fallen leaves so brown."

"No money have we, good brother," said they:
"Then," said he, "we three for money will pray:
    Singing, hey down, ho down, down, derry down:
And whatever shall come at the end of our prayer,
We three holy friars will piously share,
    All on the fallen leaves so brown."

"We will not pray with thee, good brother, God wot:
For truly, good brother, thou pleasest us not,
    Singing hey down, ho down, down, derry down:"
Then up they both started from Robin to run,
But down on their knees Robin pulled them
each one,
    All on the fallen leaves so brown.

The grey friars prayed with a doleful face,
But bold Robin prayed with a right merry grace,
    Singing, hey down, ho down, down, derry down:

And when they had prayed, their portmanteau he took,
And from it a hundred good angels he shook,
    All on the fallen leaves so brown.

"The saints," said bold Robin, "have hearkened our prayer,
And here's a good angel apiece for your share:
If more you would have, you must win ere you wear:
    Singing hey down, ho down, down, derry down:"
Then he blew his good horn with a musical cheer,
And fifty green bowmen came trooping full near,
And away the grey friars they bounded like deer,
    All on the fallen leaves so brown.

CHAPTER XIII

What can a young lassie, what shall a young lassie,
What can a young lassie do wi' an auld man?

Burns.[1]

"Here is but five shillings and a ring," said Little John, "and the young man has spoken true."

"Then," said Robin to the stranger, "if want of money be the cause of your melancholy, speak. Little John is my treasurer, and he shall disburse to you."

"It is, and it is not," said the stranger: "it is, because, had I not wanted money I had never lost my love: it is not, because now that I have lost her, money would come too late to regain her."

"In what way have you lost her?" said Robin: "let

---

1.   [In the *Book of Scottish Song* (1843), Alexander Whitelaw offers this note: "There is an old song, the burthen of which is the same as the opening of the present,—'What can a young lassie do wi' an auld man?' From this Burns took the hint, and furnished the following expressive ditty for Johnson's Museum in 1790. The tune is very old."]

us clearly know that she is past regaining, before we give up our wishes to restore her to you."

"She is to be married this day," said the stranger, "and perhaps is married by this, to a rich old knight: and yesterday I knew it not."

"What is your name?" said Robin.

"Allen," said the stranger.

"And where is the marriage to take place, Allen?" said Robin.

"At Edwinstow church," said Allen, "by the bishop of Nottingham."

"I know that bishop," said Robin: "he dined with me a month since, and paid three hundred pounds for his dinner. He has a good ear and loves music. The friar sang to him to some tune. Give me my harper's cloak, and I will play a part at this wedding."

"These are dangerous times, Robin," said Marian, "for playing pranks out of the forest."

"Fear not," said Robin: "Edwinstow lies not Nottingham-ward, and I will take my precautions."

Robin put on his harper's cloak, while Little John painted his eyebrows and cheeks, tipped his nose with red, and tied him on a comely beard. Marian confessed, that had she not been present at the metamorphosis, she should not have known her own true Robin. Robin took his harp, and went to the wedding.

Robin found the bishop and his train in the church porch, impatiently expecting the arrival of the bride and bridegroom. The clerk was observing to the bishop that the knight was somewhat gouty, and that the necessity of walking the last quarter of a mile from the road to the churchyard probably detained the lively bridegroom rather longer than had been calculated upon.

"Oh! by my fay," said the music-loving bishop, "here comes a harper in the nick of time, and now I care not how long they tarry. Ho! honest friend, are you come to play at the wedding?"

"I am come to play anywhere," answered Robin, "where I can get a cup of sack; for which I will sing the praise of the donor in lofty verse, and emblazon him with any virtue, which he may wish to have the credit of possessing, without the trouble of practising."

"A most courtly harper," said the bishop: "I will fill thee with sack, I will make thee a walking butt of sack, if thou wilt delight my ears with thy melodies."

"That will I," said Robin: "in what branch of my art shall I exert my faculty? I am passing well in all, from the anthem to the glee, and from the dirge to the coranto."

"It would be idle," said the bishop, "to give thee sack for playing me anthems, seeing that I myself do receive sack for hearing them sung. Therefore, as the occasion is festive, thou shalt play me a coranto."

Robin struck up and played away merrily, the bishop all the while, in great delight, noddling his head, and beating time with his foot, till the bride and bridegroom appeared. The bridegroom was richly apparelled, and came slowly and painfully forward, hobbling and leering, and pursing up his mouth into a smile of resolute defiance to the gout, and of tender complacency towards his lady love, who, shining like gold at the old knight's expense, followed slowly between her father and mother, her cheeks pale, her head drooping, her steps faltering, and her eyes reddened with tears.

Robin stopped his minstrelsy, and said to the bishop, "This seems to me an unfit match."

"What do you say, rascal?" said the old knight, hobbling up to him.

"I say," said Robin, "this seems to me an unfit match. What in the devil's name can you want with a young wife, who have one foot in flannels and the other in the grave?"

"What is that to thee, sirrah varlet?" said the old knight: "stand away from the porch, or I will fracture thy sconce with my cane."

"I will not stand away from the porch," said Robin, "unless the bride bid me, and tell me that you are her own true love."

"Speak," said the bride's father, in a severe tone, and with a look of significant menace. The girl looked alternately at her father and Robin. She attempted to speak, but her voice failed in the effort, and she burst into tears.

"Here is lawful cause and just impediment," said Robin, "and I forbid the banns."

"Who are you, villain?" said the old knight, stamping his sound foot with rage.

"I am the Roman law," said Robin, "which says that there shall not be more than ten years between a man and his wife; and here are five times ten: and so says the law of nature."

"Honest harper," said the bishop, "you are somewhat over-officious here, and less courtly than I deemed you. If you love sack, forbear: for this course will never bring you a drop. As to your Roman law, and your law of nature, what right have they to say any thing which the law of Holy Writ says not?"

"The law of Holy Writ does say it," said Robin: "I

expound it so to say: and I will produce sixty commentators to establish my exposition."

And so saying, he produced a horn from beneath his cloak, and blew three blasts; and threescore bowmen in green came leaping from the bushes and trees: and young Allen was the first among them to give Robin his sword, while Friar Tuck and Little John marched up to the altar. Robin stripped the bishop and clerk of their robes, and put them on the friar and Little John; and Allen advanced to take the hand of the bride. Her cheeks grew red and her eyes grew bright, as she locked her hand in her lover's, and tripped lightly with him into the church.

"This marriage will not stand," said the bishop, "for they have not been thrice asked in church."

"We will ask them seven times," said Little John, "lest three should not suffice."

"And in the meantime," said Robin, "the knight and the bishop shall dance to my harping."

So Robin sat in the church porch and played away merrily, while his foresters formed a ring, in the centre of which the knight and bishop danced with exemplary alacrity; and if they relaxed their exertions, Scarlet gently touched them up with the point of an arrow.

The knight grimaced ruefully, and begged Robin to think of his gout.

"So I do," said Robin: "this is the true antipodagron:[2] you shall dance the gout away, and be thankful

---

2. ["A remedy against gout". Podagra was a well-known term in classical and medieval medicine for gout, particularly affecting the feet. An "antipodagron" would therefore logically be something that prevents or alleviates gout, possibly a drink, medicine or herb.]

to me while you live. I told you," he added, to the bishop, "I would play at this wedding: but you did not tell me that you would dance at it. The next couple you marry, think of the Roman law."

The bishop was too much out of breath to reply, and now the young couple issued from church: and the bride having made a farewell obeisance to her parents, they departed together with the foresters, the parents storming, the attendants laughing, the bishop puffing and blowing, and the knight rubbing his gouty foot, and uttering doleful lamentations for the gold and jewels with which he had so unwittingly adorned and dowered the bride.

CHAPTER XIV

As ye came from the holy land
　　Of blessed Walsinghame,
Oh met ye not with my true love,
　　As by the way ye came?

Old Ballad.[1]

In pursuance of the arrangement recorded in the twelfth chapter, the baron, Robin, and Marian disguised themselves as pilgrims returned from Palestine, and travelling from the sea-coast of Hampshire to their home in Northumberland. By dint of staff and cockle-shell, sandal and scrip,[2] they

---

1. [The "old ballad" Peacock is referencing is "The Lover's Complaint", also known as "As Ye Came from the Holy Land of Blessed Walsingham". This is a 16th-century English ballad that was popular in the Elizabethan era. The poem has often been attributed to Sir Walter Raleigh, though its authorship remains uncertain.]

2. [A poetic way of describing the traditional attributes of a pilgrim, particularly those who undertook religious journeys during the medieval period. A walking staff, or pilgrim's staff, was a common symbol of a medieval pilgrim, providing support during long journeys and serving as a mark of their spiritual purpose. The

proceeded in safety the greater part of the way (for Robin had many sly inns and resting-places between Barnsdale and Sherwood), and were already on the borders of Yorkshire, when, one evening, they passed within view of a castle, where they saw a lady standing on a turret, and surveying the whole extent of the valley through which they were passing. A servant came running from the castle, and delivered to them a message from his lady, who was sick with expectation of news from her lord in the Holy Land, and entreated them to come to her, that she might question them concerning him. This was an awkward occurrence: but there was no pretence for refusal, and they followed the servant into the castle. The baron, who had been in Palestine in his youth, undertook to be spokesman on the occasion, and to relate his own adventures to the lady as having happened to the lord in question. This preparation enabled him to be so minute and circumstantial in his detail, and so coherent in his replies to her questions, that the lady fell implicitly into the delusion, and was delighted to find that her lord was alive and in health, and in high favour with the king, and performing prodigies of valour in the name of his lady, whose miniature he always wore in his bosom.[3] The baron guessed at this

---

scallop shell (often called a "cockle-shell") was a famous emblem of pilgrimage, especially associated with the Camino de Santiago (the Way of St James) in Spain. Pilgrims wore these shells on their hats or cloaks to signify their journey. A scrip was a small bag or pouch carried by medieval pilgrims to hold their provisions, such as bread and water.]

3. [Refers to the 18th- and 19th-century custom of wearing a miniature portrait of a loved one—often a lover, spouse or close family member—as a token of affection and remembrance. In Scott's *Ivanhoe*, Rowena (Ivanhoe's love interest) is depicted in a

circumstance from the customs of that age, and happened to be in the right.

"This miniature," added the baron, "I have had the felicity to see, and should have known you by it among a million." The baron was a little embarrassed by some questions of the lady concerning her lord's personal appearance: but Robin came to his aid, observing a picture suspended opposite to him on the wall, which he made a bold conjecture to be that of the lord in question, and making a calculation of the influences of time and war, which he weighed with a comparison of the lady's age, he gave a description of her lord sufficiently like the picture in its groundwork to be a true resemblance, and sufficiently differing from it in circumstance to be more an original than a copy. The lady was completely deceived, and entreated them to partake her hospitality for the night: but this they deemed it prudent to decline, and with many humble thanks for her kindness and representations of the necessity of not delaying their homeward course, they proceeded on their way.

As they passed over the drawbridge, they met Sir Ralph Montfaucon and his squire, who were wandering in quest of Marian, and were entering to claim that hospitality which the pilgrims had declined. Their countenances struck Sir Ralph with a kind of imperfect recognition, which would never have been matured, but that the eyes of Marian, as she passed him, encountered his, and the images of those stars of

---

noble and idealised manner, fitting the kind of romantic devotion that might inspire a lover to wear her miniature. Peacock may be parodying this idea by presenting a more exaggerated or absurd version in *Maid Marian*.]

beauty continued involuntarily twinkling in his sensorium to the exclusion of all other ideas, till memory, love, and hope concurred with imagination to furnish a probable reason for their haunting him so pertinaciously. Those eyes, he thought, were certainly the eyes of Matilda Fitzwater: and if the eyes were hers, it was extremely probable, if not logically consecutive, that the rest of the body they belonged to was hers also. Now, if it were really Matilda Fitzwater, who were her two companions? The baron? Aye, and the elder pilgrim was something like him. And the earl of Huntingdon? Very probably. The earl and the baron might be good friends again, now that they were both in disgrace together. While he was revolving these cogitations, he was introduced to the lady, and after claiming and receiving the promise of hospitality, he inquired what she knew of the pilgrims who had just departed? The lady told him they were newly returned from Palestine, having been long in the Holy Land. The knight expressed some scepticism on this point. The lady replied, that they had given her so minute a detail of her lord's proceedings, and so accurate a description of his person, that she could not be deceived in them. This staggered the knight's confidence in his own penetration; and if it had not been a heresy in knighthood to suppose for a moment that there could be *in rerum naturâ* such another pair of eyes as those of his mistress, he would have acquiesced implicitly in the lady's judgment. But while the lady and the knight were conversing, the warder blew his bugle-horn, and presently entered a confidential messenger from Palestine, who gave her to understand that her lord was well, but entered into a detail of his adventures most completely at variance with the baron's narrative, to which not the correspondence of a single incident gave the remotest colouring of similarity. It now became manifest that the pilgrims were not true men, and Sir Ralph Montfaucon sate down to supper with his head full of cogitations, which we shall leave him to chew and digest with his pheasant and canary.

Meanwhile our three pilgrims proceeded on their way. The evening set in black and lowering, when Robin turned aside from the main track, to seek an asylum for the night, along a narrow way that led between rocky and woody hills. A peasant observed the pilgrims as they entered that narrow pass, and called after them: "Whither go you, my masters? there are rogues in that direction."

"Can you show us a direction," said Robin, "in which there are none? If so we will take it in preference." The peasant grinned, and walked away whistling.

The pass widened as they advanced, and the woods grew thicker and darker around them. Their path wound along the slope of a woody declivity, which rose high above them in a thick rampart of foliage, and descended almost precipitously to the bed of a small river, which they heard dashing in its rocky channel, and saw its white foam gleaming at intervals in the last faint glimmerings of twilight. In a short time all was dark, and the rising voice of the wind foretold a coming storm. They turned a point of the valley, and saw a light below them in the depth of the hollow, shining through a cottage-casement and dancing in its reflection on the restless stream. Robin blew his horn, which was answered from below. The cottage door opened: a boy came forth with a torch, ascended the steep, showed tokens of great delight at meeting with Robin, and lighted them down a flight of steps rudely cut in the rock, and over a series of rugged stepping-stones, that crossed the channel of the river. They entered the cottage, which exhibited neatness, comfort, and plenty, being amply enriched with pots, pans, and pipkins, and adorned with flitches of bacon and sundry similar ornaments, that gave goodly promise in the firelight that gleamed upon the rafters. A woman, who seemed just old enough to be the boy's mother, had thrown down her spinning wheel in her joy at the sound of Robin's horn, and was bustling with singular alacrity to set forth her festal ware and prepare an abundant supper. Her features, though not beautiful, were agreeable and expressive, and were now lighted up with such manifest joy at the sight of Robin, that Marian could not help feeling a momentary touch of jealousy, and a half-formed suspicion that Robin had broken his forest law, and had occasionally gone out of bounds, as other great men have done upon occasion, in order to reconcile the breach of the spirit, with the preservation of the letter, of their own legislation. However, this suspicion, if it could be said to exist in a mind so generous as Marian's, was very soon dissipated by the entrance of the woman's husband, who testified as much joy as his wife had done at the sight of Robin: and in a short time the whole of the party were amicably seated round a smoking supper of river-fish and wild-wood fowl, on which the baron fell with as much alacrity as if he had been a true pilgrim from Palestine.

The husband produced some recondite flasks of wine, which were laid by in a binn consecrated to

Robin, whose occasional visits to them in his wanderings were the festal days of these warm-hearted cottagers, whose manners showed that they had not been born to this low estate. Their story had no mystery, and Marian easily collected it from the tenour of their conversation. The young man had been like Robin the victim of an usurious abbot and had been outlawed for debt, and his nut-brown maid had accompanied him to the depths of Sherwood, where they lived an unholy and illegitimate life, killing the king's deer, and never hearing mass. In this state, Robin, then earl of Huntingdon, discovered them in one of his huntings, and gave them aid and protection. When Robin himself became an outlaw, the necessary qualification or gift of continency was too hard a law for our lovers to subscribe to; and as they were thus disqualified for foresters, Robin had found them a retreat in this romantic and secluded spot. He had done similar service to other lovers similarly circumstanced, and had disposed them in various wild scenes which he and his men had discovered in their flittings from place to place, supplying them with all necessaries and comforts from the reluctant disgorgings of fat abbots and usurers. The benefit was in some measure mutual; for these cottages served him as resting-places in his removals, and enabled him to travel untraced and unmolested: and in the delight with which he was always received he found himself even more welcome than he would have been at an inn;[4] and this is saying very much for gratitude and affection together. The smiles which surrounded him were of his own creation, and he participated in the happiness he had bestowed.

The casements began to rattle in the wind, and the rain to beat upon the windows. The wind swelled to a hurricane, and the rain dashed like a flood against the glass. The boy retired to his little bed, the wife trimmed the lamp, the husband heaped logs upon the fire: Robin broached another flask; and Marian filled the baron's cup, and sweetened Robin's by touching its edge with her lips.

"Well," said the baron, "give me a roof over my

---

4. [In his poem Written at an Inn at Henley (circa 1764), William Shenstone laments that commercial hospitality (at an inn) is often warmer than what one finds in life, implying that friendships and relationships are less sincere than simple paid-for services:

"Whoe'er has travel'd life's dull round,
Where'er his stages may have been,
May sigh to think he still has found
The warmest welcome at an inn."

Peacock contrasts this idea by suggesting that Robin Hood found a more genuine welcome in the homes of the people than he would have at an inn, reversing Shenstone's melancholy observation.]

head, be it never so humble.[5] Your greenwood canopy is pretty and pleasant in sunshine, but if I were doomed to live under it, I should wish it were water-tight."

"But," said Robin, "we have tents and caves for foul weather, good store of wine and venison, and fuel in abundance."

"Ay, but," said the baron, "I like to pull off my boots of a night, which you foresters seldom do, and to ensconce myself thereafter in a comfortable bed. Your beech-root is over-hard for a couch, and your mossy stump is somewhat rough for a bolster."

"Had you not dry leaves," said Robin, "with a bishop's surplice over them? What would you have softer? And had you not an abbot's travelling cloak for a coverlet? What would you have warmer?"

"Very true," said the baron, "but that was an indulgence to a guest, and I dreamed all night of the sheriff of Nottingham. I like to feel myself safe," he added, stretching out his legs to the fire, and throwing himself back in his chair with the air of a man determined to be comfortable. "I like to feel myself safe," said the baron.

---

5. [The phrase bears a strong connection to the famous song "Home! Sweet Home!" from *Clari, the Maid of Milan,* an opera by John Howard Payne with music by Henry Bishop, first performed in 1823—just one year after *Maid Marian* was published in 1822. The most famous lines from the song "Home! Sweet Home!" are:
"Mid pleasures and palaces though we may roam,
Be it ever so humble, there's no place like home."
Peacock's phrase "be it never so humble" closely mirrors "be it ever so humble", making it highly likely that he is alluding to or foreshadowing the sentiment that became widely known through Payne's opera. Given that the song gained immense popularity in the 19th century, it's possible that the phrase was already in use in poetic or proverbial form before *Clari* made it famous.]

At that moment the woman caught her husband's arm, and all the party following the direction of her eyes, looked simultaneously to the window, where they had just time to catch a glimpse of an apparition of an armed head, with its plumage tossing in the storm, on which the light shone from within, and which disappeared immediately.

CHAPTER XV

O knight, thou lack'st a cup of canary. When did I see
thee so put down?

Twelfth Night.[1]

SEVERAL knocks, as from the knuckles of an iron glove,
were given to the door of the cottage, and a voice was
heard entreating shelter from the storm for a traveller
who had lost his way. Robin arose and went to the
door.

"What are you?" said Robin.

"A soldier," replied the voice: "an unfortunate ad-
herent of Longchamp, flying the vengeance of Prince
John."

"Are you alone?" said Robin.

"Yes," said the voice: "it is a dreadful night. Hospitable cottagers, pray give me admittance. I would
not have asked it but for the storm. I would have kept
my watch in the woods."

"That I believe," said Robin. "You did not reckon

---

1.   [Act I, Scene 3. See note on page 42.]

on the storm when you turned into this pass. Do you know there are rogues this way?"

"I do," said the voice.

"So do I," said Robin. A pause ensued, during which Robin listening attentively caught a faint sound of whispering.

"You are not alone," said Robin. "Who are your companions?"

"None but the wind and the water," said the voice, "and I would I had them not."

"The wind and the water have many voices," said Robin, "but I never before heard them say, What shall we do?"

Another pause ensued; after which,

"Look ye, master cottager," said the voice, in an altered tone, "if you do not let us in willingly, we will break down the door."

"Ho! ho!" roared the baron, "you are become plural are you, rascals? How many are there of you, thieves? What, I warrant, you thought to rob and murder a poor harmless cottager and his wife, and did not dream of a garrison? You looked for no weapon of opposition but spit, poker, and basting-ladle, wielded by unskilful hands: but, rascals, here is short sword and long cudgel in hands well tried in war, wherewith you shall be drilled into cullenders and beaten into mummy."[2]

----

2. ["Drilled into cullenders" suggests being pierced repeatedly, likely by weapons such as arrows, swords or pikes, to the point that the victim resembles a perforated colander. "Mummy" here does not refer to an Egyptian mummy but to a pulverised or mashed state. The word was sometimes used in English to describe a substance derived from ground-up embalmed remains, which were once believed to have medicinal properties. In this

No reply was made, but furious strokes from without resounded upon the door. Robin, Marian, and the baron, threw by their pilgrim's attire, and stood in arms on the defensive. They were provided with swords, and the cottager gave them bucklers and helmets, for all Robin's haunts were furnished with secret armouries. But they kept their swords sheathed, and the baron wielded a ponderous spear, which he pointed towards the door ready to run through the first that should enter, and Robin and Marian each held a bow with the arrow drawn to its head and pointed in the same direction. The cottager flourished a strong cudgel (a weapon in the use of which he prided himself on being particularly expert), and the wife seized the spit from the fire-place and held it as she saw the baron hold his spear. The storm of wind and rain continued to beat on the roof and the casement, and the storm of blows to resound upon the door, which at length gave way with a violent crash, and a cluster of armed men appeared without, seemingly not less than twelve. Behind them rolled the stream now changed from a gentle and shallow river to a mighty and impetuous torrent, roaring in waves of yellow foam, partially reddened by the light that streamed through the open door, and turning up its convulsed surface in flashes of shifting radiance from restless masses of half-visible shadow. The stepping-stones, by which the intruders must have crossed, were buried under the waters. On

---

context, "beaten into mummy" means to be pounded or crushed to a pulp, exaggerating the idea of an opponent being utterly destroyed. The grotesque and absurd imagery recalls Rabelais, who frequently described battle wounds and destruction in comically excessive detail, or Butler's *Hudibras* (1663).]

the opposite bank the light fell on the stems and boughs of the rock-rooted oak and ash tossing and swaying in the blast, and sweeping the flashing spray with their leaves.

The instant the door broke, Robin and Marian loosed their arrows. Robin's arrow struck one of the assailants in the juncture of the shoulder, and disabled his right arm: Marian's struck a second in the juncture of the knee, and rendered him unserviceable for the night. The baron's long spear struck on the mailed breastplate of a third, and being stretched to its full extent by the long-armed hero, drove him to the edge of the torrent, and plunged him into its eddies, along which he was whirled down the darkness of the descending stream, calling vainly on his comrades for aid till his voice was lost in the mingled roar of the waters and the wind. A fourth springing through the door was laid prostrate by the cottager's cudgel: but the wife being less dexterous than her company, though an Amazon in strength, missed her pass at a fifth, and drove the point of the spit several inches into the right hand door-post as she stood close to the left, and thus made a new barrier which the invaders could not pass without dipping under it and submitting their necks to the sword: but one of the assailants seizing it with gigantic rage, shook it at once from the grasp of its holder and from its lodgment in the post, and at the same time made good the irruption of the rest of his party into the cottage.

Now raged an unequal combat, for the assailants fell two to one on Robin, Marian, the baron, and the cottager; while the wife, being deprived of her spit, converted every thing that was at hand to a missile, and rained pots, pans, and pipkins on the armed heads of the enemy. The baron raged like a tiger, and the cottager laid about him like a thresher. One of the soldiers struck Robin's sword from his hand and brought him on his knee, when the boy, who had been roused by the tumult and had been peeping through the inner door, leaped forward in his shirt, picked up the sword and replaced it in Robin's hand, who instantly springing up, disarmed and wounded one of his antagonists, while the other was laid prostrate under the dint of a brass cauldron launched by the Amazonian dame. Robin now turned to the aid of Marian, who was parrying most dexterously the cuts and slashes of her two assailants, of whom Robin delivered her from one, while a well-applied blow of her sword struck off the helmet of the other, who fell on his knees to beg a boon, and she recognised Sir Ralph Montfaucon. The men who were engaged with the baron and the peasant, seeing their leader subdued, immediately laid down their arms and cried for quarter. The wife brought some strong rope, and the baron tied their arms behind them.

"Now, Sir Ralph," said Marian, "once more you are at my mercy."

"That I always am, cruel beauty," said the discomfited lover.

"Odso! courteous knight," said the baron, "is this the return you make for my beef and canary, when you kissed my daughter's hand in token of contrition for your intermeddling at her wedding? Heart, I am glad to see she has given you a bloody coxcomb. Slice him down, Mawd! slice him down, and fling him into the river."

"Confess," said Marian, "what brought you here, and how did you trace our steps?"

"I will confess nothing," said the knight.

"Then confess you, rascal," said the baron, holding his sword to the throat of the captive squire.

"Take away the sword," said the squire, "it is too near my mouth, and my voice will not come out for fear: take away the sword, and I will confess all." The baron dropped his sword, and the squire proceeded: "Sir Ralph met you, as you quitted Lady Falkland's castle, and by representing to her who you were, borrowed from her such a number of her retainers as he deemed must ensure your capture, seeing that your familiar the friar was not at your elbow. We set forth without delay, and traced you first by means of a peasant who saw you turn into this valley, and afterwards by the light from the casement of this solitary dwelling. Our design was to have laid an ambush for you in the morning, but the storm and your observation of my unlucky face through the casement made us change our purpose; and what followed you can tell better than I can, being indeed masters of the subject."

"You are a merry knave," said the baron, "and here is a cup of wine for you."

"Gramercy," said the squire, "and better late than never: but I lacked a cup of this before. Had I been pot-valiant, I had held you play."

"Sir knight," said Marian, "this is the third time you have sought the life of my lord and of me, for mine is interwoven with his. And do you think me so spiritless as to believe that I can be yours by compulsion? Tempt me not again, for the next time shall be the last, and the fish of the nearest river shall commute the flesh of a recreant knight into the fast-day dinner of an uncarnivorous friar. I spare you now, not in pity but in scorn. Yet shall you swear to a convention never more to pursue or molest my lord or me, and on this condition you shall live."

The knight had no alternative but to comply, and swore, on the honour of knighthood, to keep the convention inviolate. How well he kept his oath we shall have no opportunity of narrating: *Di lui la nostra istoria più non parla.*[3]

---

3. ["Of him, our history speaks no more." This phrase is often used in historical or literary contexts to indicate that a character or figure disappears from the narrative, because either they are no longer relevant or their fate is unknown. It is commonly found in Italian chronicles, historical narratives and literary works, particularly those influenced by medieval and Renaissance historiography, and resembles expressions used in Ariosto's *Orlando Furioso* and Boiardo's *Orlando Innamorato.*]

CHAPTER XVI

Carry me over the water, thou fine fellowe.

Old Ballad.[1]

THE pilgrims, without experiencing further molestation, arrived at the retreat of Sir Guy of Gamwell. They found the old knight a cup too low; partly from being cut off from the scenes of his old hospitality and the shouts of his Nottinghamshire vassals, who were wont to make the rafters of his ancient hall re-echo to their revelry; but principally from being parted from his son, who had long been the better half of his flask and pasty. The arrival of our visitors cheered him up; and finding that the baron was to remain with him, he testified his delight and the cordiality of his welcome by pegging him in the ribs till he made him roar.

1. [Peacock is likely referring to The Jolly Waterman, a traditional English folk song or ballad that was well known in earlier centuries. While variations of the song exist, the theme generally revolves around a ferryman or waterman helping passengers across a river, sometimes with romantic or humorous undertones.]

Robin and Marian took an affectionate leave of the baron and the old knight; and before they quitted the vicinity of Barnsdale, deeming it prudent to return in a different disguise, they laid aside their pilgrim's attire, and assumed the habits and appurtenances of wandering minstrels.

They travelled in this character safely and pleasantly, till one evening at a late hour they arrived by the side of a river, where Robin looking out for a mode of passage perceived a ferry-boat safely moored in a nook on the opposite bank; near which a chimney sending up a wreath of smoke through the thick-set willows, was the only symptom of human habitation; and Robin naturally conceiving the said chimney and wreath of smoke to be the outward signs of the inward ferryman, shouted "Over!" with much strength and clearness; but no voice replied, and no ferryman appeared. Robin raised his voice, and shouted with redoubled energy, "Over, Over, O-o-o-over!" A faint echo alone responded "Over!" and again died away into deep silence: but after a brief interval a voice from among the willows, in a strange kind of mingled intonation that was half a shout and half a song, answered:

Over, over, over, jolly, jolly rover,
Would you then come over? Over, over, over?
Jolly, jolly rover, here's one lives in clover:
Who finds the clover? The jolly, jolly rover.
He finds the clover, let him then come over,
The jolly, jolly rover, over, over, over.

"I much doubt," said Marian, "if this ferryman do

not mean by clover something more than the toll of his ferry-boat."

"I doubt not," answered Robin, "he is a levier of toll and tithe, which I shall put him upon proof of his right to receive, by making trial of his might to enforce."

The ferryman emerged from the willows and stepped into his boat. "As I live," exclaimed Robin, "the ferryman is a friar."

"With a sword," said Marian, "stuck in his rope girdle."

The friar pushed his boat off manfully, and was presently half over the river.

"It is Friar Tuck," said Marian.

"He will scarcely know us," said Robin; "and if he do not, I will break a staff with him for sport."

The friar came singing across the water: the boat touched the land: Robin and Marian stepped on board: the friar pushed off again.

"Silken doublets, silken doublets," said the friar: "slenderly lined, I trow: your wandering minstrel is always poor toll: your sweet angels of voices pass current for a bed and a supper at the house of every lord that likes to hear the fame of his valour without the trouble of fighting for it. What need you of purse or pouch? You may sing before thieves. Pedlars, pedlars: wandering from door to door with the small ware of lies and cajolery: exploits for carpet-knights; honesty for courtiers; truth for monks, and chastity for nuns: a good saleable stock that costs the vender nothing, defies wear and tear, and when it has served a hundred customers is as plentiful and as marketable as ever. But, sirrahs, I'll none of your balderdash. You pass not hence without clink of brass, or I'll knock your musical noddles together till they ring like a pair of cymbals. That will be a new tune for your minstrelships."

This friendly speech of the friar ended as they stepped on the opposite bank. Robin had noticed as they passed that the summer stream was low.

"Why, thou brawling mongrel," said Robin, "that whether thou be thief, friar, or ferryman, or an ill-mixed compound of all three, passes conjecture, though I judge thee to be simple thief, what barkest thou at thus? Villain, there is clink of brass for thee. Dost thou see this coin? Dost thou hear this music? Look and listen: for touch thou shalt not: my minstrelship defies thee. Thou shalt carry me on thy back over the water, and receive nothing but a cracked sconce for thy trouble."

"A bargain," said the friar: "for the water is low, the labour is light, and the reward is alluring." And he stooped down for Robin, who mounted his back, and the friar waded with him over the river.

"Now, fine fellow," said the friar, "thou shalt carry me back over the water, and thou shalt have a cracked sconce for thy trouble."[2]

Robin took the friar on his back, and waded with him into the middle of the river, when by a dexterous jerk he suddenly flung him off and plunged him horizontally over head and ears in the water. Robin waded to shore, and the friar half swimming and half scrambling followed.

---

2. [The word "sconce" has multiple meanings in English, but in this case, it refers to the head, a usage that was common in early modern English and persisted into the 18th and 19th centuries.]

"Fine fellow, fine fellow," said the friar, "now will I pay thee thy cracked sconce."

"Not so," said Robin, "I have not earned it: but thou hast earned it, and shalt have it."

It was not, even in those good old times, a sight of every day to see a troubadour and a friar playing at single-stick by the side of a river, each aiming with fell intent at the other's coxcomb. The parties were both so skilled in attack and defence, that their mutual efforts for a long time expended themselves in quick and loud rappings on each other's oaken staves. At length Robin by a dexterous feint contrived to score one on the friar's crown: but in the careless moment of triumph a splendid sweep of the friar's staff struck Robin's out of his hand into the middle of the river, and repaid his crack on the head with a degree of vigour that might have passed the bounds of a jest if Marian had not retarded its descent by catching the friar's arm.

"How now, recreant friar," said Marian; "what have you to say why you should not suffer instant execution, being detected in open rebellion against your liege lord? Therefore kneel down, traitor, and submit your neck to the sword of the offended law."

"Benefit of clergy," said the friar: "I plead my clergy. And is it you indeed, ye scapegraces? Ye are well disguised: I knew ye not, by my flask. Robin, jolly Robin, he buys a jest dearly that pays for it with a bloody coxcomb. But here is balm for all bruises, outward and inward. (The friar produced a flask of canary.) Wash thy wound twice and thy throat thrice with this solar concoction, and thou shalt marvel where was thy hurt. But what moved ye to this frolic? Knew ye not that ye could not appear in a mask more fashioned to move my bile than in that of these gilders and lackerers of the smooth surface of worthlessness, that bring the gold of true valour into disrepute, by stamping the baser metal with the fairer impression? I marvelled to find any such given to fighting (for they have an old instinct of self-preservation): but I rejoiced thereat, that I might discuss to them poetical justice: and therefore have I cracked thy sconce: for which, let this be thy medicine."

"But wherefore," said Marian, "do we find you here, when we left you joint lord warden of Sherwood?"

"I do but retire to my devotions," replied the friar. "This is my hermitage, in which I first took refuge when I escaped from my beloved brethren of Rubygill; and to which I still retreat at times from the vanities of the world, which else might cling to me too closely, since I have been promoted to be peer-spiritual of your forest-court. For, indeed, I do find in myself certain indications and admonitions that my day has past its noon; and none more cogent than this: that every day I grow more intolerant of bad, and have a keener and more fastidious relish of good wine. There is no surer symptom of receding years. The ferryman is my faithful varlet. I send him on some pious errand, that I may meditate in ghostly privacy, when my presence in the forest can best be spared: and when can it be better spared than now, seeing that the neighbourhood of Prince John, and his incessant perquisitions for Marian, have made the forest too hot to hold more of us than are needful to keep up a quorum, and preserve unbroken the continuity of our forest-dominion? For, in truth, without your greenwood majesties, we have hardly the wit to live in a body, and at the same time to keep our necks out of jeopardy, while that arch-rebel and traitor John infests the precincts of our territory."

The friar now conducted them to his peaceful cell, where he spread his frugal board with fish, venison, wild-fowl, fruit, and canary. Under the compound operation of this *materia medica* Robin's wounds healed apace, and the friar, who hated minstrelsy, began as usual chirping in his cups. Robin and Marian chimed in with his tuneful humour till the midnight moon peeped in upon their revelry.

It was now the very witching time of night,[3] when they heard a voice shouting, "Over!" They paused to listen, and the voice repeated "Over!" in accents clear and loud, but which at the same time either were in themselves, or seemed to be, from the place and the hour, singularly plaintive and dreary. The friar fidgetted about in his seat: fell into a deep musing: shook himself, and looked about him; first at Marian, then at Robin, then at Marian again: filled and tossed off a cup of canary, and relapsed into his reverie.

"Will you not bring your passenger over?" said Robin. The friar shook his head and looked mysterious.

"That passenger," said the friar, "will never come over. Every full moon, at midnight, that voice calls, 'Over!' I and my varlet have more than once obeyed the summons, and we have sometimes had a glimpse

---

3. [*Hamlet*, Act III, Scene 2:
   "Tis now the very witching time of night,
   When churchyards yawn and hell itself breathes out
   Contagion to this world: now could I drink hot blood,
   And do such bitter business as the day
   Would quake to look on."]

of a white figure under the opposite trees: but when the boat has touched the bank, nothing has been to be seen; and the voice has been heard no more till the midnight of the next full moon."

"It is very strange," said Robin.

"Wondrous strange," said the friar, looking solemn.

The voice again called "Over!" in a long plaintive musical cry.

"I must go to it," said the friar, "or it will give us no peace. I would all my customers were of this world. I begin to think that I am Charon, and that this river is Styx."

"I will go with you, friar," said Robin.

"By my flask," said the friar, "but you shall not."

"Then I will," said Marian.

"Still less," said the friar, hurrying out of the cell. Robin and Marian followed: but the friar outstepped them, and pushed off his boat.

A white figure was visible under the shade of the opposite trees. The boat approached the shore, and the figure glided away. The friar returned.

They re-entered the cottage, and sat some time conversing on the phenomenon they had seen. The friar sipped his wine, and after a time, said:

"There is a tradition of a damsel who was drowned here some years ago. The tradition is——-"

But the friar could not narrate a plain tale: he therefore cleared his throat, and sang with due solemnity, in a ghostly voice:

A damsel came, in midnight rain,
   And called across the ferry:
The weary wight she called in vain,

Whose senses sleep did bury.
At evening, from her father's door
   She turned to meet her lover:
At midnight, on the lonely shore,
   She shouted, "Over, over!"

She had not met him by the tree
   Of their accustomed meeting,
And sad and sick at heart was she,
   Her heart all wildly beating.
In chill suspense the hours went by,
   The wild storm burst above her:
She turned her to the river nigh,
   And shouted, "Over, over!"

A dim, discoloured, doubtful light
   The moon's dark veil permitted,
And thick before her troubled sight
   Fantastic shadows flitted.
Her lover's form appeared to glide,
   And beckon o'er the water:
Alas! his blood that morn had dyed
   Her brother's sword with slaughter.

Upon a little rock she stood,
   To make her invocation:
She marked not that the rain-swoln flood
   Was islanding her station.
The tempest mocked her feeble cry:
   No saint his aid would give her:
The flood swelled high and yet more high,
   And swept her down the river.

Yet oft beneath the pale moonlight,

When hollow winds are blowing,
The shadow of that maiden bright
  Glides by the dark stream's flowing.
And when the storms of midnight rave,
While clouds the broad moon cover,
The wild gusts waft across the wave
  The cry of, "Over, over!"

While the friar was singing, Marian was meditating: and when he had ended she said, "Honest friar, you have misplaced your tradition, which belongs to the æstuary of a nobler river, where the damsel was swept away by the rising of the tide, for which your land-flood is an indifferent substitute. But the true tradition of this stream, I think I myself possess, and I will narrate it in your own way:

It was a friar of orders free,
A friar of Rubygill:
At the greenwood-tree a vow made he,
But he kept it very ill:
A vow made he of chastity,
But he kept it very ill.
He kept it, perchance, in the conscious shade
Of the bounds of the forest wherein it was made:
But he roamed where he listed, as free as the wind,
And he left his good vow in the forest behind:
For its woods out of sight were his vow out of mind,
With the friar of Rubygill.

In lonely hut himself he shut,
The friar of Rubygill;
Where the ghostly elf absolved himself,
To follow his own good will:
And he had no lack of canary sack,
To keep his conscience still.
And a damsel well knew, when at lonely midnight
It gleamed on the waters, his signal-lamp-light:
"Over! over!" she warbled with nightingale throat,
And the friar sprang forth at the magical note,
And she crossed the dark stream in his trim ferryboat,
With the friar of Rubygill.

"Look you, now," said Robin, "if the friar does not blush. Many strange sights have I seen in my day, but never till this moment did I see a blushing friar."

"I think," said the friar, "you never saw one that blushed not, or you saw good canary thrown away. But you are welcome to laugh if it so please you. None shall laugh in my company, though it be at my expense, but I will have my share of the merriment. The world is a stage, and life is a farce, and he that laughs most has most profit of the performance. The worst thing is good enough to be laughed at, though it be good for nothing else; and the best thing, though it be good for something else, is good for nothing better."

And he struck up a song in praise of laughing and quaffing, without further adverting to Marian's insinuated accusation; being, perhaps, of opinion, that it was a subject on which the least said would be the soonest mended.

So passed the night. In the morning a forester came to the friar, with intelligence that Prince John had been compelled by the urgency of his affairs in other quarters, to disembarrass Nottingham Castle of his royal presence. Our wanderers returned joyfully to their forest-dominion, being thus relieved from the vicinity of any more formidable belligerent, than their old bruised and beaten enemy the sheriff of Nottingham.

CHAPTER XVII

Oh! this life
Is nobler than attending for a check,
Richer than doing nothing for a bribe,
Prouder than rustling in unpaid-for silk.

Cymbeline.[1]

So Robin and Marian dwelt and reigned in the forest, ranging the glades and the greenwoods from the matins of the lark to the vespers of the nightingale, and administering natural justice according to Robin's ideas of rectifying the inequalities of human condition: raising genial dews from the bags of the rich and idle, and returning them in fertilizing

---

1. [Act III, Scene 3:
    "Oh, this life
    Is nobler than attending for a check,
    Richer than doing nothing for a babe,
    Prouder than rustling in unpaid-for silk:
    Such gain the cap of him that makes him fine
    Yet keeps his book uncrossed. No life to ours!"
    "Babe" is often interpreted as a bauble.]

showers on the poor and industrious: an operation which more enlightened statesmen have happily reversed, to the unspeakable benefit of the community at large. The light footsteps of Marian were impressed on the morning dew beside the firmer step of her lover, and they shook its large drops about them as they cleared themselves a passage through the thick tall fern, without any fear of catching cold, which was not much in fashion in the twelfth century. Robin was as hospitable as Cathmor;[2] for seven men stood on seven paths to call the stranger to his feast. It is true, he superadded the small improvement of making the stranger pay for it: than which what could be more generous? For Cathmor was himself the prime giver of his feast, whereas Robin was only the agent to a series of strangers, who provided in turn for the entertainment of their successors; which is carrying the disinterestedness of hospitality to its acme. Marian often killed the deer,

> Which Scarlet dressed, and Friar Tuck blessed,
> While Little John wandered in search of a guest.

Robin was very devout, though there was great unity in his religion: it was exclusively given to our Lady the Virgin, and he never set forth in a morning till he had said three prayers, and had heard the sweet voice of his Marian singing a hymn to their mutual patroness. Each of his men had, as usual, a patron

---

2. [An allusion to Cathmor, a character in James Macpherson's Ossian poems, particularly *Temora* (1763), an epic poem attributed (falsely) to an ancient Gaelic bard named Ossian. Cathmor is a noble and generous warrior-king and the brother of Cairbar, a usurper who rules Ireland. In *Temora*, Cathmor is renowned for his hospitality and noble spirit, often depicted as a warrior with great generosity towards his followers and guests.]

saint according to his name or taste. The friar chose a saint for himself, and fixed on Saint Botolph, whom he euphonized into Saint Bottle, and maintained that he was that very Panomphic Pantagruelian saint,[3] well known in ancient France as a female divinity, by the name of La Dive Bouteille, whose oracular mono-syllable "Trincq," is celebrated and under-stood by all nations, and is expounded by the learned doctor Al-cofribas,[4] who has treated at large on the subject, to signify "drink." Saint Bottle, then, was the saint of Friar Tuck, who did not yield even to Robin and Marian in the assiduity of his devotions to his chosen patron. Such was their summer life, and in their winter caves they had sufficient furniture, ample provender, store of old wine, and assuredly no lack of fuel, with joyous music and pleasant discourse to charm away the season of darkness and storms.

Many moons had waxed and waned when on the afternoon of a lovely summer day a lusty broad-boned knight was riding through the forest of Sher-

---

3. ["Panomphic" derives from the Greek πανόμφαιος (panom-phaios), meaning "all-voiced" or "uttering oracles from all places". In classical mythology, the term was sometimes associated with Jupiter (Zeus) as a deity whose influence or pronouncements were universal. By calling Saint Bottle a "Panomphic" saint, Peacock is mocking the idea of saints as sources of universal wisdom, espe-cially in the case of a drunken, humorous Rabelaisian saint. Panta-gruel is one of the main characters in Rabelais' *Gargantua and Pantagruel*. The term "Pantagruelian" refers to something in the spirit of Pantagruel, meaning boisterous, extravagant, merry and often excessive in drinking and eating.]

4. Alcofribas Nasier: an anagram of François Rabelais, and his assumed appellation.

The reader who desires to know more about this oracular di-vinity, may consult the said doctor Alcofribas Nasier, who will usher him into the adytum through the medium of the high priestess Bacbuc.

wood. The sun shone brilliantly on the full green foliage, and afforded the knight a fine opportunity of observing picturesque effects, of which it is to be feared he did not avail himself. But he had not proceeded far, before he had an opportunity of observing something much more interesting, namely, a fine young outlaw leaning, in the true Sherwood fashion, with his back against a tree. The knight was preparing to ask the stranger a question, the answer to which, if correctly given, would have relieved him from a doubt that pressed heavily on his mind, as to whether he was in the right road or the wrong, when the youth prevented the inquiry by saying: "In God's name, sir knight, you are late to your meals. My master has tarried dinner for you these three hours."

"I doubt," said the knight, "I am not he you wot of. I am no where bidden to-day and I know none in this vicinage."

"We feared," said the youth, "your memory would be treacherous: therefore am I stationed here to refresh it."

"Who is your master?" said the knight; "and where does he abide?"

"My master," said the youth, "is called Robin Hood, and he abides hard by."

"And what knows he of me?" said the knight.

"He knows you," answered the youth, "as he does every way-faring knight and friar, by instinct."

"Gramercy," said the knight; "then I understand his bidding: but how if I say I will not come?"

"I am enjoined to bring you," said the youth. "If persuasion avail not, I must use other argument."

"Say'st thou so?" said the knight; "I doubt if thy stripling rhetoric would convince me."

"That," said the young forester, "we will see."

"We are not equally matched, boy," said the knight. "I should get less honour by thy conquest, than grief by thy injury."

"Perhaps," said the youth, "my strength is more than my seeming, and my cunning more than my strength. Therefore let it please your knighthood to dismount."

"It shall please my knighthood to chastise thy presumption," said the knight, springing from his saddle.

Hereupon, which in those days was usually the result of a meeting between any two persons anywhere, they proceeded to fight.

The knight had in an uncommon degree both strength and skill: the forester had less strength but not less skill than the knight, and showed such a mastery of his weapon as reduced the latter to great admiration.

They had not fought many minutes by the forest clock, the sun; and had as yet done each other no worse injury than that the knight had wounded the forester's jerkin, and the forester had disabled the knight's plume; when they were interrupted by a voice from a thicket, exclaiming, "Well fought, girl: well fought. Mass, that had nigh been a shrewd hit. Thou owest him for that, lass. Marry, stand by, I'll pay him for thee."

The knight turning to the voice, beheld a tall friar issuing from the thicket, brandishing a ponderous cudgel.

"Who art thou?" said the knight.

"I am the church militant of Sherwood," answered the friar. "Why art thou in arms against our lady queen?"

"What meanest thou?" said the knight.

"Truly, this," said the friar, "is our liege lady of the forest, against whom I do apprehend thee in overt act of treason. What sayest thou for thyself?"

"I say," answered the knight, "that if this be indeed a lady, man never yet held me so long."

"Spoken," said the friar, "like one who hath done execution. Hast thou thy stomach full of steel? Wilt thou diversify thy repast with a taste of my oak-graff? Or wilt thou incline thine heart to our venison, which truly is cooling? Wilt thou fight? or wilt thou dine? or wilt thou fight and dine? or wilt thou dine and fight? I am for thee, choose as thou mayest."

"I will dine," said the knight; "for with lady I never fought before, and with friar I never fought yet, and with neither will I ever fight knowingly: and if this be the queen of the forest, I will not, being in her own dominions, be backward to do her homage."

So saying, he kissed the hand of Marian, who was pleased most graciously to express her approbation.

"Gramercy, sir knight," said the friar, "I laud thee for thy courtesy, which I deem to be no less than thy valour. Now do thou follow me, while I follow my nose, which scents the pleasant odour of roast from the depth of the forest recesses. I will lead thy horse, and do thou lead my lady."

The knight took Marian's hand, and followed the friar, who walked before them, singing:

When the wind blows, when the wind blows
From where under buck the dry log glows,

What guide can you follow,
O'er brake and o'er hollow,
So true as a ghostly, ghostly nose?

158

CHAPTER XVIII

Robin and Richard were two pretty men.

Mother Goose's Melody.[1]

THEY proceeded, following their infallible guide, first along a light elastic greensward under the shade of lofty and wide-spreading trees that skirted a sunny opening of the forest, then along labyrinthine paths, which the deer, the outlaw, or the woodman had made, through the close shoots of the young cop-

---

1. [A well-known collection of English nursery rhymes that dates back to the 18th century. The full rhyme reads:
    "Robin and Richard
    Were two pretty men,
    They lay in bed.
    Till the clock struck ten,
    Then up starts Robin
    And looks at the sky:
    "Oh brother Richard,
    The sun's very high.
    You go before
    With the bottle and bag,
    And I will come after
    On little Jack nag."]

pices, through the thick undergrowth of the ancient woods, through beds of gigantic fern that filled the narrow glades and waved their green feathery heads above the plume of the knight. Along these sylvan alleys they walked in single file; the friar singing and pioneering in the van, the horse plunging and floundering behind the friar, the lady following "in maiden meditation fancy free,"[2] and the knight bringing up the rear, much marvelling at the strange company into which his stars had thrown him. Their path had expanded sufficiently to allow the knight to take Marian's hand again, when they arrived in the august presence of Robin Hood and his court.

Robin's table was spread under a high overarching canopy of living boughs, on the edge of a natural lawn of verdure starred with flowers, through which a swift transparent rivulet ran sparkling in the sun. The board was covered with abundance of choice food and excellent liquor, not without the comeliness of snow-white linen and the splendour of costly plate, which the sheriff of Nottingham had unwillingly contributed to supply, at the same time with an excellent cook, whom Little John's art had spirited away to the forest with the contents of his master's silver scullery.

An hundred foresters were here assembled overready for their dinner, some seated at the table and some lying in groups under the trees.

Robin bade courteous welcome to the knight, who took his seat between Robin and Marian at the festal board; at which was already placed one strange guest in the person of a portly monk, sitting between

---

2. [*A Midsummer Night's Dream*, Act II, Scene 1.]

Little John and Scarlet, with his rotund physiognomy elongated into an unnatural oval by the conjoint influence of sorrow and fear: sorrow for the departed contents of his travelling treasury, a good-looking valise which was hanging empty on a bough; and fear for his personal safety, of which all the flasks and pasties before him could not give him assurance. The appearance of the knight, however, cheered him up with a semblance of protection, and gave him just sufficient courage to demolish a cygnet and a numble-pie, which he diluted with the contents of two flasks of canary sack.

But wine, which sometimes creates and often increases joy, doth also, upon occasion, heighten sorrow: and so it fared now with our portly monk, who had no sooner explained away his portion of provender, than he began to weep and bewail himself bitterly.

"Why dost thou weep, man?" said Robin Hood. "Thou hast done thine embassy justly, and shalt have thy Lady's grace."

"Alack! alack!" said the monk: "no embassy had I, luckless sinner, as well thou wottest, but to take to my abbey in safety the treasure whereof thou hast despoiled me."

"Propound me his case," said Friar Tuck, "and I will give him ghostly counsel."

"You well remember," said Robin Hood, "the sorrowful knight who dined with us here twelve months and a day gone by."

"Well do I," said Friar Tuck. "His lands were in jeopardy with a certain abbot, who would allow him no longer day for their redemption. Whereupon you lent to him the four hundred pounds which he needed, and which he was to repay this day, though he had no better security to give than our Lady the Virgin."

"I never desired better," said Robin, "for she never yet failed to send me my pay; and here is one of her own flock, this faithful and well-favoured monk of St. Mary's, hath brought it me duly, principal and interest to a penny, as Little John can testify, who told it forth. To be sure, he denied having it, but that was to prove our faith. We sought and found it."

"I know nothing of your knight," said the monk: "and the money was our own, as the Virgin shall bless me."

"She shall bless thee," said Friar Tuck, "for a faithful messenger."

The monk resumed his wailing. Little John brought him his horse. Robin gave him leave to depart. He sprang with singular nimbleness into the saddle, and vanished without saying, God give you good day.

The stranger knight laughed heartily as the monk rode off.

"They say, sir knight," said Friar Tuck, "they should laugh who win: but thou laughest who art likely to lose."

"I have won," said the knight, "a good dinner, some mirth, and some knowledge: and I cannot lose by paying for them."

"Bravely said," answered Robin. "Still it becomes thee to pay: for it is not meet that a poor forester should treat a rich knight. How much money hast thou with thee?"

"Troth, I know not," said the knight. "Sometimes much, sometimes little, sometimes none. But search, and what thou findest keep: and for the sake of thy kind heart and open hand, be it what it may, I shall wish it were more."

"Then, since thou sayest so," said Robin, "not a penny will I touch. Many a false churl comes hither, and disburses against his will: and till there is lack of these, I prey not on true men."

"Thou art thyself a true man, right well I judge, Robin," said the stranger knight, "and seemest more like one bred in court than to thy present outlaw life."

"Our life," said the friar, "is a craft, an art, and a mystery. How much of it, think you, could be learned at court?"

"Indeed, I cannot say," said the stranger knight: "but I should apprehend very little."

"And so should I," said the friar: "for we should find very little of our bold open practice, but should hear abundance of praise of our principles. To live in seeming fellowship and secret rivalry; to have a hand for all, and a heart for none; to be everybody's acquaintance, and nobody's friend; to meditate the ruin of all on whom we smile, and to dread the secret stratagems of all who smile on us; to pilfer honours and despoil fortunes, not by fighting in daylight, but by sapping in darkness: these are arts which the court can teach, but which we, by 'r Lady, have not learned. But let your court-minstrel tune up his throat to the praise of your court-hero, then come our principles into play: then is our practice extolled: not by the same name, for their Richard is a hero, and our Robin is a thief: marry, your hero guts an exchequer, while your thief disembowels a portmanteau; your hero sacks a city, while your thief sacks a cellar: your hero marauds on a larger scale, and that is all the difference, for the principle and the virtue are one: but two of a trade cannot agree: therefore your hero makes laws to get rid of your thief, and gives him an ill name that he may hang him: for might is right, and the strong make laws for the weak, and they that make laws to serve their own turn do also make morals to give colour to their laws."

"Your comparison, friar," said the stranger, "fails in this: that your thief fights for profit, and your hero for honour. I have fought under the banners of Richard, and if, as you phrase it, he guts exchequers, and sacks cities, it is not to win treasure for himself, but to furnish forth the means of his greater and more glorious aim."

"Misconceive me not, sir knight," said the friar. "We all love and honour King Richard, and here is a deep draught to his health: but I would show you, that we foresters are miscalled by opprobrious names, and that our virtues, though they follow at humble distance, are yet truly akin to those of Cœur-de-Lion. I say not that Richard is a thief, but I say that Robin is a hero: and for honour, did ever yet man, miscalled thief, win greater honour than Robin? Do not all men grace him with some honourable epithet? The most gentle thief, the most courteous thief, the most bountiful thief, yea and the most honest thief? Richard is courteous, bountiful, honest, and valiant: but so also is Robin: it is the false word that makes the unjust distinction. They are twin-spirits, and should be friends but that fortune hath differently cast their lot: but their names shall descend together to the latest days, as the flower of their age and of England: for in the pure principles of freebootery have they excelled all men; and to the principles of freebootery, diversely developed, belong all the qualities to which song and story concede renown."

"And you may add, friar," said Marian, "that Robin, no less than Richard, is king in his own dominion; and that if his subjects be fewer, yet are they more uniformly loyal."

"I would, fair lady," said the stranger, "that thy latter observation were not so true. But I nothing doubt, Robin, that if Richard could hear your friar, and see you and your lady, as I now do, there is not a man in England whom he would take by the hand more cordially than yourself."

"Gramercy, sir knight," said Robin—But his speech was cut short by Little John calling, "Hark!"

All listened. A distant trampling of horses was heard. The sounds approached rapidly, and at length a group of horsemen glittering in holyday dresses was visible among the trees.

"God's my life!" said Robin, "what means this? To arms, my merrymen all."

"No arms, Robin," said the foremost horseman, riding up and springing from his saddle: "have you forgotten Sir William of the Lee?"

"No, by my fay," said Robin; "and right welcome again to Sherwood."

Little John bustled to re-array the disorganized economy of the table, and replace the dilapidations of the provender.

"I come late, Robin," said Sir William, "but I came by a wrestling, where I found a good yeoman wrongfully beset by a crowd of sturdy varlets, and I staid to do him right."

"I thank thee for that, in God's name," said Robin, "as if thy good service had been to myself."

"And here," said the knight, "is thy four hundred pound; and my men have brought thee an hundred bows and as many well-furnished quivers; which I beseech thee to receive and to use as a poor token of my grateful kindness to thee: for me and my wife and children didst thou redeem from beggary."

"Thy bows and arrows," said Robin, "will I joyfully receive: but of thy money, not a penny. It is paid already. My Lady, who was thy security, hath sent it me for thee."

Sir William pressed, but Robin was inflexible.

"It is paid," said Robin, "as this good knight can testify, who saw my Lady's messenger depart but now."

Sir William looked round to the stranger knight, and instantly fell on his knee, saying, "God save King Richard."

The foresters, friar and all, dropped on their knees together, and repeated in chorus: "God save King Richard."

"Rise, rise," said Richard, smiling: "Robin is king here, as his lady hath shown. I have heard much of thee, Robin, both of thy present and thy former state. And this, thy fair forest-queen, is, if tales say true, the lady Matilda Fitzwater."

Marian signed acknowledgment.

"Your father," said the king, "has approved his fidelity to me, by the loss of his lands, which the newness of my return, and many public cares, have not yet given me time to restore: but this justice shall be done to him, and to thee also Robin, if thou wilt leave thy forest-life and resume thy earldom, and be a peer of Cœur-de-Lion: for braver heart and juster hand I never yet found."

Robin looked round on his men.

"Your followers," said the king, "shall have free pardon, and such of them as thou wilt part with, shall have maintenance from me; and if ever I confess to priest, it shall be to thy friar."

"Gramercy to your majesty," said the friar; "and my inflictions shall be flasks of canary; and if the number be (as in grave cases I may, peradventure, make it) too great for one frail mortality, I will relieve you by vicarious penance, and pour down my own throat the redundancy of the burden."

Robin and his followers embraced the king's proposal. A joyful meeting soon followed with the baron and Sir Guy of Gamwell: and Richard himself honoured with his own presence a formal solemnization of the nuptials of our lovers, whom he constantly distinguished with his peculiar regard.

The friar could not say, Farewell to the forest, without something of a heavy heart: and he sang as he turned his back upon its bounds, occasionally reverting his head:

Ye woods, that oft at sultry noon
   Have o'er me spread your massy shade:
Ye gushing streams, whose murmured tune
   Has in my ear sweet music made,
While, where the dancing pebbles show
   Deep in the restless fountain-pool
The gelid water's upward flow,
   My second flask was laid to cool:

Ye pleasant sights of leaf and flower:
   Ye pleasant sounds of bird and bee:
Ye sports of deer in sylvan bower:

Ye feasts beneath the greenwood tree:
Ye baskings in the vernal sun:
Ye slumbers in the summer dell:
Ye trophies that this arm has won:
And must ye hear your friar's farewell?

But the friar's farewell was not destined to be eternal. He was domiciled as the family confessor of the earl and countess of Huntingdon, who led a discreet and courtly life, and kept up old hospitality in all its munificence, till the death of King Richard and the usurpation of John, by placing their enemy in power, compelled them to return to their greenwood sovereignty; which, it is probable, they would have before done from choice, if their love of sylvan liberty had not been counteracted by their desire to retain the friendship of Cœur-de-Lion. Their old and tried adherents, the friar among the foremost, flocked again round their forest-banner; and in merry Sherwood they long lived together, the lady still retaining her former name of Maid Marian, though the appellation was then as much a misnomer as that of Little John.

THE END

THE MISFORTUNES OF ELPHIN

by

THE AUTHOR OF HEADLONG HALL.

Quod non exspectes ex transverso fit,
Et suprà nos Fortuna negotia curat:
Quare da nobis vina Falerna, puer.[1]
PETRONIUS ARBITER.

---

1. ["The unexpected will turn up;
    Our whole lives Fortune bungles up.
    Falernian, boy, hand round the cup."
    Satyricon, Vol. II. Ch. LV, as translated by W. C. Firebaugh. Peacock's more lyrical translation appears on page 177.]

CONTENTS

INDEX TO THE POETRY

INTRODUCTION

The Misfortunes of Elphin (1829) is one of Thomas Love Peacock's most distinctive works, a remarkable blend of historical romance, political satire and whimsical humour. Set in 6th-century Wales during the reign of King Arthur, the novella intertwines ancient British legend with Peacock's sharp wit and his characteristic irreverence towards literary and historical conventions. Drawing on sources from Welsh mythology and medieval chronicles, Peacock crafts a narrative that is both steeped in the romance of the past and strikingly modern in its satirical critique of contemporary society.

At the heart of the novella is the story of Elphin ap Gwythno, a hapless yet noble-spirited prince whose fortunes rise and fall in tandem with the whimsical turns of fate. Elphin is married to the wise and virtuous Angharad, whose unwavering loyalty and sharp intellect provide a steady counterbalance to her husband's misadventures. The tale also features the legendary bard Taliesin, a figure from Welsh mythology renowned for his poetic genius and prophetic insight. In Peacock's hands, Taliesin becomes both a mystic seer and a sardonic commentator, reflecting the author's own dual role as storyteller and satirist.

Peacock draws heavily from medieval Welsh sources, particularly the *Mabinogion* and the *Historia Brittonum*, but he filters these legends through a lens of playful scepticism. The mythical inundation of the land of Gwaelod, a great flood said to have submerged a fertile kingdom beneath the sea, serves as a central event in the story. Yet Peacock treats even this cataclysm with a lightness that deflates its tragic potential, turning what could have been an epic disaster into a backdrop for comic misadventure and philosophical musing.

The origins of *The Misfortunes of Elphin* can be traced to Peacock's deep fascination with Celtic mythology and his broader engagement with Romantic literary trends. While he was critical of the Romantic movement's excesses, Peacock shared its interest in the revival of ancient legends and national myths. His government role with the East India Company also provided him with a unique perspective on the machinations of power and governance, themes that seep into the narrative's satirical undertones. The work was conceived during a period of political turbulence in Britain, and Peacock's sharp observations on the absurdities of leadership and the follies of reform reflect his disillusionment with contemporary politics.

As in his other works, Peacock's true interest lies not in the mechanics of plot but in the interplay of ideas. *The Misfortunes of Elphin* is as much a vehicle for satirical dialogue as it is a narrative. Characters engage in spirited debates about politics, religion, war and poetry, often with anachronistic flourishes that highlight the absurdities of both the ancient world and Peacock's own time. The contrast between the lofty ideals of chivalry and the mundane realities of human folly is a recurring theme, handled with Peacock's signature blend of erudition and humour.

One of the novella's most striking features is its treatment of King Arthur, who appears not as the noble paragon of legend but as a flawed, bumbling ruler presiding over a court rife with incompetence and vanity. This portrayal is a deliberate subversion of Romantic and Victorian ideals of Arthurian heroism, reflecting Peacock's scepticism toward the idealisation of history and national myth. Instead of celebrating the grandeur of Britain's legendary past, Peacock exposes its contradictions and invites readers to laugh at its pretensions.

The satire extends beyond historical targets to encompass the political landscape of Peacock's own era. Written during a period of intense debate over parliamentary reform in Britain, *The Misfortunes of Elphin* uses its ancient setting to comment on the follies of contemporary governance. Peacock, through his post at the East India Company, was intimately familiar with the bureaucratic absurdities of his time, and his experiences colour the novella's depiction of political incompetence and moral hypocrisy.

Stylistically, *The Misfortunes of Elphin* showcases Peacock's mastery of language and literary pastiche. His prose is rich with classical allusions, poetic interludes and mock-heroic flourishes that parody the conventions of epic storytelling. The novella is also peppered with verses attributed to Taliesin, blending genuine fragments of Welsh poetry with Peacock's own compositions. This fusion of the authentic and the invented reflects Peacock's playful approach to historical fiction, where fact and fantasy coexist in a tapestry of wit and whimsy.

Despite its light-hearted tone, *The Misfortunes of Elphin* is not without depth. Beneath the satire lies a meditation on the capriciousness of fortune and the resilience of the human spirit. Elphin's misfortunes, though often absurd, are tempered by his steadfastness and the loyalty of those around him. The novella suggests that while individuals may be powerless against the tides of fate, they can still find meaning in friendship, love and the pursuit of knowledge.

For modern readers, *The Misfortunes of Elphin* offers both entertainment and insight. It is a work that delights in the absurdities of history and human nature, challenging us to question the myths we inherit and the values we uphold. Peacock's wit remains as sharp today as it was in his time, and his satirical vision continues to resonate in an age that is no less susceptible to the follies of pride, power, and pretence.

Whether approached as a parody of Arthurian romance, a political satire or a whimsical philosophical tale, *The Misfortunes of Elphin* stands as a testament to Thomas Love Peacock's unique voice in English literature—irreverent, erudite and endlessly entertaining.

L.A.D.

THE MISFORTUNES OF ELPHIN

Unlooked-for good betides us still,
And unanticipated ill:
Blind Fortune rules the hours that roll:
Then fill with good old wine the bowl.

THE PROSPERITY OF GWAELOD.

Regardless of the sweeping whirlwind's sway,
That, hush'd in grim repose, expects his evening prey.[1]

In the beginning of the sixth century, when Uther Pendragon held the nominal sovereignty of Britain over a number of petty kings, Gwythno Garanhir was king of Caredigion. The most valuable portion of his dominions was the Great Plain of Gwaelod, an extensive tract of level land, stretching along that part of the sea-coast which now belongs to the counties of Merioneth and Cardigan. This district was populous and highly cultivated. It contained sixteen fortified towns, superior to all the towns and cities of the Cymry, excepting Caer Lleon upon Usk; and, like Caer

---

1. [*The Bard: A Pindaric Ode*, II.2:
    "Fair laughs the Morn, and soft the Zephyr blows,
    While proudly riding o'er the azure realm
    In gallant trim the gilded vessel goes;
    Youth on the prow, and Pleasure at the helm;
    Regardless of the sweeping Whirlwind's sway,
    That, hush'd in grim repose, expects his evening prey."]

Lleon, they bore in their architecture, their language, and their manners, vestiges of past intercourse with the Roman lords of the world. It contained also one of the three privileged ports of the isle of Britain, which was called the Port of Gwythno. This port, we may believe if we please, had not been unknown to the Phœnicians and Carthaginians, when they visited the island for metal, accommodating the inhabitants, in return, with luxuries which they would not otherwise have dreamed of, and which they could very well have done without; of course, in arranging the exchange of what they denominated equivalents, imposing on their simplicity, and taking advantage of their ignorance, according to the approved practice of civilized nations; which they called imparting the blessings of Phœnician and Carthaginian light.

An embankment of massy stone protected this lowland country from the sea, which was said, in traditions older than the embankment, to have, in occasional spring-tides, paid short but unwelcome visits to the interior inhabitants, and to have, by slow aggressions, encroached considerably on the land. To prevent the repetition of the first of these inconveniences, and to check the progress of the second, the people of Gwaelod had built the stony rampart, which had withstood the shock of the waves for centuries, when Gwythno began his reign.

Gwythno, like other kings, found the business of governing too light a matter to fill up the vacancy of either his time or his head, and took to the more solid pursuits of harping and singing; not forgetting feasting, in which he was glorious; nor hunting, wherein he was mighty. His several pursuits composed a very harmonious triad. The chace[2] conduced to the good cheer of the feast, and to the good appetite which consumed it; the feast inspired the song; and the song gladdened the feast, and celebrated the chace.

Gwythno and his subjects went on together very happily. They had little to do with him but to pay him revenue, and he had little to do with them but to receive it. Now and then they were called on to fight for the protection of his sacred person, and for the privilege of paying revenue to him rather than to any of the kings in his vicinity, a privilege of which they were particularly tenacious. His lands being far more fertile, and his people, consequently, far more numerous, than those of the rocky dwellers on his borders, he was always victorious in the defensive warfare to which he restricted his military achievements; and, after the invaders of his dominions had received two or three inflictions of signal chastisement, they limited their aggressions to coming quietly in the night, and vanishing, before morning, with cattle: an heroic operation, in which the pre-eminent glory of Scotland renders the similar exploits of other nations not worth recording.

Gwythno was not fond of the sea: a moonstruck bard had warned him to beware of the oppression of

---

2. ["Chase" in modern English. The word derives from the Old French "chacier" (to hunt), which entered Middle English as "chace" or "chase". In the 16th and 17th centuries, both spellings were common, with "chace" typically found in more formal or literary contexts. By the time Peacock was writing *The Misfortunes of Elphin*, "chase" had become the more common spelling in everyday usage. However, "chace" persisted in literary, poetic, and heraldic contexts, where it conveyed an archaic tone, especially when referring to hunting traditions or classical allusions.]

Gwenhidwy;[3] and he thought he could best do so by keeping as far as possible out of her way. He had a palace built of choice slate stone on the rocky banks of the Mawddach, just above the point where it quitted its native mountains, and entered the Plain of Gwaelod. Here, among green woods and sparkling waters, he lived in festal munificence, and expended his revenue in encouraging agriculture, by consuming a large quantity of produce.

Watchtowers were erected along the embankment, and watchmen were appointed to guard against the first approaches of damage or decay. The whole of these towers, and their companies of guards, were subordinate to a central castle, which commanded the sea-port already mentioned, and wherein dwelt Prince Seithenyn ap Seithyn Saidi, who held the office of Arglwyd Gorwarcheidwad yr Argae Breninawl, which signifies, in English, Lord High Commissioner of Royal Embankment; and he executed it as a personage so denominated might be expected to do: he drank the profits, and left the embankment to his deputies, who left it to their assistants, who left it to itself.

The condition of the head, in a composite as in a simple body, affects the entire organization to the extremity of the tail, excepting that, as the tail in the figurative body usually receives the largest share in the distribution of punishment, and the smallest in the distribution of reward, it has the stronger stimulus to ward off evil, and the smaller supply of means to indulge in diversion; and it sometimes happens

---

3. *Gwen-hudiw*, "the white alluring one:" the name of a mermaid. Used figuratively for the elemental power of the sea.

that one of the least regarded of the component parts of the said tail will, from a pure sense of duty, or an inveterate love of business, or an oppressive sense of ennui, or a development of the organ of order, or some other equally cogent reason, cheerfully undergo all the care and labour, of which the honour and profit will redound to higher quarters.

Such a component portion of the Gwaelod High Commission of Royal Embankment was Teithrin ap Tathral, who had the charge of a watchtower where the embankment terminated at the point of Mochres, in the high land of Ardudwy. Teithrin kept his portion of the embankment in exemplary condition, and paced with daily care the limits of his charge; but one day, by some accident, he strayed beyond them, and observed symptoms of neglect that filled him with dismay. This circumstance induced him to proceed till his wanderings brought him round to the embankment's southern termination in the high land of Caredigion. He met with abundant hospitality at the towers of his colleagues, and at the castle of Seithenyn: he was supposed to be walking for his amusement; he was asked no questions, and he carefully abstained from asking any. He examined and observed in silence; and, when he had completed his observations, he hastened to the palace of Gwythno.

Preparations were making for a high festival, and Gwythno was composing an ode. Teithrin knew better than to interrupt him in his *awen*.[4]

Gwythno had a son named Elphin, who is celebrated in history as the most expert of fishers.

---

4. The rapturous and abstracted state of poetical inspiration.

Teithrin, finding the king impracticable, went in search of the young prince.

Elphin had been all the morning fishing in the Mawddach, in a spot where the river, having quitted the mountains and not yet entered the plain, ran in alternate streams and pools sparkling through a pastoral valley. Elphin sat under an ancient ash, enjoying the calm brightness of an autumnal noon, and the melody and beauty of the flying stream, on which the shifting sunbeams fell chequering through the leaves. The monotonous music of the river, and the profound stillness of the air, had contributed to the deep abstraction of a meditation into which Elphin had fallen. He was startled into attention by a sudden rush of the wind through the trees, and during the brief interval of transition from the state of reverie to that of perfect consciousness, he heard, or seemed to hear, in the gust that hurried by him, the repetition of the words, "Beware of the oppression of Gwenhidwy." The gust was momentary: the leaves ceased to rustle, and the deep silence of nature returned.

The prophecy, which had long haunted the memory and imagination of his father, had been often repeated to Elphin, and had sometimes occupied his thoughts, but it had formed no part of his recent meditation, and he could not persuade himself that the words had not been actually spoken near him. He emerged from the shade of the trees that fringed the river, and looked round him from the rocky bank.

At this moment Teithrin ap Tathral discovered and approached him.

Elphin knew him not, and inquired his name. He answered, "Teithrin ap Tathral."

"And what seek you here?" said Elphin.

"I seek," answered Teithrin, "the Prince of Gwaelod, Elphin ap Gwythno Garanhir."

"You spoke," said Elphin, "as you approached." Teithrin answered in the negative.

"Assuredly you did," said Elphin. "You repeated the words, 'Beware of the oppression of Gwenhidwy.'"

Teithrin denied having spoken the words; but their mysterious impression made Elphin listen readily to his information and advice; and the result of their conference was a determination, on the part of the Prince, to accompany Teithrin ap Tathral on a visit of remonstrance to the Lord High Commissioner.

They crossed the centre of the enclosed country to the privileged port of Gwythno, near which stood the castle of Seithenyn. They walked towards the castle along a portion of the embankment, and Teithrin pointed out to the Prince its dilapidated condition. The sea shone with the glory of the setting sun; the air was calm; and the white surf, tinged with the crimson of sunset, broke lightly on the sands below. Elphin turned his eyes from the dazzling splendour of ocean to the green meadows of the Plain of Gwaelod; the trees, that in the distance thickened into woods; the wreaths of smoke rising from among them, marking the solitary cottages, or the populous towns; the massy barrier of mountains beyond, with the forest rising from their base; the precipices frowning over the forest; and the clouds resting on their summits, reddened with the reflection of the west. Elphin gazed earnestly on the peopled plain, reposing in the calm of evening between the mountains and the sea, and thought, with deep feelings of secret pain, how much of life and human happiness was intrusted to the ruinous mound on which he stood.

188

CHAPTER 2
THE DRUNKENNESS OF SEITHENYN.

The three immortal drunkards of the isle of Britain:
Ceraint of Essyllwg; Gwrtheyrn Gwrthenau; and Seithenyn ap Seithyn Saidi.

TRIADS OF THE ISLE OF BRITAIN.[1]

THE sun had sunk beneath the waves when they
reached the castle of Seithenyn. The sound of the
harp and the song saluted them as they approached
it. As they entered the great hall, which was already
blazing with torchlight, they found his highness, and
his highness's household, convincing themselves and
each other with wine and wassail, of the excellence of

---

1. [A collection of traditional Welsh wisdom literature known as
The Triads of the Island of Britain (*Trioedd Ynys Prydein*) that pre-
serves early Welsh folklore, history and mythology, structured in
groups of three related items (hence the name *triads*). They cover a
wide range of topics, such as heroes, battles, historical events,
virtues and legendary objects. The triads likely originated in oral
tradition. Written versions dating from the 13th century, though
the material is often much older. The most significant collection of
the triads comes from manuscripts like the *Red Book of Hergest*
(14th century), which also contains parts of the *Mabinogion*.]

their system of virtual superintendence; and the following jovial chorus broke on the ears of the visitors:

THE CIRCLING OF THE MEAD-HORNS[2]

Fill the blue horn, the blue buffalo horn:
Natural is mead in the buffalo horn:
As the cuckoo in spring, as the lark in the morn,
So natural is mead in the buffalo horn.

As the cup of the flower to the bee when he sips,
Is the full cup of mead to the true Briton's lips:
From the flower-cups of summer, on field and on tree,
Our mead cups are filled by the vintager bee.

Seithenyn[3] ap Seithyn, the generous, the bold,
Drinks the wine of the stranger from vessels of gold;[4]
But we from the horn, the blue silver-rimmed horn,

---

2.   [These verses echo the spirit and style of the Welsh musical and poetic traditions popularised in the early 19th century in part by John Parry (Bardd Alaw), a Welsh harpist, composer, and collector of traditional Welsh music. His work, particularly *Welsh Melodies* (published around 1809–1811), with lyrics by Thomas Dibdin, sought to preserve and adapt traditional Welsh tunes for a wider British audience during the Romantic era's fascination with Celtic revivalism.]
3.   The accent is on the second syllable: Seithényn.
4.   Gwin...o eur... ANEURIN. [The Welsh poet Aneurin (or Aneirin), of the Brythonic-speaking kingdoms of early Britain, who was likely associated with the court of Gododdin (in modern-day southern Scotland and northern England). He flourished around the time of the Battle of Catraeth (c. 600 CE), the subject of his famous work, *Y Gododdin*, an elegy for the warriors of Gododdin who fought and died at Catraeth. The poem is filled with vivid imagery of heroism, feasting and drinking, particularly of mead and wine, which were symbolic of both warrior culture and ritualistic camaraderie before battle.]

Drink the ale and the mead in our fields that were
born.

The ale-froth is white, and the mead sparkles bright;
They both smile apart, and with smiles they unite:[5]
The mead from the flower, and the ale from the corn,
Smile, sparkle, and sing in the buffalo horn.

The horn, the blue horn, cannot stand on its tip;
Its path is right on from the hand to the lip:
Though the bowl and the wine-cup our tables adorn,
More natural the draught from the buffalo horn.

But Seithenyn ap Seithyn, the generous, the bold,
Drinks the bright-flowing wine from the far-
gleaming gold:
The wine, in the bowl by his lip that is worn,
Shall be glorious as mead in the buffalo horn.

The horns circle fast, but their fountains will last,
As the stream passes ever, and never is past:
Exhausted so quickly, replenished so soon,
They wax and they wane like the horns of the moon.

Fill high the blue horn, the blue buffalo horn;
Fill high the long silver-rimmed buffalo horn:
While the roof of the hall by our chorus is torn,
Fill, fill to the brim, the deep silver-rimmed horn.

Elphin and Teithrin stood some time on the floor
of the hall before they attracted the attention of

---

5. The mixture of ale and mead made *bradawd*, a favourite drink
of the Ancient Britons.

Seithenyn, who, during the chorus, was tossing and flourishing his golden goblet. The chorus had scarcely ended when he noticed them, and immediately roared aloud, "You are welcome all four."

Elphin answered, "We thank you: we are but two."

"Two or four," said Seithenyn, "all is one. You are welcome all. When a stranger enters, the custom in other places is to begin by washing his feet. My custom is, to begin by washing his throat. Seithenyn ap Seithyn Saidi bids you welcome."

Elphin, taking the wine-cup, answered, "Elphin ap Gwythno Garanhir thanks you."

Seithenyn started up. He endeavoured to straighten himself into perpendicularity, and to stand steadily on his legs. He accomplished half his object by stiffening all his joints but those of his ancles, and from these the rest of his body vibrated upwards with the inflexibility of a bar. After thus oscillating for a time, like an inverted pendulum, finding that the attention requisite to preserve his rigidity absorbed all he could collect of his dissipated energies, and that he required a portion of them for the management of his voice, which he felt a dizzy desire to wield with peculiar steadiness in the presence of the son of the king, he suddenly relaxed the muscles that perform the operation of sitting, and dropped into his chair like a plummet. He then, with a gracious gesticulation, invited Prince Elphin to take his seat on his right hand, and proceeded to compose himself into a dignified attitude, throwing his body back into the left corner of his chair, resting his left elbow on its arm and his left cheekbone on the middle of the back of his left hand, placing his left foot on a footstool, and stretching out his right leg as straight and as far as his position allowed. He had thus his right hand at liberty, for the ornament of his eloquence and the conduct of his liquor.

Elphin seated himself at the right hand of Seithenyn. Teithrin remained at the end of the hall: on which Seithenyn exclaimed, "Come on, man, come on. What, if you be not the son of a king, you are the guest of Seithenyn ap Seithyn Saidi. The most honourable place to the most honourable guest, and the next most honourable place to the next most honourable guest; the least honourable guest above the most honourable inmate; and, where there are but two guests, be the most honourable who he may, the least honourable of the two is next in honour to the most honourable of the two, because they are no more but two; and, where there are only two, there can be nothing between. Therefore sit, and drink. GWIN O EUR: wine from gold."

Elphin motioned Teithrin to approach, and sit next to him.

Prince Seithenyn, whose liquor was "his eating and his drinking solely,"[6] seemed to measure the gastronomy of his guests by his own; but his groom of the pantry thought the strangers might be disposed to eat, and placed before them a choice of provision, on which Teithrin ap Tathral did vigorous execution.

"I pray your excuses," said Seithenyn, "my

---

6. [Cf. Beaumont and Fletcher, *The Scornful Lady*, Act IV, Scene 2:
    "Ale is their eating and their drinking surely,
    Which keeps their bodies clear and soluble.
    Bread is a binder, and for that abolished,
    Even in their ale, whose lost room fills an apple,
    Which is more airy, and of subtler nature."]

stomach is weak, and I am subject to dizziness in the head, and my memory is not so good as it was, and my faculties of attention are somewhat impaired, and I would dilate more upon the topic, whereby you should hold me excused, but I am troubled with a feverishness and parching of the mouth, that very much injures my speech, and impedes my saying all I would say, and will say before I have done, in token of my loyalty and fealty to your highness and your highness's house. I must just moisten my lips, and I will then proceed with my observations. Cupbearer, fill."

"Prince Seithenyn," said Elphin, "I have visited you on a subject of deep moment. Reports have been brought to me, that the embankment, which has been so long intrusted to your care, is in a state of dangerous decay."

"Decay," said Seithenyn, "is one thing, and danger is another.[7] Every thing that is old must decay. That the embankment is old, I am free to confess; that it is somewhat rotten in parts, I will not altogether deny; that it is any the worse for that, I do most sturdily gainsay. It does its business well: it works well: it keeps out the water from the land, and it lets in the wine upon the High Commission of Embankment. Cupbearer, fill. Our ancestors were wiser than we:

---

7. [A satirical reference to contemporary arguments against political reform during Peacock's time, particularly relating to the debates surrounding the Reform movement in early 19th-century Britain, culminating in the Reform Act of 1832. The Reform movement aimed to address issues such as rotten boroughs, lack of representation in industrial cities and broader electoral corruption. Conservative opponents of reform often argued that changing traditional institutions would lead to instability, chaos or even revolution—fears rooted in the memory of the French Revolution.]

they built it in their wisdom; and, if we should be so rash as to try to mend it, we should only mar it."

"The stonework," said Teithrin, "is sapped and mined: the piles are rotten, broken, and dislocated: the floodgates and sluices are leaky and creaky."

"That is the beauty of it," said Seithenyn. "Some parts of it are rotten, and some parts of it are sound."

"It is well," said Elphin, "that some parts are sound: it were better that all were so."

"So I have heard some people say before," said Seithenyn; "perverse people, blind to venerable antiquity: that very unamiable sort of people, who are in the habit of indulging their reason. But I say, the parts that are rotten give elasticity to those that are sound: they give them elasticity, elasticity, elasticity. If it were all sound, it would break by its own obstinate stiffness: the soundness is checked by the rottenness, and the stiffness is balanced by the elasticity. There is nothing so dangerous as innovation. See the waves in the equinoctial storms, dashing and clashing, roaring and pouring, spattering and battering, rattling and battling against it. I would not be so presumptuous as to say, I could build any thing that would stand against them half an hour; and here this immortal old work, which God forbid the finger of modern mason should bring into jeopardy, this immortal work has stood for centuries, and will stand for centuries more, if we let it alone. It is well: it works well: let well alone. Cupbearer, fill. It was half rotten when I was born, and that is a conclusive reason why it should be three parts rotten when I die."

The whole body of the High Commission roared approbation.

"And after all," said Seithenyn, "the worst that

could happen would be the overflow of a springtide, for that was the worst that happened before the embankment was thought of; and, if the high water should come in, as it did before, the low water would go out again, as it did before. We should be no deeper in it than our ancestors were, and we could mend as easily as they could make."

"The level of the sea," said Teithrin, "is materially altered."

"The level of the sea!" exclaimed Seithenyn. "Who ever heard of such a thing as altering the level of the sea? Alter the level of that bowl of wine before you, in which, as I sit here, I see a very ugly reflection of your very goodlooking face. Alter the level of that: drink up the reflection: let me see the face without the reflection, and leave the sea to level itself."

"Not to level the embankment," said Teithrin.

"Good, very good," said Seithenyn. "I love a smart saying, though it hits at me. But, whether yours is a smart saying or no, I do not very clearly see; and, whether it hits at me or no, I do not very sensibly feel. But all is one. Cupbearer, fill."

"I think," pursued Seithenyn, looking as intently as he could at Teithrin ap Tathral, "I have seen something very like you before. There was a fellow here the other day very like you: he stayed here some time: he would not talk: he did nothing but drink: he used to drink till he could not stand, and then he went walking about the embankment. I suppose he thought it wanted mending; but he did not say any thing. If he had, I should have told him to embank his own throat, to keep the liquor out of that. That would have posed him: he could not have answered that: he would not have had a word to say for himself after that."

"He must have been a miraculous person," said Teithrin, "to walk when he could not stand."

"All is one for that," said Seithenyn. "Cupbearer, fill."

"Prince Seithenyn," said Elphin, "if I were not aware that wine speaks in the silence of reason, I should be astonished at your strange vindication of your neglect of duty, which I take shame to myself for not having sooner known and remedied. The wise bard has well observed, 'Nothing is done without the eye of the king.'"[8]

"I am very sorry," said Seithenyn, "that you see things in a wrong light: but we will not quarrel for three reasons: first, because you are the son of the king, and may do and say what you please, without any one having a right to be displeased: second, because I never quarrel with a guest, even if he grows riotous in his cups: third, because there is nothing to quarrel about; and perhaps that is the best reason of the three; or rather the first is the best, because you are the son of the king; and the third is the second, that is, the second best, because there is nothing to quarrel about; and the second is nothing to the purpose, because, though guests will grow riotous in their cups, in spite of my good orderly example, God forbid I should say, that is the case with you. And I completely agree in the truth of your remark, that reason speaks in the silence of wine."

Seithenyn accompanied his speech with a

---

8. [A reference to the Welsh bardic traditions concerning royal authority and oversight.]

vehement swinging of his right hand: in so doing, at this point, he dropped his cup: a sudden impulse of rash volition, to pick it dexterously up before he resumed his discourse, ruined all his devices for maintaining dignity; in stooping forward from his chair, he lost his balance, and fell prostrate on the floor.

The whole body of the High Commission arose in simultaneous confusion, each zealous to be the foremost in uplifting his fallen chief. In the vehemence of their uprise, they hurled the benches backward and the tables forward; the crash of cups and bowls accompanied their overthrow; and rivulets of liquor ran gurgling through the hall. The household wished to redeem the credit of their leader in the eyes of the Prince; but the only service they could render him was to participate his discomfiture; for Seithenyn, as he was first in dignity, was also, as was fitting, hardest in skull; and that which had impaired his equilibrium had utterly destroyed theirs. Some fell, in the first impulse, with the tables and benches; others were tripped up by the rolling bowls; and the remainder fell at different points of progression, by jostling against each other, or stumbling over those who had fallen before them.

CHAPTER 3

THE OPPRESSION OF GWENHIDWY.

Nid meddw y dyn a allo
Cwnu ei hun a rhodio,
Ac yved rhagor ddiawd:
Nid yw hyny yn veddwdawd.

Not drunk is he, who from the floor
Can rise alone, and still drink more;
But drunk is he, who prostrate lies,
Without the power to drink or rise.[1]

A SIDE door, at the upper end of the hall, to the left of
Seithenyn's chair, opened, and a beautiful young girl
entered the hall, with her domestic bard, and her attendant maidens.

It was Angharad, the daughter of Seithenyn. The
tumult had drawn her from the solitude of her chamber, apprehensive that some evil might befall her father in that incapability of self-protection to which he

---

1.   [Reflects the style and content of Welsh proverbial or bardic
poetry, particularly related to drinking culture and moral observations often found in gnomic verses (traditional Welsh maxims).]

made a point of bringing himself by set of sun. She gracefully saluted Prince Elphin, and directed the cupbearers, (who were bound, by their office, to remain half sober till the rest of the company were finished off, after which they indemnified themselves at leisure,) she directed the cupbearers to lift up Prince Seithenyn, and bear him from the hall. The cupbearers reeled off with their lord, who had already fallen asleep, and who now began to play them a pleasant march with his nose, to inspirit their progression.

Elphin gazed with delight on the beautiful apparition, whose gentle and serious loveliness contrasted so strikingly with the broken trophies and fallen heroes of revelry that lay scattered at her feet.

"Stranger," she said, "this seems an unfitting place for you: let me conduct you where you will be more agreeably lodged."

"Still less should I deem it fitting for you, fair maiden," said Elphin.

She answered, "The pleasure of her father is the duty of Angharad."

Elphin was desirous to protract the conversation, and this very desire took from him the power of speaking to the purpose. He paused for a moment to collect his ideas, and Angharad stood still, in apparent expectation that he would show symptoms of following, in compliance with her invitation.

In this interval of silence, he heard the loud dashing of the sea, and the blustering of the wind through the apertures of the walls.

This supplied him with what has been, since Britain was Britain, the alpha and omega of British conversation. He said, "It seems a stormy night."

She answered, "We are used to storms: we are far from the mountains, between the lowlands and the sea, and the winds blow round us from all quarters."

There was another pause of deep silence. The noise of the sea was louder, and the gusts pealed like thunder through the apertures. Amidst the fallen and sleeping revellers, the confused and littered hall, the low and wavering torches, Angharad, lovely always, shone with single and surpassing loveliness. The gust died away in murmurs, and swelled again into thunder, and died away in murmurs again; and, as it died away, mixed with the murmurs of the ocean, a voice, that seemed one of the many voices of the wind, pronounced the ominous words, "Beware of the oppression of Gwenhidwy."

They looked at each other, as if questioning whether all had heard alike.

"Did you not hear a voice?" said Angharad, after a pause.

"The same," said Elphin, "which has once before seemed to say to me, 'Beware of the oppression of Gwenhidwy.'"

Teithrin hurried forth on the rampart: Angharad turned pale, and leaned against a pillar of the hall. Elphin was amazed and awed, absorbed as his feelings were in her. The sleepers on the floor made an uneasy movement, and uttered an inarticulate cry.

Teithrin returned. "What saw you?" said Elphin.

Teithrin answered, "A tempest is coming from the west. The moon has waned three days, and is half hidden in clouds, just visible above the mountains: the bank of clouds is black in the west; the scud is flying before them; and the white waves are rolling to the shore."

"This is the highest of the springtides," said Angharad, "and they are very terrible in the storms from the west, when the spray flies over the embankment, and the breakers shake the tower which has its foot in the surf."

"Whence was the voice," said Elphin, "which we heard erewhile? Was it the cry of a sleeper in his drink, or an error of the fancy, or a warning voice from the elements?"

"It was surely nothing earthly," said Angharad, "nor was it an error of the fancy, for we all heard the words, 'Beware of the oppression of Gwenhidwy.' Often and often, in the storms of the springtides, have I feared to see her roll her power over the fields of Gwaelod."

"Pray heaven she do not tonight," said Teithrin.

"Can there be such a danger?" said Elphin.

"I think," said Teithrin, "of the decay I have seen, and I fear the voice I have heard."

A long pause of deep silence ensued, during which they heard the intermitting peals of the wind, and the increasing sound of the rising sea, swelling progressively into wilder and more menacing tumult, till, with one terrific impulse, the whole violence of the equinoctial tempest seemed to burst upon the shore. It was one of those tempests which occur once in several centuries, and which, by their extensive devastations, are chronicled to eternity; for a storm that signalizes its course with extraordinary destruction, becomes as worthy of celebration as a hero for the same reason. The old bard seemed to be of this opinion; for the turmoil which appalled Elphin, and terrified Angharad, fell upon his ears as the sound of inspiration: the *awen* came upon him; and, seizing his

harp, he mingled his voice and his music with the up-
roar of the elements:

THE SONG OF THE FOUR WINDS[2]

Wind from the north: the young spring day
Is pleasant on the sunny mead;
The merry harps at evening play;
The dance gay youths and maidens lead:
The thrush makes chorus from the thorn:
The mighty drinker fills his horn.

Wind from the east: the shore is still;
The mountain-clouds fly tow'rds the sea;
The ice is on the winter-rill;
The great hall fire is blazing free:
The prince's circling feast is spread:
Drink fills with fumes the brainless head.

Wind from the south: in summer shade
'Tis sweet to hear the loud harp ring;
Sweet is the step of comely maid,
Who to the bard a cup doth bring:
The black crow flies where carrion lies:
Where pignuts[3] lurk, the swine will work.

---

2. This poem is a specimen of a numerous class of ancient Welsh
poems, in which each stanza begins with a repetition of the prom-
inent idea, and terminates with a proverb, more or less applicable
to the subject. In some poems, the sequency of the main images is
regular and connected, and the proverbial terminations strictly
appropriate: in others, the sequency of the main images is loose
and incoherent, and the proverbial termination has little or
nothing to do with the subject of the stanza. The basis of the poem
in the text is in the *Englynion* of Llwyarch Hên.
3. [The underground edible tubers of the plant *Conopodium*

Wind from the west: the autumnal deep
Rolls on the shore its billowy pride:
He, who the rampart's watch must keep,
Will mark with awe the rising tide:
The high springtide, that bursts its mound,
May roll o'er miles of level ground.

Wind from the west: the mighty wave
Of ocean bounds o'er rock and sand;
The foaming surges roar and rave
Against the bulwarks of the land:
When waves are rough, and winds are high,
Good is the land that's high and dry.

Wind from the west: the storm-clouds rise;
The breakers rave; the whirlblasts roar;
The mingled rage of seas and skies
Bursts on the low and lonely shore:
When safety's far, and danger nigh,
Swift feet the readiest aid supply.

Wind from the west—

His song was cut short by a tremendous crash. The tower, which had its foot in the sea, had long been sapped by the waves; the storm had prematurely perfected the operation, and the tower fell into the surf, carrying with it a portion of the wall of the main building, and revealing, through the chasm, the white raging of the breakers beneath the blackness of

---

majus, commonly known as the pignut, which is native to Europe, including Britain. The plant is part of the carrot family (Apiaceae) and typically grows in woodlands, meadows and grassy areas.]

the midnight storm. The wind rushed into the hall, extinguishing the torches within the line of its course, tossing the grey locks and loose mantle of the bard, and the light white drapery and long black tresses of Angharad. With the crash of the falling tower, and the simultaneous shriek of the women, the sleepers started from the floor, staring with drunken amazement; and, shortly after, reeling like an Indian from the wine-rolling Hydaspes,[4] in staggered Seithenyn ap Seithyn.

Seithenyn leaned against a pillar, and stared at the sea through the rifted wall, with wild and vacant surprise. He perceived that there was an innovation, and he felt that he was injured: how, or by whom, he did not quite so clearly discern. He looked at Elphin and Teithrin, at his daughter, and at the members of his household, with a long and dismal aspect of blank and mute interrogation, modified by the struggling consciousness of puzzled self-importance, which seemed to require from his chiefship some word of command in this incomprehensible emergency. But the longer he looked, the less clearly he saw; and the longer he pondered, the less he understood. He felt the rush of the wind; he saw the white foam of the sea; his ears were dizzy with their mingled roar. He remained at length motionless, leaning against the

---

4. In the fourteenth and fifteenth books of the *Dionysiaca* of Nonnus, Bacchus changes the river Astacis into wine; and the multitudinous army of water-drinking Indians, proceeding to quench their thirst in the stream, become franticly drunk, and fall an easy prey to the Bacchic invaders. In the thirty-fifth book, the experiment is repeated on the Hydaspes. "*Ainsi conquesta Bacchus l'Inde,*" ["Thus did Bacchus conquer India"] as Rabelais has it.

pillar, and gazing on the breakers with fixed and glaring vacancy.

"The sleepers of Gwaelod," said Elphin, "they who sleep in peace and security, trusting to the vigilance of Seithenyn, what will become of them?"

"Warn them with the beacon fire," said Teithrin, "if there be fuel on the summit of the landward tower."

"That of course has been neglected too," said Elphin.

"Not so," said Angharad, "that has been my charge."

Teithrin seized a torch, and ascended the eastern tower, and, in a few minutes, the party in the hall beheld the breakers reddening with the reflected fire, and deeper and yet deeper crimson tinging the whirling foam, and sheeting the massy darkness of the bursting waves.

Seithenyn turned his eyes on Elphin. His recollection of him was extremely faint, and the longer he looked on him he remembered him the less. He was conscious of the presence of strangers, and of the occurrence of some signal mischief, and associated the two circumstances in his dizzy perceptions with a confused but close connexion. He said at length, looking sternly at Elphin, "I do not know what right the wind has to blow upon me here; nor what business the sea has to show itself here; nor what business you have here: but one thing is very evident, that either my castle or the sea is on fire; and I shall be glad to know who has done it, for terrible shall be the vengeance of Seithenyn ap Seithyn. Show me the enemy," he pursued, drawing his sword furiously, and flourishing it over his head, "Show me the enemy; show me the enemy."

An unusual tumult mingled with the roar of the waves; a sound, the same in kind, but greater in degree, with that produced by the loose stones of the beach, which are rolled to and fro by the surf.

Teithrin rushed into the hall, exclaiming, "All is over! the mound is broken; and the springtide is rolling through the breach."

Another portion of the castle wall fell into the mining waves, and, by the dim and thickly-clouded moonlight, and the red blaze of the beacon fire, they beheld a torrent pouring in from the sea upon the plain, and rushing immediately beneath the castle walls, which, as well as the points of the embankment that formed the sides of the breach, continued to crumble away into the waters.

"Who has done this?" vociferated Seithenyn, "Show me the enemy."

"There is no enemy but the sea," said Elphin, "to which you, in your drunken madness, have abandoned the land. Think, if you can think, of what is passing in the plain. The storm drowns the cries of your victims; but the curses of the perishing are upon you."

"Show me the enemy," vociferated Seithenyn, flourishing his sword more furiously.

Angharad looked deprecatingly at Elphin, who abstained from further reply.

"There is no enemy but the sea," said Teithrin, "against which your sword avails not."

"Who dares to say so?" said Seithenyn. "Who dares to say that there is an enemy on earth against whom the sword of Seithenyn ap Seithyn is unavailing? Thus, thus I prove the falsehood."

And, springing suddenly forward, he leaped into the torrent, flourishing his sword as he descended.

"Oh, my unhappy father!" sobbed Angharad, veiling her face with her arm on the shoulder of one of her female attendants, whom Elphin dexterously put aside, and substituted himself as the supporter of the desolate beauty.

"We must quit the castle," said Teithrin, "or we shall be buried in its ruins. We have but one path of safety, along the summit of the embankment, if there be not another breach between us and the high land, and if we can keep our footing in this hurricane. But there is no alternative. The walls are melting away like snow."

The bard, who was now recovered from his *awen*, and beginning to be perfectly alive to his own personal safety, conscious at the same time that the first duty of his privileged order was to animate the less-gifted multitude by examples of right conduct in trying emergencies, was the first to profit by Teithrin's admonition, and to make the best of his way through the door that opened to the embankment, on which he had no sooner set his foot than he was blown down by the wind, his harp-strings ringing as he fell. He was indebted to the impediment of his harp, for not being rolled down the mound into the waters which were rising within.

Teithrin picked him up, and admonished him to abandon his harp to its fate, and fortify his steps with a spear. The bard murmured objections: and even the reflection that he could more easily get another harp than another life, did not reconcile him to parting with his beloved companion. He got over the difficulty by slinging his harp, cumbrous as it was, to his left side, and taking a spear in his right hand.

Angharad, recovering from the first shock of Seithenyn's catastrophe, became awake to the imminent danger. The spirit of the Cymric female, vigilant and energetic in peril, disposed her and her attendant maidens to use their best exertions for their own preservation. Following the advice and example of Elphin and Teithrin, they armed themselves with spears, which they took down from the walls.

Teithrin led the way, striking the point of his spear firmly into the earth, and leaning from it on the wind: Angharad followed in the same manner: Elphin followed Angharad, looking as earnestly to her safety as was compatible with moderate care of his own: the attendant maidens followed Elphin; and the bard, whom the result of his first experiment had rendered unambitious of the van, followed the female train. Behind them went the cupbearers, whom the accident of sobriety had qualified to march: and behind them reeled and roared those of the bacchanal rout who were able and willing to move; those more especially who had wives or daughters to support their tottering steps. Some were incapable of locomotion, and others, in the heroic madness of liquor, sat down to await their destiny, as they finished the half-drained vessels.

The bard, who had somewhat of a picturesque eye, could not help sparing a little leisure from the care of his body, to observe the effects before him: the volumed blackness of the storm; the white bursting of the breakers in the faint and scarcely-perceptible moonlight; the rushing and rising of the waters within the mound; the long floating hair and waving drapery of the young women; the red light of the beacon fire falling on them from behind; the surf rolling up the side of the embankment, and breaking almost at their feet; the spray flying above their heads; and the resolution with which they impinged the stony ground with their spears, and bore themselves up against the wind.

Thus they began their march. They had not proceeded far, when the tide began to recede, the wind to abate somewhat of its violence, and the moon to look on them at intervals through the rifted clouds, disclosing the desolation of the inundated plain, silvering the tumultuous surf, gleaming on the distant mountains, and revealing a lengthened prospect of their solitary path, that lay in its irregular line like a ribbon on the deep.

CHAPTER 4
THE LAMENTATIONS OF GWYTHNO.

Οὐ παύσομαι τὰς Χάριτας
Μούσαις ουγκαταμγνύς
ʽΗδίσταν συζυγίαν

EURIPIDES.[1]

Not, though grief my ages defaces,
Will I cease, in concert dear,
Blending still the gentle graces
With the muses more severe.

KING GWYTHNO had feasted joyously, and had sung his new ode to a chosen party of his admiring subjects, amidst their, of course, enthusiastic applause. He heard the storm raging without, as he laid himself down to rest: he thought it a very hard case for those who were out in it, especially on the sea; congratulated himself on his own much more comfortable condition; and went to sleep with a pious reflection on the goodness of Providence to himself.

---

1. [*Heracles*, line 674.]

He was roused from a pleasant dream by a confused and tumultuous dissonance, that mingled with the roar of the tempest. Rising with much reluctance, and looking forth from his window, he beheld in the moonlight a half-naked multitude, larger than his palace thrice multiplied could have contained, pressing round the gates, and clamouring for admission and shelter; while beyond them his eye fell on the phænomenon of stormy waters, rolling in the place of the fertile fields from which he derived his revenue.

Gwythno, though a king and his own laureate, was not without sympathy for the people who had the honour and happiness of victualling his royal house, and he issued forth on his balcony full of perplexities and alarms, stunned by the sudden sense of the half-understood calamity, and his head still dizzy from the effects of abruptly-broken sleep, and the vapours of the overnight's glorious festival.

Gwythno was altogether a reasonably good sort of person, and a poet of some note. His people were somewhat proud of him on the latter score, and very fond of him on the former; for even the tenth part of those homely virtues, that decorate the memories of "husbands kind and fathers dear" in every church-yard, are matters of plebeian admiration in the persons of royalty; and every tangible point in every such virtue so located, becomes a convenient peg for the suspension of love and loyalty. While, therefore, they were unanimous in consigning the soul of Seithenyn to a place that no well-bred divine will name to a polite congregation, they overflowed, in the abundance of their own griefs, with a portion of sympathy for Gwythno, and saluted him, as he issued forth on his balcony, with a hearty *Duw cadw y Brenin*, or God save the King, which he returned with a benevolent wave of the hand; but they followed it up by an intense vociferation for food and lodging, which he received with a pitiful shake of the head.

Meanwhile the morning dawned: the green spots, that peered with the ebbing tide above the waste of waters, only served to indicate the irremediableness of the general desolation.

Gwythno proceeded to hold a conference with his people, as deliberately as the stormy state of the weather and their minds, and the confusion of his own, would permit. The result of the conference was, that they should use their best exertions to catch some stray beeves, which had escaped the inundation, and were lowing about the rocks in search of new pastures. This measure was carried into immediate effect: the victims were killed and roasted, carved, distributed, and eaten, in a very Homeric fashion, and washed down with a large portion of the contents of the royal cellars; after which, having more leisure to dwell on their losses, the fugitives of Gwaelod proceeded to make loud lamentation, all collectively for home and for country, and severally for wife or husband, parent or child, whom the flood had made its victims.

In the midst of these lamentations arrived Elphin and Angharad, with her bard and attendant maidens, and Teithrin ap Tathral. Gwythno, after a con sultation, despatched Teithrin and Angharad's domestic bard on an embassy to the court of Uther Pendragon, and to such of the smaller kings as lay in the way, to solicit such relief as their several majesties might be able and willing to afford to a king in distress. It is said, that the bard, finding a royal bardship vacant in a more prosperous court, made the most of himself in the market, and stayed where he was better fed and lodged than he could expect to be in Caredigion; but that Teithrin returned, with many valuable gifts, and most especially one from Merlin, being a hamper, which multiplied an hundredfold by morning whatever was put into it overnight, so that, for a ham and a flask put by in the evening, an hundred hams and an hundred flasks were taken out in the morning. It is at least certain that such a hamper is enumerated among the thirteen wonders of Merlin's art, and, in the authentic catalogue thereof, is called the Hamper of Gwythno.[2]

Be this as it may, Gwythno, though shorn of the beams of his revenue, kept possession of his palace. Elphin married Angharad, and built a salmon-weir on the Mawddach, the produce of which, with that of a

---

2. [The "Hamper of Gwythno" (*Basged Gwythno Garanhir*) refers to a legendary object from Welsh mythology associated with Gwythno Garanhir (meaning Gwythno the Tall Crane or Long-Legged), who is said to have been a king of a fertile kingdom known as Cantre'r Gwaelod that supposedly existed in what is now Cardigan Bay off the coast of Wales. According to legend, Cantre'r Gwaelod was a rich, low-lying land protected by sea walls, with sluice gates to control the sea's flow. When these defences failed due to negligence—often attributed to the drunken gatekeeper Seithenyn—the kingdom was flooded and lost beneath the waves. The "Hamper of Gwythno" is listed among the legendary "Thirteen Treasures of the Island of Britain" (*Tri Thlws ar Ddeg Ynys Prydain*), a collection of magical items from Welsh mythology. The hamper had the extraordinary ability to magically provide food. Specifically, it could produce enough food for one hundred men whenever it was opened, regardless of how many times it was used. This made it a symbol of abundance and prosperity, reflecting the legendary richness of Gwythno's kingdom, Cantre'r Gwaelod, before its downfall.]

series of beehives, of which his princess and her maidens made mead, constituted for some time the principal wealth and subsistence of the royal family of Caredigion.

King Gwythno, while his son was delving or fishing, and his daughter spinning or making mead, sat all day on the rocks, with his harp between his knees, watching the rolling of ocean over the locality of his past dominion, and pouring forth his soul in pathetic song on the change of his own condition, and the mutability of human things. Two of his songs of lamentation have been preserved by tradition: they are the only relics of his muse which time has spared.

GWYDDNAU EI CANT,

PAN DDOAI Y MOR DROS CANTREV Y GWAELAWD.

A SONG OF GWYTHNO GARANHIR,

ON THE INUNDATION OF THE SEA OVER THE PLAIN OF GWAELOD.

Stand forth, Seithenyn: winds are high:
Look down beneath the lowering sky;
Look from the rock: what meets thy sight?
Nought but the breakers rolling white.

Stand forth, Seithenyn: winds are still:
Look from the rock and heathy hill
For Gwythno's realm: what meets thy view?
Nought but the ocean's desert blue.

Curst be the treacherous mound, that gave
A passage to the mining wave:
Curst be the cup, with mead-froth crowned,

That charmed from thought the trusted mound.

A tumult, and a cry to heaven!
The white surf breaks; the mound is riven:
Through the wide rift the ocean-spring
Bursts with tumultuous ravaging.

The western ocean's stormy might
Is curling o'er the rampart's height:
Destruction strikes with want and scorn
Presumption, from abundance born.

The tumult of the western deep
Is on the winds, affrighting sleep:
It thunders at my chamber-door;
It bids me wake, to sleep no more.

The tumult of the midnight sea
Swells inland, wildly, fearfully:
The mountain-caves respond its shocks
Among the unaccustomed rocks.

The tumult of the vext sea-coast
Rolls inland like an armed host:
It leaves, for flocks and fertile land,
But foaming waves and treacherous sand.

The wild sea rolls where long have been
Glad homes of men, and pastures green:
To arrogance and wealth succeed
Wide ruin and avenging need.

Seithenyn, come: I call in vain:
The high of birth and weak of brain

Sleeps under ocean's lonely roar
Between the rampart and the shore.

The eternal waste of waters, spread
Above his unrespected head,
The blue expanse, with foam besprent,
Is his too glorious monument.

ANOTHER SONG OF GWYTHNO

I love the green and tranquil shore;
I hate the ocean's dizzy roar,
Whose devastating spray has flown
High o'er the monarch's barrier-stone.

Sad was the feast, which he who spread
Is numbered with the inglorious dead;
The feast within the torch-lit hall,
While stormy breakers mined the wall.

To him repentance came too late:
In cups the chatterer met his fate:
Sudden and sad the doom that burst
On him and me, but mine the worst.

I love the shore, and hate the deep:
The wave has robbed my nights of sleep:
The heart of man is cheered by wine;
But now the wine-cup cheers not mine.

The feast, which bounteous hands dispense,
Makes glad the soul, and charms the sense:
But in the circling feast I know
The coming of my deadliest foe.

Blest be the rock, whose foot supplied
A step to them that fled the tide;
The rock of bards, on whose rude steep
I bless the shore, and hate the deep.

"The sigh of Gwythno Garanhir when the breakers ploughed up his land"[3] is the substance of a proverbial distich, which may still be heard on the coast of Merioneth and Cardigan, to express the sense of an overwhelming calamity. The curious investigator may still land on a portion of the ancient stony rampart; which stretches, off the point of Mochres, far out into Cardigan Bay, nine miles of the summit being left dry, in calm weather, by the low water of the springtides; and which is now called Sarn Badrig, or St. Patrick's Causeway.

Thus the kingdom of Caredigion fell into ruin: its people were destroyed, or turned out of house and home; and its royal family were brought to a condition in which they found it difficult to get loaves to their fishes. We, who live in more enlightened times, amidst the "gigantic strides of intellect," when offices of public trust are so conscientiously and zealously discharged, and so vigilantly checked and superintended, may wonder at the wicked negligence of Seithenyn; at the sophisms with which, in his liquor, he vindicated his system, and pronounced the eulogium of his old dilapidations, and at the blind confidence of Gwythno and his people in this virtual guardian of their lives and property: happy that our own public guardians are too virtuous to act or talk like Sei-

---

3. Ochenaid Gwyddnau Garanhir
   Pan droes y don dros ei dir.

thenyn, and that we ourselves are too wise not to perceive, and too free not to prevent it, if they should be so disposed.

CHAPTER 5

THE PRIZE OF THE WEIR.

Weave a circle round him thrice,
And close your eyes with holy dread;
For he on honey-dew hath fed,
And drank the milk of paradise.

COLERIDGE.[1]

PRINCE ELPHIN constructed his salmon-weir on the Mawddach at the point where the fresh water met the top of the springtides. He built near it a dwelling for himself and Angharad, for which the old king Gwythno gradually deserted his palace. An amphitheatre of rocky mountains enclosed a pastoral valley. The meadows gave pasture to a few cows; and the flowers of the mountain-heath yielded store of honey to the bees of many hives, which were tended by Angharad and her handmaids. Elphin had also some sheep, which wandered on the mountains. The worst was, they often wandered out of reach; but, when he could not find his sheep, he brought down a

---

1.   [The final four lines of *Kubla Khan*.]

wild goat, the venison of Gwyneth. The woods and turbaries supplied unlimited fuel. The straggling cultivators, who had escaped from the desolation of Gwaelod, and settled themselves above the level of the sea, on a few spots propitious to the plough, still acknowledged their royalty, and paid them tribute in corn. But their principal wealth was fish. Elphin was the first Briton who caught fish on a large scale, and salted them for other purposes than home consumption.

The weir was thus constructed: a range of piles crossed the river from shore to shore, slanting upwards from both shores, and meeting at an angle in the middle of the river. A little down the stream a second range of piles crossed the river in the same manner, having towards the middle several wide intervals with light wicker gates, which, meeting at an angle, were held together by the current, but were so constructed as to yield easily to a very light pressure from below. These gates gave all fish of a certain magnitude admission to a chamber, from which they could neither advance nor retreat, and from which, standing on a narrow bridge attached to the lower piles, Elphin bailed them up at leisure. The smaller fish passed freely up and down the river through the interstices of the piles. This weir was put together in the early summer, and taken to pieces and laid by in the autumn.

Prince Elphin, one fine July night, was sleepless and troubled in spirit. His fishery had been beyond all precedent unproductive, and the obstacle which this circumstance opposed to his arrangements for victualling his little garrison kept him for the better half of the night vigilant in unprofitable cogitation. Soon after the turn of midnight, when dreams are true, he was startled from an incipient doze by a sudden cry of Angharad, who had been favoured with a vision of a miraculous draught of fish. Elphin, as a drowning man catches at a straw, caught at the shadowy promise of Angharad's dream, and at once, beneath the clear light of the just-waning moon, he sallied forth with his princess to examine his weir.

The weir was built across the stream of the river, just above the flow of the ordinary tides; but the springtide had opened the wicker gates, and had floated up a coracle[2] between a pair of them, which closing, as the tide turned, on the coracle's nose, re-tained it within the chamber of the weir, at the same time that it kept the gates sufficiently open to permit the escape of any fish that might have entered the chamber. The great prize, which undoubtedly might have been there when Angharad dreamed of it, was gone to a fish.

Elphin, little pleased, stepped on the narrow bridge, and opened the gates with a pole that termi-nated piscatorially in a hook. The coracle began drop-ping down the stream. Elphin arrested its course, and guided it to land.

In the coracle lay a sleeping child, clothed in splendid apparel. Angharad took it in her arms. The child opened its eyes, and stretched its little arms to-wards her with a smile; and she uttered, in delight and wonder at its surpassing beauty, the exclamation of "Taliesin!" "Radiant brow!"

Elphin, nevertheless, looked very dismal on

---

2. A small boat of basketwork, sheathed with leather.

finding no food, and an additional mouth;[3] so dismal, that his physiognomy on that occasion passed into a proverb: "As rueful as Elphin when he found Taliesin."[4]

In after years, Taliesin, being on the safe side of prophecy, and writing after the event, addressed a poem to Elphin, in the character of the foundling of the coracle, in which he supposes himself, at the moment of his discovery, to have addressed Elphin as follows:

DYHUDDIANT ELFFIN.
THE CONSOLATION OF ELPHIN.

Lament not, Elphin: do not measure
By one brief hour thy loss or gain:
Thy weir tonight has borne a treasure,
Will more than pay thee years of pain.
St. Cynllo's aid will not be vain:
Smooth thy bent brow, and cease to mourn:
Thy weir will never bear again
Such wealth as it tonight has borne.

The stormy seas, the silent rivers,

---

3. [This episode closely parallels a story from *The Mabinogion*, specifically from the tale of Elphin and Taliesin found in the *Hanes Taliesin* (The *Tale of Taliesin*). Elphin discovers the infant Taliesin while inspecting his fishing weirs, which belonged to his father, Gwyddno Garanhir. Elphin, expecting to find a good catch of fish, instead discovers a mysterious child floating in the weir. Initially, Elphin is disappointed because there's no fish to show for the day —only this unexpected child. After Elphin lifts the boy, Taliesin immediately recites prophetic and poetic verses, revealing his extraordinary wisdom and talent despite being an infant.]
4. Mor drist ac Elffin pan gavod Taliesin.

The torrents down the steeps that spring,
Alike of weal or woe are givers,
As pleases heaven's immortal king.
Though frail I seem, rich gifts I bring,
Which in Time's fulness shall appear,
Greater than if the stream should fling
Three hundred salmon in thy weir.

Cast off this fruitless sorrow, loading
With heaviness the unmanly mind:
Despond not; mourn not; evil boding
Creates the ill it fears to find.
When fates are dark, and most unkind
Are they who most should do thee right,
Then wilt thou know thine eyes were blind
To thy good fortune of tonight.

Though, small and feeble, from my coracle
To thee my helpless hands I spread,
Yet in me breathes a holy oracle
To bid thee lift thy drooping head.
When hostile steps around thee tread,
A spell of power my voice shall wield,
That, more than arms with slaughter red,
Shall be thy refuge and thy shield.[5]

Two years after this event, Angharad presented
Elphin with a daughter, whom they named

---

5. In the medieval Welsh tale *Hanes Taliesin*, Elphin, son of
Gwyddno Garanhir, discovers the infant Taliesin in a salmon weir.
Upon finding the child, Elphin laments his misfortune, believing
the weir has yielded nothing of value. In response, the infant Taliesin speaks for the first time, delivering a poem to console Elphin
and predict his future prosperity.

Melanghel. The fishery prospered; and the progress of cultivation and population among the more fertile parts of the mountain districts brought in a little revenue to the old king.

CHAPTER 6

THE EDUCATION OF TALIESIN.

The three objects of intellect: the true, the beautiful, and the beneficial.

The three foundations of wisdom: youth, to acquire learning; memory, to retain learning; and genius, to illustrate learning.

TRIADS OF WISDOM.[1]

The three primary requisites of poetical genius: an eye, that can see nature; a heart, that can feel nature; and a resolution, that dares follow nature.

TRIADS OF POETRY.[2]

---

1.   [The Triads of Wisdom (*Trioedd Doethineb*) are moral or philosophical triads, offering insights into life, virtue, leadership, and human behaviour. They are more didactic than The Triads of the Island of Britain and focus on ethical lessons rather than historical figures.]

2.   [The Triads of Poetry (*Trioedd Cerddwriaeth*) focus on poetic composition, bardic knowledge and the role of poets in Welsh society. They reflect the bardic tradition of medieval Wales, offering rules, techniques, and principles for poets and singers.]

As Taliesin grew up, Gwythno instructed him in all the knowledge of the age, which was of course not much, in comparison with ours. The science of political economy was sleeping in the womb of time. The advantage of growing rich by getting into debt and paying interest was altogether unknown: the safe and economical currency, which is produced by a man writing his name on a bit of paper, for which other men give him their property, and which he is always ready to exchange for another bit of paper, of an equally safe and economical manufacture, being also equally ready to render his own person, at a moment's notice, as impalpable as the metal which he promises to pay, is a stretch of wisdom to which the people of those days had nothing to compare. They had no steam-engines, with fires as eternal as those of the nether world, wherein the squalid many, from infancy to age, might be turned into component portions of machinery for the benefit of the purple-faced few. They could neither poison the air with gas, nor the waters with its dregs: in short, they made their money of metal, and breathed pure air, and drank pure water, like unscientific barbarians.

Of moral science they had little; but morals, without science, they had about the same as we have. They had a number of fine precepts, partly from their religion, partly from their bards, which they remembered in their liquor, and forgot in their business.

Political science they had none. The blessings of virtual representation were not even dreamed of; so that, when any of their barbarous metallic currency got into their pockets or coffers, it had a chance to remain there, subjecting them to the inconvenience of unemployed capital. Still they went to work politically much as we do. The powerful took all they could get from their subjects and neighbours; and called something or other sacred and glorious, when they wanted the people to fight for them. They repressed disaffection by force, when it showed itself in an overt act; but they encouraged freedom of speech, when it was, like Hamlet's reading, "words, words, words."[3]

There was no liberty of the press, because there was no press; but there was liberty of speech to the bards, whose persons were inviolable, and the general motto of their order was Y GWIR YN ERBYN Y BYD: the Truth against the World.[4] If many of them, instead of acting up to this splendid profession, chose to advance their personal fortunes by appealing to the selfishness, the passions, and the prejudices, of kings, factions, and the rabble, our free press gentry may afford them a little charity out of the excess of their own virtue.

In physical science, they supplied the place of knowledge by converting conjectures into dogmas; an art which is not yet lost. They held that the earth was the centre of the universe; that an immense ocean surrounded the earth; that the sky was a vast frame resting on the ocean; that the circle of their contact was a mystery of infinite mist; with a great deal more

---

3. [Act 2, Scene 2:

Polonius: What do you read, my lord?

Hamlet: Words, words, words.]

4. [A maxim closely associated with Druidic and bardic traditions, as well as later Welsh nationalism and philosophical idealism. It also appears at the start of Part II of Peacock's *Memoirs of Percy Bysshe Shelley*, in which he defends the memory of Harriet Shelley.]

of cosmogony and astronomy, equally correct and profound, which answered the same purpose as our more correct and profound astronomy answers now, that of elevating the mind, as the eidouranion[5] lecturers have it, to sublime contemplations.

Medicine was cultivated by the Druids, and it was just as much a science with them as with us; but they had not the wit or the means to make it a flourishing trade; the principal means to that end being women with nothing to do, articles which especially belong to a high state of civilization.

The laws lay in a small compass: every bard had those of his own community by heart. The king, or chief, was the judge; the plaintiff and defendant told their own story; and the cause was disposed of in one hearing. We may well boast of the progress of light, when we turn from this picture to the statutes at large, and the Court of Chancery; and we may indulge in a pathetic reflection on our sweet-faced myriads of "learned friends," who would be under the unpleasant necessity of suspending themselves by the neck, if this barbaric "practice of the courts" were suddenly revived.

The religion of the time was Christianity grafted on Druidism. The Christian faith had been very early

---

5. [A type of mechanical astronomical device used in the 18th and 19th centuries to demonstrate the movements of celestial bodies. It was essentially a large orrery, an apparatus that represented the solar system with moving parts to illustrate planetary orbits and relationships. The term was popularised by Adam Walker (1730–1821), a British astronomer and lecturer, who built a massive orrery called the "Eidouranion" and used it for public astronomy lectures in London. It was described as a grand, illuminated mechanical representation of the heavens, capable of simulating planetary motion, eclipses and celestial phenomena.]

preached in Britain. Some of the Welsh historians are of opinion that it was first preached by some of the apostles: most probably by St. John. They think the evidence inconclusive with respect to St. Paul. But, at any rate, the faith had made considerable progress among the Britons at the period of the arrival of Hengist;[6] for many goodly churches, and, what was still better, richly-endowed abbeys, were flourishing in many places. The British clergy were, however, very contumacious towards the see of Rome, and would only acknowledge the spiritual authority of the archbishopric of Caer Lleon, which was, during many centuries, the primacy of Britain. St. Augustin, when he came over, at a period not long subsequent to that of the present authentic history, to preach Christianity to the Saxons, who had for the most part held fast to their Odinism, had also the secondary purpose of making them instruments for teaching the British clergy submission to Rome: as a means to which end, the newly-converted Saxons set upon the monastery of Bangor Iscoed, and put its twelve hundred monks to the sword. This was the first overt act in which the Saxons set forth their new sense of a religion of peace. It is alleged, indeed, that these twelve hundred monks supported themselves by the labour of their own hands. If they did so, it was, no doubt, a gross heresy; but whether it deserved the castigation it received from St. Augustin's proselytes, may be a question in polemics.

------

6. [A reference to the spread of Christianity among the Britons before the arrival of Hengist, the legendary 5th-century Saxon leader who, according to mediaeval sources, played a key role in the Anglo-Saxon conquest of Britain.]

As the people did not read the Bible, and had no religious tracts, their religion, it may be assumed, was not very pure. The rabble of Britons must have seen little more than the superficial facts, that the lands, revenues, privileges, and so forth, which once belonged to Druids and so forth, now belonged to abbots, bishops, and so forth, who, like their extruded precursors, walked occasionally in a row, chanting unintelligible words, and never speaking in common language but to exhort the people to fight; having, indeed, better notions than their predecessors of building, apparel, and cookery; and a better knowledge of the means of obtaining good wine, and of the final purpose for which it was made.

They were observant of all matters of outward form, and tradition even places among them personages who were worthy to have founded a society for the suppression of vice. It is recorded, in the Triads, that "Gwrgi Garwlwyd killed a male and female of the Cymry daily, and devoured them; and, on the Saturday, he killed two of each, that he might not kill on the Sunday." This can only be a type of some sanctimonious hero, who made a cloak of piety for oppressing the poor.

But, even among the Britons, in many of the least populous and most mountainous districts, Druidism was still struggling with Christianity. The lamb had driven the wolf from the rich pastures of the vallies to the high places of the wilderness, where the rites and mysteries of the old religion flourished in secrecy, and where a stray proselyte of the new light was occasionally caught and roasted for the glory of Andraste.[7]

---

7. [A reference to the persecution of early Christian converts

Taliesin, worshipping Nature in her wildest solitudes, often strayed away for days from the dwelling of Elphin, and penetrated the recesses of Eryri,[8] where one especial spot on the banks of Lake Ceirionydd became the favourite haunt of his youth. In these lonely recesses, he became familiar with Druids, who initiated him in their mysteries, which, like all other mysteries, consisted of a quantity of allegorical mummery, pretending to be symbolical of the immortality of the soul, and of its progress through various stages of being; interspersed with a little, too literal, ducking and singeing of the aspirant, by way of trying his mettle, just enough to put him in fear, but not in risk, of his life.

That Taliesin was thoroughly initiated in these mysteries is evident from several of his poems, which have neither head nor tail, and which, having no sense in any other point of view, must necessarily, as a learned mythologist has demonstrated, be assigned to the class of theology, in which an occult sense can be found or made for them, according to the views of the expounder. One of them, a shade less obscure than its companions, unquestionably adumbrates the Druidical doctrine of transmigration. According to this poem, Taliesin had been with the cherubim at the fall of Lucifer, in Paradise at the fall of man, and with Alexander at the fall of Babylon; in the ark with Noah, and in the milky-way with Tetragrammaton;[9]

("proselytes") by pagan Britons, specifically Druidic or warrior-class Britons who remained devoted to their old gods; in this case, Andraste.]

8. Snowdon.

9. [A Greek term meaning "four letters", used to describe the divine name of God in the Hebrew Bible. The name YHWH (יהוה) is

and in many other equally marvellous or memorable conditions: showing that, though the names and histories of the new religion were adopted, its doctrines had still to be learned; and, indeed, in all cases of this description, names are changed more readily than doctrines, and doctrines more readily than ceremonies.

When any of the Romans or Saxons, who invaded the island, fell into the hands of the Britons, before the introduction of Christianity, they were handed over to the Druids, who sacrificed them, with pious ceremonies, to their goddess Andraste. These human sacrifices have done much injury to the Druidical character, amongst us, who never practise them in the same way. They lacked, it must be confessed, some of our light, and also some of our prisons. They lacked some of our light, to enable them to perceive that the act of coming, in great multitudes, with fire and sword, to the remote dwellings of peaceable men, with the premeditated design of cutting their throats, ravishing their wives and daughters, killing their children, and appropriating their worldly goods, belongs, not to the department of murder and robbery, but to that of legitimate war, of which all the practitioners are gentlemen, and entitled to be treated like gentlemen. They lacked some of our prisons, in which our

---

found in the Old Testament and is traditionally not spoken aloud in Jewish practice, out of reverence. In Kabbalah (Jewish mysticism), it holds mystical significance, representing the fundamental structure of divine existence. In Christian theology, the Tetragrammaton is sometimes associated with Jesus (Yeshua) as a divine extension of YHWH. In Renaissance magic and alchemy, the Tetragrammaton was often used in mystical and esoteric texts, sometimes inscribed on amulets or magical symbols.]

philanthropy has provided accommodation for so large a portion of our own people, wherein, if they had left their prisoners alive, they could have kept them from returning to their countrymen, and being at their old tricks again immediately. They would also, perhaps, have found some difficulty in feeding them, from the lack of the county rates, by which the most sensible and amiable part of our nation, the country squires, contrive to coop up, and feed, at the public charge, all who meddle with the wild animals of which they have given themselves the monopoly. But as the Druids could neither lock up their captives, nor trust them at large, the darkness of their intellect could suggest no alternative to the process they adopted, of putting them out of the way, which they did with all the sanctions of religion and law. If one of these old Druids could have slept, like the seven sleepers of Ephesus,[10] and awaked, in the nineteenth century, some fine morning near Newgate,[11] the exhi-

---

10. [A Christian and Islamic legend about seven young men from Ephesus, an ancient Greek city in modern-day Turkey, who were accused of being Christians during the Roman persecution of Christians, either under Emperor Decius (c. 250 CE) or Diocletian (c. 303 CE). To escape execution, they fled to a cave and fell asleep. The emperor ordered the cave to be sealed. Centuries later, during the reign of Christian Emperor Theodosius II (5th century CE), the cave was reopened, and the Seven Sleepers woke up. They were astonished to find that Christianity was now the dominant religion, and one of the Sleepers went into the city and was bewildered by the changes in society.]

11. [Newgate Prison, originally built in the 12th century and located near Newgate in the old city wall, was one of London's most notorious prisons. By the 19th century, it had become synonymous with crime, punishment, and public executions. It housed debtors, thieves, murderers and political prisoners, and was infamous for its squalid conditions and harsh treatment of inmates. Public hangings took place outside its gates, drawing large crowds.]

bition of some half-dozen funipendulous[12] forgers might have shocked the tender bowels of his humanity, as much as one of his wicker baskets of captives in the flames shocked those of Cæsar;[13] and it would, perhaps, have been difficult to convince him that paper credit was not an idol, and one of a more sanguinary character than his Andraste. The Druids had their view of these matters, and we have ours; and it does not comport with the steam-engine speed of our march of mind to look at more than one side of a question.

The people lived in darkness and vassalage. They were lost in the grossness of beef and ale. They had no pamphleteering societies to demonstrate that reading and writing are better than meat and drink; and they were utterly destitute of the blessings of those "schools for all," the house of correction, and the treadmill, wherein the autochthonal justice of our agrestic kakistocracy[14] now castigates the heinous sins which were then committed with impunity, of treading on old footpaths, picking up dead wood, and moving on the face of the earth within sound of the whirr of a partridge.

The learning of the time was confined to the

---

12. ["Hanging by a rope".]

13. [Julius Caesar, in his first-hand account of the Gallic War (*Commentarii de Bello Gallico* [Commentaries on the Gallic War] Book VI, Chapter 16), describes the Celts (Gauls and Britons) engaging in human sacrifice, particularly burning captives alive as offerings to their gods. He writes that the Druids would construct large wicker effigies, fill them with prisoners or criminals and then set them on fire as a mass sacrifice, although the historical accuracy of his claims is questionable.]

14. [A government of the worst people, particularly of a rustic or uncultured nature.]

bards. It consisted in a somewhat complicated art of versification; in a great number of pithy apophthegms, many of which have been handed down to posterity under the title of the Wisdom of Catog; in an interminable accumulation of Triads, in which form they bound up all their knowledge, physical, traditional, and mythological; and in a mighty condensation of mysticism, being the still-cherished relics of the Druidical rites and doctrines.

The Druids were the sacred class of the bardic order. Before the change of religion, it was by far the most numerous class; for the very simple reason, that there was most to be got by it: all ages and nations having been sufficiently enlightened to make the trade of priest more profitable than that of poet. During this period, therefore, it was the only class that much attracted the notice of foreigners. After the change of religion, the denomination was retained as that of the second class of the order. The Bardd Braint, or Bard of Presidency, was of the ruling order, and wore a robe of sky-blue. The Derwydd, or Druid, wore a robe of white. The Ovydd, or Ovate, was of the class of initiation, and wore a robe of green. The Awenyddion, or disciples, the candidates for admission into the Bardic order, wore a variegated dress of the three colours, and were passed through a very severe moral and intellectual probation.

Gwythno was a Bardd Braint, or Bard of Presidency, and as such he had full power in his own person, without the intervention of a Bardic Congress, to make his Awenydd or disciple, Taliesin, an Ovydd or Ovate, which he did accordingly. Angharad, under the old king's instructions, prepared the green robe of the young aspirant's investiture. He afterwards acquired the white robe amongst the Druids of Eryri.

In all Bardic learning, Gwythno was profound. All that he knew he taught to Taliesin. The youth drew in the draughts of inspiration among the mountain forests and the mountain streams, and grew up under the roof of Elphin, in the perfection of genius and beauty.

CHAPTER 7

THE HUNTINGS OF MAELGON.

Αἰεὶ τὸ μὲν ζῇ, τὸ δὲ μεθίσταται κακόν,
Τὸ δ' ἐκπεφήμεν αὐτίκ' ἐξ ἀρχῆς νέον.

EURIPEDES.[1]

One ill is ever clinging;
One treads upon its heels;
A third, in distance springing,
Its fearful front reveals.

GWYTHNO slept, not with his fathers, for they were under the sea, but as near to them as was found convenient, within the sound of the breakers that rolled over their ancient dwellings. Elphin was now king of Caredigion, and was lord of a large but thinly-peopled tract of rock, mountain, forest, and bog. He held his sovereignty, however, not, as Gwythno had done during the days of the glory of Gwaelod, by that most indisputable sort of right which consists in might, but by the more precarious tenure of the absence of incli-

---

1. [*Æolus Nauck*, 35.]

nation in any of his brother kings to take away any thing he had.

Uther Pendragon, like Gwythno, went the way of all flesh, and Arthur reigned in Caer Lleon, as king of the kings of Britain. Maelgon Gwyneth was then king of that part of North Wales which bordered on the kingdom of Caredigion.

Maelgon was a mighty hunter, and roused the echoes of the mountains with horn and with hound. He went forth to the chace as to war, provisioned for days and weeks, and supported by bard and butler, and all the apparel of princely festivity. He pitched his tents in the forest of Snowdon, by the shore of lake or torrent; and, after hunting all the day, he feasted half the night. The light of his torches gleamed on the foam of the cataracts, and the sound of harp and song was mingled with their midnight roar.

When not thus employed, he was either feasting in his Castle of Diganwy, on the Conwy, or fighting with any of the neighbouring kings, who had any thing which he wanted, and which he thought himself strong enough to take from them.

Once, towards the close of autumn, he carried the tumult of the chace into the recesses of Meirion. The consonance, or dissonance, of men and dogs, outpealed the noise of the torrents among the rocks and woods of the Mawddach. Elphin and Teithrin were gone after the sheep or goats in the mountains; Taliesin was absent on the borders of his favourite lake; Angharad and Melanghel were alone. The careful mother, alarmed at the unusual din, and knowing, by rumour, of what materials the Nimrods of Britain were made, fled, with her daughter and handmaids, to the refuge of a deeply-secluded cavern, which they had long before noted as a safe retreat from peril. As they ascended the hills that led to the cavern, they looked back, at intervals, through the openings of the woods, to the growing tumult on the opposite side of the valley. The wild goats were first seen, flying in all directions, taking prodigious leaps from crag to crag, now and then facing about, and rearing themselves on their hind legs, as if in act to butt, and immediately thinking better of it, and springing away on all fours among the trees. Next, the more rare spectacle of a noble stag presented itself on the summit of a projecting rock, pausing a moment to snuff the air, then bounding down the most practicable slope to the valley. Next, on the summit which the stag had just deserted, appeared a solitary huntsman, sitting on a prancing horse, and waking a hundred echoes with the blast of his horn. Next rushed into view the main body of the royal company, and the two-legged and four-legged avalanche came thundering down on the track of the flying prey: not without imminent hazard of broken necks; though the mountain-bred horses, which possessed by nature almost the sure-footedness of mules, had finished their education under the first professors of the age.

The stag swam the river, and stood at bay before the dwelling of Elphin, where he was in due time despatched by the conjoint valour of dog and man. The royal train burst into the solitary dwelling, where, finding nothing worthy of much note, excepting a large store of salt salmon and mead, they proceeded to broil and tap, and made fearful havoc among the family's winter provision. Elphin and Tei-thrin, returning to their expected dinner, stood aghast on the threshold of their plundered sanctuary.

Maelgon condescended to ask them who they were; and, learning Elphin's name and quality, felt himself bound to return his involuntary hospitality by inviting him to Diganwy. So strong was his sense of justice on this head, that, on Elphin's declining the invitation, which Maelgon ascribed to modesty, he desired two of his grooms to take him up and carry him off.

So Elphin was impressed into royal favour, and was feasted munificently in the castle of Diganwy. Teithrin brought home the ladies from the cavern, and, during the absence of Elphin, looked after the sheep and goats, and did his master's business as well as his own.

One evening, when the royal "nowle" was "tottie of the must,"[2] while the bards of Maelgon were singing the praises of their master, and of all and every thing that belonged to him, as the most eximious and transcendent persons and things of the superficial garniture of the earth, Maelgon said to Elphin, "My bards say that I am the best and bravest of kings, that my queen is the most beautiful and chaste of women, and that they themselves, by virtue of belonging to me, are the best and wisest of bards. Now what say you, on these heads?"

This was a perplexing question to Elphin, who,

---

2. ["Nowle" is an archaic word for "head" derived from Middle English "noll", meaning the crown of the head or the head itself. Used humorously, it describes someone's mental state, particularly in relation to drunkenness. "Tottie" means unsteady, dizzy, or tipsy. "Must" refers to freshly fermented wine or grape juice, which still contains natural yeast and is in the process of turning into alcohol. Together, "tottie of the must" means "giddy or tipsy from drinking young wine".]

nevertheless, answered: "That you are the best and bravest of kings I do not in the least doubt; yet I cannot think that any woman surpasses my own wife in beauty and chastity; or that any bard equals my bard in genius and wisdom."

"Hear you him, Rhûn?" said Maelgon.

"I hear," said Rhûn, "and mark."

Rhûn was the son of Maelgon, and a worthy heir apparent of his illustrious sire. Rhûn set out the next morning on an embassy very similar to Tarquin's,[3] accompanied by only one attendant. They lost their way and each other, among the forests of Meirion. The attendant, after riding about some time in great trepidation, thought he heard the sound of a harp, mixed with the roar of the torrents, and following its indications, came at length within sight of an oak-fringed precipice, on the summit of which stood Taliesin, playing and singing to the winds and waters. The attendant could not approach him without dismounting; therefore, tying his horse to a branch, he ascended the rock, and, addressing the young bard, inquired his way to the dwelling of Elphin. Taliesin, in return, inquired his business there; and, partly by examination, partly by divination, ascertained his master's name, and the purport of his visit.

Taliesin deposited his harp in a dry cavern of the rock, and undertook to be the stranger's guide. The attendant remounted his horse, and Taliesin preceded him on foot. But the way by which he led him

---

3.   [An allusion to Sextus Tarquinius, son of Lucius Tarquinius Superbus, the last king of Rome, and his infamous raping of Lucretia, the virtuous wife of Collatinus. This led to Lucretia's suicide, which in turn sparked the overthrow of the Roman monarchy and the foundation of the Roman Republic (509 BCE).]

grew more and more rugged, till the stranger called out, "Whither lead you, my friend? My horse can no longer keep his footing." "There is no other way," said Taliesin. "But give him to my management, and do you follow on foot." The attendant consented. Taliesin mounted the horse, and presently struck into a more practicable track; and immediately giving the horse the reins, he disappeared among the woods, leaving the unfortunate equerry to follow as he might, with no better guide than the uncertain recollection of the sound of his horse's heels.

Taliesin reached home before the arrival of Rhûn, and warned Angharad of the mischief that was designed her.

Rhûn, arriving at his destination, found only a handmaid dressed as Angharad, and another officiating as her attendant. The fictitious princess gave him a supper, and everything else he asked for; and, at parting in the morning, a lock of her hair, and a ring, which Angharad had placed on her finger.

After riding a short distance on his return, Rhûn met his unlucky attendant, torn, tired, and half-starved, and cursing some villain who had stolen his horse. Rhûn was too happy in his own success to have a grain of sympathy for his miserable follower, whom he left to find his horse and his way, or either, or neither, as he might, and returned alone to Diganwy.

Maelgon exultingly laid before Elphin the proofs of his wife's infidelity.[4] Elphin examined the lock of

---

4. [Parallels an episode from *The Mabinogion*, specifically from the tale of Taliesin, which is often included in later versions, such as Lady Charlotte Guest's translation. In the legend of Elphin and Taliesin, Elphin (the historical Elffin ap Gwyddno) is imprisoned by Maelgwn Gwynedd, the King of Gwynedd, after boasting that

hair, and listened to the narration of Rhûn. He divined at once the trick that had been put upon the prince; but he contented himself with saying, "I do not believe that Rhûn has received the favours of Angharad; and I still think that no wife in Britain, not even the queen of Maelgon Gwyneth, is more chaste or more beautiful than mine."

Hereupon Maelgon waxed wroth. Elphin, in a point which much concerned him, held a belief of his own, different from that which his superiors in worldly power required him to hold. Therefore Maelgon acted as the possessors of worldly power usually act in similar cases: he locked Elphin up within four stone walls, with an intimation that he should keep him there till he pronounced a more orthodox opinion on the question in dispute.

---

his wife is more virtuous and that he possesses the greatest bard, Taliesin. Maelgwn attempts to prove Elphin wrong by claiming that Elphin's wife has been unfaithful and showing false evidence to support the accusation. However, with the help of Taliesin, Elphin's wife's innocence is proven, and he is ultimately vindicated.]

CHAPTER 8

THE LOVE OF MELANGHEL

Ἀλλὰ ταῖς παλάμαισι μαχέμονα θύρσον αἴρων,
Αἰθέρος ἀξία ῥέξον· ἐπεί Διὸς ἀμβροτος αὐλὴ
Οὐ σε πόνων ἀπανευθε δέδεξεται· οὐδέ σοι Ὦραι
Μηπώ ἀθλησαντι πύλας πετάσωσιν Ὀλύμπου.

Grasp the bold thyrsus; seek the field's array;
And do things worthy of ethereal day:
Not without toil to earthborn man befalls
To tread the floors of Jove's immortal halls:
Never to him, who not by deeds has striven,
Will the bright Hours roll back the gates of heaven.

Iris to Bacchus, in the thirteenth book of the
Dionysiaca of Nonnus.[1]

---

1. [Part of the poem *Dionysiaca*, a 48-book Greek epic written by Nonnus of Panopolis in late antiquity (5th century CE). It is the longest surviving epic poem from antiquity, dedicated to the life, conquests, and divine nature of Dionysus (Bacchus), the god of wine, revelry, and chaos. The 13th Book of the *Dionysiaca* primarily deals with the conflict between Dionysus and the Indian king Deriades, as part of the Indian War, a mythological campaign in which Dionysus conquers India—a theme that was also refer-

THE household of Elphin was sufficiently improsperous during the absence of its chief. The havoc which Maelgon's visitation had made in their winter provision, it required the utmost exertions of their collective energies to repair. Even the young princess Melanghel sallied forth, in the garb of a huntress, to strike the deer or the wild goat among the wintry forests, on the summits of the bleak crags, or in the vallies of the flooded streams.

Taliesin, on these occasions, laid aside his harp, and the robe of his order, and accompanied the princess with his hunting spear, and more succinctly apparelled.

Their retinue, it may be supposed, was neither very numerous nor royal, nor their dogs very thoroughbred. It sometimes happened that the deer went one way, the dogs another; the attendants, losing sight of both, went a third, leaving Taliesin, who never lost sight of Melanghel, alone with her among the hills.

One day, the ardour of the chace having carried them far beyond their ordinary bounds, they stood alone together on Craig Aderyn, the Rock of Birds, which overlooks the river Dysyni. This rock takes its name from the flocks of birds which have made it their dwelling, and which make the air resonant with their multitudinous notes. Around, before, and above them, rose mountain beyond mountain, soaring above the leafless forests, to lose their heads in mist; beneath them lay the silent river; and along the

---

enced in Peacock's use of the line "Ainsi conquesta Bacchus l'Inde." See page 203.]

opening of its narrow valley, they looked to the not-distant sea.

"Prince Llywarch," said Taliesin, "is a bard and a warrior: he is the son of an illustrious line. Taliesin is neither prince nor warrior: he is the unknown child of the waters."

"Why think you of Llywarch?" said Melanghel, to whom the name of the prince was known only from Taliesin, who knew it only from fame.

"Because," said Taliesin, "there is that in my soul which tells me that I shall have no rival among the bards of Britain: but, if its princes and warriors seek the love of Melanghel, I shall know that I am but a bard, and not as Llywarch."

"You would be Prince Taliesin," said Melanghel, smiling, "to make me your princess. Am I not a princess already? and such an one as is not on earth, for the land of my inheritance is under the sea, under those very waves that now roll within our view; and, in truth, you are as well qualified for a prince as I am for a princess, and have about as valuable a dominion in the mists and the clouds as I have under the waters."

Her eyes sparkled with affectionate playfulness, while her long black hair floated loosely in the breeze that pressed the folds of her drapery against the matchless symmetry of her form.

"Oh, maid!" said Taliesin, "what shall I do to win your love?"

"Restore me my father," said Melanghel, with a seriousness as winning as her playfulness had been fascinating.

"That will I do," said Taliesin, "for his own sake. What shall I do for yours?"

"Nothing more," said Melanghel, and she held out her hand to the youthful bard. Taliesin seized it with rapture, and pressed it to his lips; then, still grasping her hand, and throwing his left arm round her, he pressed his lips to hers.

Melanghel started from him, blushing, and looked at him a moment with something like severity; but he blushed as much as she did, and seemed even more alarmed at her displeasure than she was at his momentary audacity. She reassured him with a smile; and, pointing her spear in the direction of her distant home, she bounded before him down the rock.

This was the kiss of Taliesin to the daughter of Elphin, which is celebrated in an inedited triad, as one of "the Three Chaste Kisses of the island of Britain."

CHAPTER 9
THE SONGS OF DIGANWY.

Three things that will always swallow, and never be satisfied: the sea; a burial ground; and a king.

TRIADS OF WISDOM.

THE hall of Maelgon Gwyneth was ringing with music and revelry, when Taliesin stood on the floor, with his harp, in the midst of the assembly, and, without introduction or preface, struck a few chords, that, as if by magic, suspended all other sounds, and fixed the attention of all in silent expectation. He then sang as follows:

CANU Y MEDD.
THE MEAD SONG OF TALIESIN.

The King of kings upholds the heaven,
And parts from earth the billowy sea:
By Him all earthly joys are given;
He loves the just, and guards the free.
Round the wide hall, for thine and thee,
With purest draughts the mead-horns foam,

Maelgon of Gwyneth! Can it be
That here a prince bewails his home?

The bee tastes not the sparkling draught
Which mortals from his toils obtain;
That sends, in festal circles quaffed,
Sweet tumult through the heart and brain.
The timid, while the horn they drain,
Grow bold; the happy more rejoice;
The mourner ceases to complain;
The gifted bard exalts his voice.

To royal Elphin life I owe,
Nurture and name, the harp, and mead:
Full, pure, and sparkling be their flow,
The horns to Maelgon's lips decreed:
For him may horn to horn succeed,
Till, glowing with their generous fire,
He bid the captive chief be freed,
Whom at his hands my songs require.

Elphin has given me store of mead,
Mead, ale, and wine, and fish, and corn;
A happy home; a splendid steed,
Which stately trappings well adorn.
Tomorrow be the auspicious morn
That home the expected chief shall lead;
So may King Maelgon drain the horn
In thrice three million feasts of mead.

"I give you," said Maelgon, "all the rights of hospitality, and as many horns as you please of the mead
you so well and justly extol. If you be Elphin's bard, it
must be confessed he spoke truth with respect to you,

for you are a much better bard than any of mine, as they are all free to confess: I give them that liberty."

The bards availed themselves of the royal indulgence, and confessed their own inferiority to Taliesin, as the king had commanded them to do.[1] Whether they were all as well convinced of it as they professed to be, may be left to the decision of that very large class of literary gentlemen who are in the habit of favouring the reading public with their undisguised opinions.

"But," said Maelgon, "your hero of Caredigion indulged himself in a very unjustifiable bravado with respect to his queen; for he said she was as beautiful and as chaste as mine. Now Rhûn has proved the contrary, with small trouble, and brought away trophies of his triumph; yet still Elphin persists in his first assertion, wherein he grossly disparages the queen of Gwyneth; and for this I hold him in bondage, and will do, till he make recantation."

"That he will never do," said Taliesin. "Your son received only the favours of a handmaid, who was willing, by stratagem, to preserve her lady from violence. The real Angharad was concealed in a cavern."

Taliesin explained the adventure of Rhûn, and pronounced an eulogium on Angharad, which put the king and prince into a towering passion.

Rhûn secretly determined to set forth on a second quest; and Maelgon swore by his mead-horn he would keep Elphin till doomsday. Taliesin struck his

---

1. [Impressed by Taliesin's performance and perhaps recognising the divine inspiration attributed to him, the king commands the court bards to concede their inferiority to Taliesin. This act not only secures Elphin's freedom but also cements Taliesin's reputation as the pre-eminent bard of his time.]

harp again, and, in a tone of deep but subdued feeling, he poured forth the

SONG OF THE WIND[2]

The winds that wander far and free,
Bring whispers from the shores they sweep;
Voices of feast and revelry;
Murmurs of forests and the deep;

Low sounds of torrents from the steep
Descending on the flooded vale;
And tumults from the leaguered keep,
Where foes the dizzy rampart scale.

The whispers of the wandering wind
Are borne to gifted ears alone;
For them it ranges unconfined,
And speaks in accents of its own.

It tells me of Deheubarth's throne;
The spider weaves not in its shield:[3]

---

2. This poem has little or nothing of Taliesin's Canu y Gwynt, with the exception of the title. That poem is apparently a fragment; and, as it now stands, is an incoherent and scarcely-intelligible rhapsody. It contains no distinct or explicit idea, except the proposition that is an unsafe booty to carry off fat kine, which may be easily conceded in a case where nimbleness of heel, both in man and beast, must have been of great importance. The idea from which, if from any thing in the existing portion of the poem, it takes its name, that the whispers of the wind bring rumours of war from Deheubarth, is rather implied than expressed.
3. The spider weaving in suspended armour, is an old emblem of peace and inaction. Thus Bacchylides, in his fragment on Peace:
   Ἐν δὲ σιδηροδέτοις πόρπαξιν
   Αἴθαν ἀράχναν ἔργα πελόνται.

Already from its towers is blown
The blast that bids the spoiler yield.

Ill with his prey the fox may wend,
When the young lion quits his lair:
Sharp sword, strong shield, stout arm, should tend
On spirits that unjustly dare.

To me the wandering breezes bear
The war-blast from Caer Lleon's brow;
The avenging storm is brooding there

[And on iron-bound shields,
A fiery spider weaves its works.]
Euripides, in a fragment of *Erechtheus*:
Κείσθω δόρυ μοι μίτον ἀμφιπλέκειν
Ἀράχναις.
[Let the spear lie for me, to entwine thread
With spiders.]
And Nonnus, whom no poetical image escaped: (*Dionysiaca*, L. xxxviii.)
Οὐ φόνος, οὐ τότ᾽ ἔρις· ἔκειτο δὲ τέλοθι χάρης
Βακχίας ἐξαετέρος ἀραχνιόωσα βοείη.
[No murder, no strife at that time; there lay at the end of joy
A six-year-old Bacchic one, weaving a spider's web of shouts.]
And Beaumont and Fletcher, in the *Wife for a Month*:
"Would'st thou live so long, till thy sword hung by,
And lazy spiders filled the hilt with cobwebs?"
[A contraction of several lines from Act II, Sc. I; Valerio to Menallo:
...Would'st thou live so long, till thy strength forsook thee?
Till thou grew'st only a long tedious story
Of what thou hadst been? till thy sword hang by,
And lazie spiders fill'd the hilt with cobwebs?"]
A Persian poet says, describing ruins:
"The spider spreads the veil in the palace of the Cæsars."
And among the most felicitous uses of this emblem, must never be forgotten Hogarth's cobweb over the lid of the charity-box.

To which Diganwy's towers shall bow.[4]

"If the wind talks to you," said Maelgon, "I may say, with the proverb, you talk to the wind; for I am not to be sung, or cajoled, or vapoured, or bullied out of my prisoner. And as to your war-blasts from Caer Lleon, which I construe into a threat that you will stir up King Arthur against me, I can tell you for your satisfaction, and to spare you the trouble of going so far, that he has enough to do with seeking his wife, who has been carried off by some unknown marauder, and with fighting the Saxons, to have much leisure or inclination to quarrel with a true Briton, who is one of his best friends, and his heir presumptive; for, though he is a man of great prowess, and moreover, saving his reverence and your presence, a cuckold, he has not yet favoured his kingdom with an heir apparent. And I request you to understand, that when I extolled you above my bards, I did so only in respect of your verse and voice, melody and execution, figure and action, in short, of your manner; for your matter is naught; and I must do my own bards the justice to say, that, however much they may fall short of you in the requisites aforesaid, they know much better than you do, what is fitting for bards to sing, and kings to hear."

The bards, thus encouraged, recovered from the first shock of Maelgon's ready admission of Taliesin's manifest superiority, and struck up a sort of consecutive chorus, in a series of pennillion, or stanzas, in praise of Maelgon and his heirship presumptive,

---

4. [Peacock's literal translation of Taliesin's Canu y Gwynt first printed in The Halliford Edition of the *Works of Thomas Love Peacock*, edited by H.F.B. Brett-Smith & C.E. Jones (1934).]

giving him credit for all the virtues of which the reputation was then in fashion; and, amongst the rest, they very loftily celebrated his justice and magnanimity.

Taliesin could not reconcile his notions of these qualities with Maelgon's treatment of Elphin. He changed his measure and his melody, and pronounced, in impassioned numbers, the poem which a learned Welsh historian calls "The Indignation of the Bards," though, as the indignation was Taliesin's, and not theirs, he seems to have made a small mistake in regard to the preposition.

THE INDIGNATION OF TALIESIN
WITH THE
BARDS OF MAELGON GWYNETH.

False bards the sacred fire pervert,
Whose songs are won without desert;
Who falsehoods weave in specious lays,
To gild the base with virtue's praise.

From court to court, from tower to tower,
In warrior's tent, in lady's bower,
For gold, for wine, for food, for fire,
They tune their throats at all men's hire.

Their harps re-echo wide and far
With sensual love, and bloody war,
And drunkenness, and flattering lies:
Truth's light may shine for other eyes.

In palaces they still are found,
At feasts, promoting senseless sound:

He is their demigod at least,
Whose only virtue is his feast.

They love to talk: they hate to think:
All day they sing; all night they drink:
No useful toils their hands employ;
In boisterous throngs is all their joy.

The bird will fly, the fish will swim,
The bee the honied flowers will skim;
Its food by toil each creature brings,
Except false bards and worthless kings.

Learning and wisdom claim to find
Homage and succour from mankind;
But learning's right, and wisdom's due,
Are falsely claimed by slaves like you.

True bards know truth, and truth will show;
Ye know it not, nor care to know:
Your king's weak mind false judgment warps;
Rebuke his wrong, or break your harps.

I know the mountain and the plain;
I know where right and justice reign;
I from the tower will Elphin free;
Your king shall learn his doom from me.

A spectre of the marsh shall rise,
With yellow teeth, and hair, and eyes,
From whom your king in vain aloof
Shall crouch beneath the sacred roof.

He through the half-closed door shall spy

The Yellow Spectre sweeping by;
To whom the punishment belongs
Of Maelgon's crimes and Elphin's wrongs.

By the name of the Yellow Spectre, Taliesin designated a pestilence, which afterwards carried off great multitudes of the people, and, amongst them, Maelgon Gwyneth, then sovereign of Britain, who had taken refuge from it in a church.

Maelgon paid little attention to Taliesin's prophecy, but he was much incensed by the general tenor of his song.

"If it were not," said Maelgon, "that I do not choose to add to the number of the crimes of which you so readily accuse me, that of disregarding the inviolability of your bardship, I would send you to keep company with your trout-catching king, and you might amuse his salmon-salting majesty with telling him as much truth as he is disposed to listen to; which, to judge by his reception of Rhûn's story of his wife, I take to be exceedingly little. For the present, you are welcome to depart; and, if you are going to Caer Lleon, you may present my respects to King Arthur, and tell him, I hope he will beat the Saxons, and find his wife; but I hope, also, that the cutting me off with an heir apparent will not be the consequence of his finding her, or (which, by the by, is more likely,) of his having lost her."

Taliesin took his departure from the hall of Diganwy, leaving the bards biting their lips at his rebuke, and Maelgon roaring with laughter at his own very excellent jest.

CHAPTER 10

THE DISAPPOINTMENT OF RHÛN.

Παρθένε, πῶς μεταμείψας ἐρυθαλῆν σεο μορφήν;
Εἰαρινὴν δ' ἀκτίνα τίς ἔσβεσε σεῖο προσώπου;
Οὐκέτι σῶν μελέων ἀμαρύσσεται ἀργυφὸς αἴγλη
Οὐκέτι δ', ὡς τὸ πρόσθε, τεαὶ γελῶσιν ὀπῶπαι.

Sweet maid, what grief has changed thy roseate
grace,
And quenched the vernal sunshine of thy face?
No more thy light form sparkles as it flies,
Nor laughter flashes from thy radiant eyes.

VENUS TO PASITHEA, in the thirty third book of
the *Dionysiaca* of NONNUS.[1]

TALIESIN returned to the dwelling of Elphin, auguring that, in consequence of his information, Rhûn would pay it another visit. In this anticipation he was not mistaken, for Rhûn very soon appeared, with a numerous retine, determined, apparently, to carry his

---

1. [See page 243.]

point by force of arms. He found, however, no inmate in the dwelling but Taliesin and Teithrin ap Tathral.

Rhûn stormed, entreated, promised, and menaced, without success. He perlustrated the vicinity, and found various caverns, but not the one he sought. He passed many days in the search, and, finally, departed; but, at a short distance, he dismissed all his retinue, except his bard of all work, or laureate expectant, and, accompanied by this worthy, returned to the banks of Mawddach, where they resolved themselves into an ambuscade. It was not long before they saw Taliesin issue from the dwelling, and begin ascending the hill. They followed him, at a cautious distance; first up a steep ascent of the forest-covered rocks; then along a small space of densely-wooded tableland, to the edge of a dingle; and, again, by a slight descent, to the bed of a mountain stream, in a spot where the torrent flung itself, in a series of cataracts, down the rift of a precipitous rock, that towered high above their heads. About half way up the rock, near the base of one of these cataracts, was a projecting ledge, or natural platform of rock, behind which was seen the summit of the opening of a cave. Taliesin paused, and looked around him, as if to ascertain that he was unobserved; and then, standing on a projection of the rock below, he mingled, in spontaneous song, the full power of his voice with the roar of the waters.

TALIESIN.

Maid of the rock! though loud the flood,
My voice will pierce thy cell:
No foe is in the mountain wood;

No danger in the dell:
The torrents bound along the glade;
Their path is free and bright;
Be thou as they, oh mountain maid!
In liberty and light.

Melanghel appeared on the rocky platform, and answered the song of her lover:

MELANGHEL.

The cataracts thunder down the steep;
The woods all lonely wave:
Within my heart the voice sinks deep
That calls me from my cave.
The voice is dear, the song is sweet,
And true the words must be:
Well pleased I quit the dark retreat,
To wend away with thee.

TALIESIN.

Not yet; not yet: let nightdews fall,
And stars be bright above,
Ere to her long deserted hall
I guide my gentle love.
When torchlight flashes on the roof,
No foe will near thee stray:
Even now his parting courser's hoof
Rings from the rocky way.

MELANGHEL.

Yet climb the path, and comfort speak,

To cheer the lonely cave,
Where woods are bare, and rocks are bleak,
And wintry torrents rave.
A dearer home my memory knows,
A home I still deplore;
Where firelight glows, while winds and snows
Assail the guardian door.

Taliesin vanished a moment from the sight of Rhûn, and almost immediately reappeared by the side of Melanghel, who had now been joined by her mother. In a few minutes he returned, and Angharad and Melanghel withdrew.

Rhûn watched him from the dingle, and then proceeded to investigate the path by which he had gained the platform. After some search he discovered it, ascended to the platform, and rushed into the cavern.

They here found a blazing fire, a half-finished dinner, materials of spinning and embroidering, and other signs of female inhabitancy; but they found not the inhabitants. They searched the cavern to its depth, which was not inconsiderable; much marvelling how the ladies had vanished. While thus engaged, they heard a rushing sound, and a crash on the rocks, as of some ponderous body. The mystery of this noise was very soon explained to them, in a manner that gave an unusual length to their faces, and threw a deep tinge of blue into their rosy complexions. A ponderous stone, which had been suspended like a portcullis at the mouth of the cavern, had been dropped by some unseen agency, and made them as close prisoners as Elphin.

They were not long kept in suspense as to how

this matter had been managed. The hoarse voice of Teithrin ap Tathral sounded in their ears from without, "Foxes! you have been seen through, and you are fairly trapped. Eat and drink. You shall want nothing but to get out; which you must want some time; for it is sworn that no hand but Elphin's shall raise the stone of your captivity."

"Let me out," vociferated Rhûn, "and on the word of a prince—" but, before he could finish the sentence, the retreating steps of Teithrin were lost in the roar of the torrent.

CHAPTER II
THE HEROES OF DINAS VAWR.

L'ombra sua torna ch'era dipartita.

DANTE.[1]

While there is life there is hope.

English Proverb.

PRINCE RHÛN being safe in schistous bastile, Taliesin commenced his journey to the court of King Arthur. On his way to Caer Lleon, he was received with all hospitality, entertained with all admiration, and dismissed with all honour, at the castles of several petty kings, and, amongst the rest, at the castle of Dinas Vawr, on the Towy, which was then garrisoned by King Melvas, who had marched with a great force out of his own kingdom, on the eastern shores of the Severn, to levy contributions in the country to the westward, where, as the pleasure of his company had been

---

1. ["Its shade returns, which had departed." *Inferno*, Canto IV, 81.]

altogether unlooked for, he had got possession of a good portion of moveable property. The castle of Dinas Vawr presenting itself to him as a convenient hold, he had taken it by storm; and having cut the throats of the former occupants, thrown their bodies into the Towy, and caused a mass to be sung for the good of their souls, he was now sitting over his bowl, with the comfort of a good conscience, enjoying the fruits of the skill and courage with which he had planned and accomplished his scheme of ways and means for the year.

The hall of Melvas was full of magnanimous heroes, who were celebrating their own exploits in sundry chorusses, especially in that which follows, which is here put upon record as being the quintessence of all the war-songs that ever were written, and the sum and substance of all the appetencies, tendencies, and consequences of military glory:

THE WAR-SONG OF DINAS VAWR

The mountain sheep are sweeter,
But the valley sheep are fatter;
We therefore deemed it meeter[2]
To carry off the latter.
We made an expedition;
We met a host, and quelled it;
We forced a strong position,
And killed the men who held it.

On Dyfed's richest valley,
Where herds of kine were brousing,

---

2. ["More suitable" or "more fitting".]

We made a mighty sally,
To furnish our carousing.
Fierce warriors rushed to meet us;
We met them, and o'erthrew them:
They struggled hard to beat us;
But we conquered them, and slew them.

As we drove our prize at leisure,
The king marched forth to catch us:
His rage surpassed all measure,
But his people could not match us.
He fled to his hall-pillars;
And, ere our force we led off,
Some sacked his house and cellars,
While others cut his head off.

We there, in strife bewild'ring,
Spilt blood enough to swim in:
We orphaned many children,
And widowed many women.
The eagles and the ravens
We glutted with our foemen;
The heroes and the cravens,
The spearmen and the bowmen.

We brought away from battle,
And much their land bemoaned them,
Two thousand head of cattle,
And the head of him who owned them:
Ednyfed, king of Dyfed,
His head was borne before us;
His wine and beasts supplied our feasts,
And his overthrow, our chorus.

As the doughty followers of Melvas, having sung themselves hoarse with their own praises, subsided one by one into drunken sleep, Taliesin, sitting near the great central fire, and throwing around a scrutinizing glance on all the objects in the hall, noticed a portly and somewhat elderly personage, of an aspect that would have been venerable, if it had been less rubicund and Bacchic, who continued plying his potations with undiminished energy, while the heroes of the festival dropped round him, like the leaves of autumn. This figure excited Taliesin's curiosity. The features struck him with a sense of resemblance to objects which had been somewhere familiar to him; but he perplexed himself in vain, with attempts at definite recollections. At length, when these two were almost the sole survivors of the evening, the stranger approached him with a golden goblet, which he had just replenished with the choicest wine of the vaults of Dinas Vawr, and pronounced the oracular monosyllable, "Drink!" to which he subjoined emphatically "Gwin O Eur: Wine from gold. That is my taste. Ale is well; mead is better; wine is best. Horn is well; silver is better; gold is best."

Taliesin, who had been very abstemious during the evening, took the golden goblet, and drank to please the inviter; in the hope that he would become communicative, and satisfy the curiosity his appearance had raised.

The stranger sat down near him, evidently in that amiable state of semi-intoxication which inflates the head, warms the heart, lifts up the veil of the inward man, and sets the tongue flying, or rather tripping, in the double sense of nimbleness and titubancy.

The stranger repeated, taking a copious draught, "My taste is wine from gold."

"I have heard those words," said Taliesin, "Gwin O Eur, repeated as having been the favourite saying of a person whose memory is fondly cherished by one as dear to me as a mother, though his name, with all others, is the by-word of all that is disreputable."

"I cannot believe," said the stranger, "that a man whose favourite saying was Gwin O Eur, could possibly be a disreputable person, or deserve any other than that honourable remembrance, which, you say, only one person is honest enough to entertain for him."

"His name," said Taliesin, "is too unhappily notorious throughout Britain, by the terrible catastrophe of which his Gwin O Eur was the cause."

"And what might that be?" said the stranger.

"The inundation of Gwaelod," said Taliesin.

"You speak then," said the stranger, taking an enormous potation, "of Seithenyn, Prince Seithenyn, Seithenyn ap Seithyn Saidi, Arglwyd Gorwarcheidwad yr Argae Breninawl."

"I seldom hear his name," said Taliesin, "with any of those sounding additions; he is usually called Seithenyn the Drunkard."

The stranger goggled about his eyes in an attempt to fix them steadily on Taliesin, screwed up the corners of his mouth, stuck out his nether lip, pursed up his chin, thrust forward his right foot, and elevated his golden goblet in his right hand; then, in a tone which he intended to be strongly becoming of his impressive aspect and imposing attitude, he muttered, "Look at me."

Taliesin looked at him accordingly, with as much gravity as he could preserve.

After a silence, which he designed to be very dignified and solemn, the stranger spoke again: "I am the man."

"What man?" said Taliesin.

"The man," replied his entertainer, "of whom you have spoken so disparagingly; Seithenyn ap Seithyn Saidi."

"Seithenyn," said Taliesin, "has slept twenty years under the waters of the western sea, as King Gwythno's Lamentations have made known to all Britain."

"They have not made it known to me," said Seithenyn, "for the best of all reasons, that one can only know the truth; for, if that which we think we know is not truth, it is something which we do not know. A man cannot know his own death; for, while he knows any thing, he is alive; at least, I never heard of a dead man who knew any thing, or pretended to know any thing: if he had so pretended, I should have told him to his face he was no dead man."

"Your mode of reasoning," said Taliesin, "unquestionably corresponds with what I have heard of Seithenyn's: but how is it possible Seithenyn can be living?"

"Every thing that is, is possible, says Catog the Wise;" answered Seithenyn, with a look of great sapience. "I will give you proof that I am not a dead man; for, they say, dead men tell no tales: now I will tell you a tale, and a very interesting one it is. When I saw the sea sapping the tower, I jumped into the water, and just in the nick of time. It was well for me that I had been so provident as to empty so many barrels, and that somebody, I don't know who, but I suppose it was my daughter, had been so provident as to put the bungs into them, to keep them sweet; for the beauty of it was that, when there was so much water in the case, it kept them empty; and when I jumped into the sea, the sea was just making a great hole in the cellar, and they were floating out by dozens. I don't know how I managed it, but I got one arm over one, and the other arm over another: I nipped them pretty tight; and, though my legs were under water, the good liquor I had in me kept me warm. I could not help thinking, as I had nothing else to think of just then that touched me so nearly, that if I had left them full, and myself empty, as a sober man would have done, we should all three, that is, I and the two barrels, have gone to the bottom together, that is to say, separately; for we should never have come together, except at the bottom, perhaps; when no one of us could have done the other any good; whereas they have done me much good, and I have requited it; for, first, I did them the service of emptying them; and then they did me the service of floating me with the tide, whether the ebb, or the flood, or both, is more than I can tell, down to the coast of Dyfed, where I was picked up by fishermen; and such was my sense of gratitude, that, though I had always before detested an empty barrel, except as a trophy, I swore I would not budge from the water unless my two barrels went with me; so we were all marched inland together, and were taken into the service of King Ednyfed, where I stayed till his castle was sacked, and his head cut off, and his beeves marched away with, by the followers of King Melvas, of whom I killed two or three; but they were too many for us: therefore, to make the best of a bad bargain, I followed leisurely in the train of the beeves, and presented myself to King Melvas, with this golden goblet, saying GWIN O EUR. He was struck with my deportment, and made me his chief butler; and now my two barrels are the two pillars of his cellar, where I regularly fill them from affection, and as regularly empty them from gratitude, taking care to put the bungs in them, to keep them sweet."

"But all this while," said Taliesin, "did you never look back to the Plain of Gwaelod, to your old king, and, above all, to your daughter?"

"Why yes," said Seithenyn, "I did in a way! But as to the Plain of Gwaelod, that was gone, buried under the sea, along with many good barrels, which I had been improvident enough to leave full: then, as to the old king, though I had a great regard for him, I thought he might be less likely to feast me in his hall, than to set up my head on a spike over his gate: then, as to my daughter—"

Here he shook his head, and looked maudlin; and dashing two or three drops from his eye, he put a great many into his mouth.

"Your daughter," said Taliesin, "is the wife of King Elphin, and has a daughter, who is now as beautiful as her mother was."

"Very likely," said Seithenyn, "and I should be very glad to see them all; but I am afraid King Elphin, as you call him, (what he is king of, you shall tell me at leisure,) would do me a mischief. At any rate, he would stint me in liquor. No! If they will visit me, here I am. Fish, and water, will not agree with me. I am growing old, and need cordial nutriment. King Melvas will never want for beeves and wine; nor, indeed, for any thing else that is good. I can tell you what," he added, in a very low voice, cocking his eye, and putting his finger on his lips, "he has got in this very castle the finest woman in Britain."

"That I doubt," said Taliesin.

"She is the greatest, at any rate," said Seithenyn, "and ought to be the finest."

"How the greatest?" said Taliesin.

Seithenyn looked round, to observe if there were any listener near, and fixed a very suspicious gaze on a rotund figure of a fallen hero, who lay coiled up like a maggot in a filbert, and snoring with an energy that, to the muddy apprehensions of Seithenyn, seemed to be counterfeit. He determined, by a gentle experiment, to ascertain if his suspicions were well founded; and proceeded, with what he thought great caution, to apply the point of his foot to the most bulging portion of the fat sleeper's circumference. But he greatly miscalculated his intended impetus, for he impinged his foot with a force that overbalanced himself, and hurled him headlong over his man, who instantly sprang on his legs, shouting "To arms!" Numbers started up at the cry; the hall rang with the din of arms, and with the vociferation of questions, which there were many to ask, and none to answer. Some stared about for the enemy; some rushed to the gates; others to the walls. Two or three, reeling in the tumult and the darkness, were jostled over the parapet, and went rolling down the precipitous slope of the castle hill, crashing through the bushes, and bellowing for some one to stop them, till their clamours were cut short by a plunge into the Towy, where the conjoint weight of their armour and their liquor carried them at once to the bottom. The rage which would have fallen on the enemy, if there had been one, was turned against the author of the false alarm; but, as none could point him out, the tumult subsided by degrees, through a descending scale of imprecations, into the last murmured malediction of him whom the intensity of his generous anger kept longest awake. By this time, the rotund hero had again coiled himself up into his ring; and Seithenyn was stretched in a right line, as a tangent to the circle, in a state of utter incapacity to elucidate the mystery of King Melvas's possession of the finest woman in Britain.

THE SPLENDOUR OF CAER LLEON.

The three principal cities of the isle of Britain: Caer Llion upon Wysg in Cymru; Caer Llundain in Lloegr; and Caer Evrawg in Deifr and Brynaich.

TRIADS OF THE ISLE OF BRITAIN.[1]

THE sunset of a bright December day was glittering on the waves of the Usk, and on the innumerable roofs, which, being composed chiefly of the glazed tiles of the Romans, reflected the light almost as vividly as the river; when Taliesin descended one of the hills that border the beautiful valley in which

---

1. Caer Lleon upon Usk in Cambria: London in Loegria: and York in Deïra and Bernicia. [Cambria is the Latinised name for Wales. It derives from the Welsh word *Cymry*. Loegria refers to England, specifically the southern and central regions. Deïra and Bernicia were two early medieval Anglo-Saxon kingdoms in what is now northern England and southern Scotland. Together, they formed the larger kingdom of Northumbria in the 7th century. By referencing Caer Lleon, London, and York as key centres of these regions, Peacock blends Roman, Arthurian, and Anglo-Saxon elements, reflecting both the historical richness and the mythological traditions surrounding Britain.]

then stood Caer Lleon, the metropolis of Britain, and in which now stands, on a small portion of the self-same space, a little insignificant town, possessing nothing of its ancient glory but the unaltered name of Caer Lleon.

The rapid Usk flowed then, as now, under the walls: the high wooden bridge, with its slender piles, was then much the same as it is at this day: it seems to have been never regularly rebuilt, but to have been repaired, from time to time, on the original Roman model. The same green and fertile meadows, the same gently-sloping wood-covered hills, that now meet the eye of the tourist, then met the eye of Taliesin; except that the woods on one side of the valley, were then only the skirts of an extensive forest, which the nobility and beauty of Caer Lleon made frequently re-echo to the clamours of the chace.

The city, which had been so long the centre of the Roman supremacy, which was now the seat of the most illustrious sovereign that had yet held the sceptre of Britain, could not be approached by the youthful bard, whose genius was destined to eclipse that of all his countrymen, without feelings and reflections of deep interest. The sentimental tourist, (who, perching himself on an old wall, works himself up into a soliloquy of philosophical pathos, on the vicissitudes of empire and the mutability of all sublunary things, interrupted only by an occasional peep at his watch, to ensure his not overstaying the minute at which his fowl, comfortably roasting at the nearest inn, has been promised to be ready,) has, no doubt, many fine thoughts well worth recording in a dapper volume; but Taliesin had an interest in the objects before him too deep to have a thought to spare, even for his dinner. The monuments of Roman magnificence, and of Roman domination, still existing in comparative freshness; the arduous struggle, in which his countrymen were then engaged with the Saxons, and which, notwithstanding the actual triumphs of Arthur, Taliesin's prophetic spirit told him would end in their being dispossessed of all the land of Britain, except the wild region of Wales, (a result which political sagacity might have apprehended from their disunion, but which, as he told it to his countrymen in that memorable prophecy which every child of the Cymry knows, has established for him, among them, the fame of the prophet;) the importance to himself and his benefactors of the objects of his visit to the city, on the result of which depended the liberation of Elphin, and the success of his love for Melanghel; the degree in which these objects might be promoted by the construction he had put on Seithenyn's imperfect communication respecting the lady in Dinas Vawr; furnished, altogether, more materials for absorbing thought, than the most zealous peregrinator, even if he be at once poet, antiquary, and philosopher, is likely to have at once in his mind, on the top of the finest old wall on the face of the earth.

Taliesin passed, in deep musing, through the gates of Caer Lleon; but his attention was speedily drawn to the objects around him. From the wild solitudes in which he had passed his earlier years, the transition to the castles and cities he had already visited, furnished much food to curiosity: but the ideas of them sunk into comparative nothingness before the magnificence of Caer Lleon.

He did not stop in the gateway to consider the knotty question, which has since puzzled so many antiquaries, whether the name of Caer Lleon signifies the City of Streams, the City of Legions, or the City of King Lleon? He saw a river filled with ships, flowing through fine meadows, bordered by hills and forests; walls of brick, as well as of stone; a castle, of impregnable strength; stately houses, of the most admirable architecture; palaces, with gilded roofs; Roman temples, and Christian churches; a theatre, and an amphitheatre. The public and private buildings of the departed Romans were in excellent preservation; though the buildings, and especially the temples, were no longer appropriated to their original purposes. The king's butler, Bedwyr, had taken possession of the Temple of Diana, as a cool place of deposit for wine: he had recently effected a stowage of vast quantities therein, and had made a most luminous arrangement of the several kinds; under the judicious and experienced superintendence of Dyvrig, the Ex-Archbishop of Caer Lleon; who had just then nothing else to do, having recently resigned his see in favour of King Arthur's uncle, David, who is, to this day, illustrious as the St. David in whose honour the Welshmen annually adorn their hats with a leek. This David was a very respectable character in his way: he was a man of great sanctity and simplicity; and, in order to eschew the vanities of the world, which were continually present to him in Caer Lleon, he removed the metropolitan see, from Caer Lleon, to the rocky, barren, woodless, streamless, meadowless, tempest-beaten point of Mynyw, which was afterwards called St. David's. He was the mirror and pattern of a godly life; teaching by example, as by precept; admirable in words, and excellent in deeds; tall in stature, handsome in aspect, noble in deportment, affable in address, eloquent and learned, a model to his followers, the life of the poor, the protector of widows, and the father of orphans. This makes altogether a very respectable saint; and it cannot be said, that the honourable leek is unworthily consecrated. A long series of his Catholic successors maintained, in great magnificence, a cathedral, a college, and a palace; keeping them all in repair, and feeding the poor into the bargain, from the archiepiscopal, or, when the primacy of Caer Lleon had merged in that of Canterbury, from the episcopal, revenues: but these things were reformed altogether by one of the first Protestant bishops, who, having a lady that longed for the gay world, and wanting more than all the revenues for himself and his family, first raised the wind by selling off the lead from the roof of his palace, and then obtained permission to remove from it, on the plea that it was not watertight. The immediate successors of this bishop, whose name was Barlow, were in every way worthy of him; the palace and college have, consequently, fallen into incurable dilapidation, and the cathedral has fallen partially into ruins, and, most impartially, into neglect and defacement.[2]

To return to Taliesin, in the streets of Caer Lleon. Plautus and Terence were not heard in the theatre, nor to be heard of in its neighbourhood; but it was

---

2. [William Barlow (c. 1498–1568), who was Bishop of St David's (1536–1548) during the reign of Henry VIII. A strong supporter of the Reformation, aligning with Thomas Cranmer and Thomas Cromwell, he was notorious for selling off church lands and relocating the bishopric's headquarters. He later served as Bishop of Bath and Wells, where he continued to face accusations of mismanagement and neglect of ecclesiastical buildings. Barlow was historically blamed for dismantling St David's Cathedral's wealth.]

thought an excellent place for an Eisteddfod, or Bardic Congress, and was made the principal place of assembly of the Bards of the island of Britain. This is what Ross of Warwick means, when he says there was a noble university of students in Caer Lleon.[3]

The mild precepts of the new religion had banished the ferocious sports to which the Romans had dedicated the amphitheatre, and, as Taliesin passed, it was pouring forth an improved and humanized multitude, who had been enjoying the pure British pleasure of baiting a bear.

The hot baths and aqueducts, the stoves of "wonderful artifice," as Giraldus has it,[4] which diffused hot air through narrow spiracles, and many other wonders of the place, did not all present themselves to a first observation. The streets were thronged with people, especially of the fighting order, of whom a greater number flocked about Arthur, than he always found it convenient to pay. Horsemen, with hawks and hounds, were returning from the neighbouring forest, accompanied by beautiful huntresses, in scarlet and gold.

Taliesin, having perlustrated the city, proceeded

---

3. [John Ross (or Rous) of Warwick was a 15th-century English historian and antiquary, best known for his work *Historia Regum Angliae* (The History of the Kings of England), and who often mixed up legend with historical fact. Nevertheless, Caer Lleon (Caerleon) in South Wales was an important Roman fortress (Isca Augusta) and later became associated with Arthurian legend. Medieval chroniclers, including Geoffrey of Monmouth in his *Historia Regum Britanniae* (c. 1136) described Caerleon as a major centre of learning and Arthurian splendour.

4. [Giraldus Cambrensis (Gerald of Wales, c. 1146–1223), a medieval chronicler who described Roman remains in Britain, particularly in Caerleon (Caer Lleon).]

to the palace of Arthur. At the gates he was challenged by a formidable guard, but passed by his bardic privilege. It was now very near Christmas, and when Taliesin entered the great hall, it was blazing with artificial light, and glowing with the heat of the Roman stoves.

Arthur had returned victorious from the great battle of Badon hill, in which he had slain with his own hand four hundred and forty Saxons; and was feasting as merrily as an honest man can be supposed to do while his wife is away. Kings, princes, and soldiers of fortune, bards and prelates, ladies superbly apparelled, and many of them surpassingly beautiful; and a most gallant array of handsome young cup-bearers, marshalled and well drilled by the king's butler, Bedwyr, who was himself a petty king, were the chief components of the illustrious assembly.

Amongst the ladies were the beautiful Tegau Eurvron; Dywir the Golden-haired; Enid, the daughter of Yniwl; Garwen, the daughter of Henyn; Gwyl, the daughter of Enddaud; and Indeg, the daughter of Avarwy Hir, of Maelienydd. Of these, Tegau Eurvron, or Tegau of the Golden Bosom, was the wife of Caradoc, and one of the Three Chaste Wives of the island of Britain. She is the heroine, who, as the lady of Sir Cradock, is distinguished above all the ladies of Arthur's court, in the ballad of the Boy and the Mantle.[5]

Amongst the bards were Prince Llywarch, then in his youth, afterwards called Llywarch Hên, or Llywarch the Aged; Aneurin, the British Homer, who

---

5. ["The Boy and the Mantle" in Bishop Thomas Percy's *Reliques of Ancient British Poetry* Series III, Book I (1765).]

sang the fatal battle of Cattraëth, which laid the foundation of the Saxon ascendancy, in heroic numbers, which the gods have preserved to us, and who was called the Monarch of the Bards, before the days of the glory of Taliesin; and Merddin Gwyllt, or Merlin the Wild, who was so deep in the secrets of nature, that he obtained the fame of a magician, to which he had at least as good a title as either Friar Bacon or Cornelius Agrippa.

Amongst the petty kings, princes, and soldiers of fortune, were twenty-four marchawg, or cavaliers, who were the counsellors and champions of Arthur's court. This was the heroic band, illustrious, in the songs of chivalry, as the Knights of the Round Table. Their names and pedigrees would make a very instructive and entertaining chapter; and would include the interesting characters of Gwalchmai ap Gwyar the Courteous, the nephew of Arthur; Caradoc, "Colofn Cymry," the Pillar of Cambria, whose lady, as above noticed, was the mirror of chastity; and Trystan ap Tallwch, the lover of the beautiful Essyllt, the daughter, or, according to some, the wife, of his uncle March ap Meirchion; persons known to all the world, as Sir Gawain, Sir Cradock, and Sir Tristram.

On the right hand of King Arthur sate the beautiful Indeg, and on his left the lovely Garwen. Taliesin advanced, along the tesselated floor, towards the upper end of the hall, and, kneeling before King Arthur, said, "What boon will King Arthur grant to him who brings news of his queen?"

"Any boon," said Arthur, "that a king can give."

"Queen Gwenyvar," said Taliesin, "is the prisoner of King Melvas, in the castle of Dinas Vawr."

The mien and countenance of his informant satisfied the king that he knew what he was saying; therefore, without further parlance, he broke up the banquet, to make preparations for assailing Dinas Vawr.

But, before he began his march, King Melvas had shifted his quarters, and passed beyond the Severn to the isle of Avallon, where the marshes and winter-floods assured him some months of tranquillity and impunity.

King Arthur was highly exasperated, on receiving the intelligence of Melvas's movement; but he had no remedy, and was reduced to the alternative of making the best of his Christmas with the ladies, princes, and bards who crowded his court.

The period of the winter solstice had been always a great festival with the northern nations, the commencement of the lengthening of the days being, indeed, of all points in the circle of the year, that in which the inhabitants of cold countries have most cause to rejoice. This great festival was anciently called Yule; whether derived from the Gothic *Iola*, to make merry; or from the Celtic *Hiaul*, the sun; or from the Danish and Swedish *Hiul*, signifying wheel or revolution, December being *Hiul-month*, or the month of return; or from the Cimbric word *Ol*, which has the important signification of ALE, is too knotty a controversy to be settled here: but Yule had been long a great festival, with both Celts and Saxons; and, with the change of religion, became the great festival of Christmas, retaining most of its ancient characteristics while England was Merry England; a phrase which must be a mirifical puzzle to any one who looks for the first time on its present most lugubrious inhabitants.

The mistletoe of the oak was gathered by the Druids with great ceremonies, as a symbol of the season. The mistletoe continued to be so gathered, and to be suspended in halls and kitchens, if not in temples, implying an unlimited privilege of kissing; which circumstance, probably, led a learned antiquary to opine that it was the forbidden fruit.

The Druids, at this festival, made, in a capacious cauldron, a mystical brewage of carefully-selected ingredients, full of occult virtues, which they kept from the profane, and which was typical of the new year and of the transmigration of the soul. The profane, in humble imitation, brewed a bowl of spiced ale, or wine, throwing therein roasted crabs; the hissing of which, as they plunged, piping hot, into the liquor, was heard with much unction at midwinter, as typical of the conjunct benignant influences of fire and strong drink. The Saxons called this the Wassail-bowl, and the brewage of it is reported to have been one of the charms with which Rowena fascinated Vortigern.

King Arthur kept his Christmas so merrily, that the memory of it passed into a proverb:[6] "As merry as Christmas in Caer Lleon."

Caer Lleon was the merriest of places, and was commonly known by the name of Merry Caer Lleon; which the English ballad-makers, for the sake of the smoother sound, and confounding Cambria with Cumbria, most ignorantly or audaciously turned into Merry Carlisle; thereby emboldening a northern antiquary to set about proving that King Arthur was a Scotchman; according to the old principles of harry

---

6. Mor llawen ag Ngdolig yn Nghaerlleon.

and foray, which gave Scotchmen a right to whatever they could find on the English border; though the English never admitted their title to any thing there, excepting a halter in Carlisle.[7]

The chace, in the neighbouring forest; tilting in the amphitheatre; trials of skill in archery, in throwing the lance and riding at the quintain, and similar amusements of the morning, created good appetites for the evening feasts; in which Prince Cei, who is well known as Sir Kay, the seneschal, superintended the viands, as King Bedwyr did the liquor; having each a thousand men at command, for their provision, arrangement, and distribution; and music worthy of the banquet was provided and superintended by the king's chief harper, Geraint, of whom a contemporary poet observes, that when he died, the gates of heaven were thrown wide open, to welcome the ingress of so divine a musician.

7. [Carlisle was a key site of executions for captured Scottish rebels, especially after the Jacobite Rising of 1745, when Bonnie Prince Charlie and his supporters attempted to reclaim the British throne. After the Battle of Culloden (1746), many Scottish prisoners were tried and executed in Carlisle, often by hanging (a halter being a noose or hanging rope).]

CHAPTER 13

THE GHOSTLINESS OF AVALLON.

Poco più, poco meno, tutti al mondo vivono d'impostura: e chi è di buon gusto, dissimula quando occorre, gode quando può, crede quel che vuole, ride de' pazzi, e figura un mondo a suo gusto.

GOLDONI.[1]

"WHERE is the young bard," said Arthur, after some nights of Christmas had passed by, "who brought me the news of my queen, and to whom I promised a boon, which he has not yet claimed?"

None could satisfy the king's curiosity. Taliesin had disappeared from Caer Lleon. He knew the power and influence of Maelgon Gwyneth; and he was aware that King Arthur, however favourably he might receive his petition, would not find leisure to compel the liberation of Elphin, till he had enforced from

---

1.   ["All in the world live by deception, some to a greater extent, some to a lesser: and the full-blooded man dissimulates when necessary, rejoices when he can, believes what he wants to believe, laughs at the fools, and pictures the world as he desires."]

Melvas the surrender of his queen. It occurred to him that her restoration might be effected by peaceable means; and he knew that, if he could be in any degree instrumental to this result, it would greatly strengthen his claims on the king. He engaged a small fishing-vessel, which had just landed a cargo for the Christmas feasts of Caer Lleon, and set sail for the isle of Avallon. At that period, the springtides of the sea rolled round a cluster of islands, of which Avallon was one, over the extensive fens, which wiser generations have embanked and reclaimed.

The abbey of Avallon, afterwards called Glaston-bury, was, even then, a comely and commodious pile, though not possessing any of that magnificence which the accumulated wealth of ages subsequently gave to it. A large and strongly fortified castle, almost adjoining the abbey, gave to the entire place the air of a strong hold of the church militant. King Melvas was one of the pillars of the orthodoxy of those days: he was called the Scourge of the Pelagians; and extended the shield of his temporal might over the spiritual brotherhood of Avallon, who, in return, made it a point of conscience not to stint him in absolutions.

Some historians pretend that a comfortable nun-nery was erected at a convenient distance from the abbey, that is to say, close to it; but this involves a nice question in monastic antiquity, which the cu-rious may settle for themselves.

It was about midway between nones and vespers when Taliesin sounded, on the gate of the abbey, a notice of his wish for admission. A small trapdoor in the gate was cautiously opened, and a face, as round and as red as the setting sun in November, shone forth in the aperture.

The topographers who have perplexed themselves about the origin of the name Ynys Avallon, "the island of apples," had not the advantage of this piece of meteoroscopy: if they could have looked on this archetype of a Norfolk beefin, with the knowledge that it was only a sample of a numerous fraternity, they would at once have perceived the fitness of the appellation. The brethren of Avallon were the apples of the church. It was the oldest monastic establishment in Britain; and consequently, as of reason, the most plump, succulent, and rosy. It had, even in the sixth century, put forth the fruits of good living, in a manner that would have done honour to a more enlightened age. It went on steadily improving in this line till the days of its last abbot, Richard Whiting, who built the stupendous kitchen, which has withstood the ravages of time and the Reformation; and who, as appears by authentic documents, and, amongst others, by a letter signed with the honoured name of Russell, was found guilty, by a right worshipful jury, of being suspected of great riches, and of an inclination to keep them; and was accordingly sentenced to be hanged forthwith, along with his treasurer and subtreasurer, who were charged with aiding and abetting him in the safe custody of his cash and plate; at the same time that the Abbot of Peterborough was specially reprieved from the gallows, on the ground that he was the said Russell's particular friend. This was a compendium of justice and mercy according to the new light of King Henry the Eighth. The abbot's kitchen is the most interesting and perfect portion of the existing ruins. These ruins were overgrown with the finest ivy in England, till it was, not long since, pulled down by some Vandal, whom the Society of Antiquaries had sent down to make drawings of the walls, which he executed literally, by stripping them bare, that he might draw the walls, and nothing else.[2] Its shade no longer waves over the musing moralist, who, with folded arms, and his back against a wall, dreams of the days that are gone; or the sentimental cockney, who, seating himself with much gravity on a fallen column, produces a flute from his pocket, and strikes up "I'd be a butterfly."[3]

From the phænomenon of a blushing fruit that was put forth in the abbey gate of Avallon issued a deep, fat, gurgling voice, which demanded of Taliesin his name and business.

"I seek the abbot of Avallon," said Taliesin.

"He is confessing a penitent," said the ghostly brother, who was officiating in turn as porter.

"I can await his leisure," said Taliesin, "but I must see him."

---

2. [Glastonbury Abbey, once one of the most important monasteries in England, was dissolved in 1539 under Henry VIII's Dissolution of the Monasteries. By the 18th and 19th centuries, the ruins were a major subject of antiquarian interest, with artists, historians and archaeologists documenting and studying them. Ivy had heavily covered the ruins, making them a picturesque sight, often depicted in Romantic landscape paintings. Some antiquarians and preservationists have argued that removing ivy from ruins can prevent further structural decay, while others believe it contributes to their decline.]

3. [A reference to the popular song "I'd Be a Butterfly" (1827) by Thomas Haynes Bayly (1797–1839), a British poet and songwriter known for his sentimental and light-hearted lyrics. The song became immensely popular in the 1820s and 1830s, reflecting the Romantic fascination with nature, freedom and fleeting beauty. It begins:

"I'd be a butterfly, born in a bower,
Where roses and lilies and violets meet."]

"Are you alone?" said the brother.

"I am," said Taliesin.

The gate unclosed slowly, just wide enough to give him admittance. It was then again barred and barricadoed.

The ghostly brother, of whom Taliesin had now a full view, had a figure corresponding with his face, and wanted nothing but a pair of horns and a beard in ringlets, to look like an avatar of Bacchus. He maintained, however, great gravity of face, and decorum of gesture, as he said to Taliesin, "Hospitality is the rule of our house; but we are obliged to be cautious in these times, though we live under powerful protection. Those bloody Nimrods, the Saxons, are athirst for the blood of the righteous. Monsters that are born with tails."

Taliesin had not before heard of this feature of Saxon conformation, and expressed his astonishment accordingly.

"How?" said the monk. "Did not a rabble of them fasten goats' tails to the robe of the blessed preacher in Riw, and did he not, therefore, pray that their posterity might be born with tails? And it is so. But let that pass.[4] Have they not sacked monasteries, plun-

---

4. [An allusion to stories associated with both John Horne Tooke and Lord Monboddo, particularly their discussions of folklore, evolution, and human appendages. John Horne Tooke (1736–1812) was an English radical, philologist and political thinker. He was known for his interest in etymology and provocative political and linguistic theories. Tooke was associated with satirical and polemical writings, and tales of people being born with tails were often cited in discussions of folklore, superstition and social satire. James Burnett, Lord Monboddo (1714–1799) was a Scottish judge and philosopher best known for his proto-evolutionary ideas. He argued that humans were originally more animal-like and had

dered churches, and put holy brethren to the sword? The blood of the saints calls for vengeance."

"And will have it," said Taliesin, "from the hand of Arthur."

The name of Arthur evidently discomposed the monk, who, desiring Taliesin to follow him, led the way across the hall of the abbey, and along a short wide passage, at the end of which was a portly door.

The monk disappeared through this door, and, presently returning, said, "The abbot requires your name and quality."

"Taliesin, the bard of Elphin ap Gwythno Garanhir," was the reply.

The monk disappeared again, and, returning, after a longer pause than before, said, "You may enter."

The abbot was a plump and comely man, of middle age, having three roses in his complexion; one in full blossom on each cheek, and one in bud on the tip of his nose.

He was sitting at a small table, on which stood an enormous vase, and a golden goblet; and opposite to him sat the penitent of whom the round-faced brother had spoken, and in whom Taliesin recognised his acquaintance of Dinas Vawr, who called himself Seithenyn ap Seithyn.

The abbot and Seithenyn sat with their arms folded on the table, leaning forward towards each other, as if in momentous discussion.

---

tails in earlier stages of evolution, making him one of the first thinkers to anticipate aspects of Darwinian theory. His ideas were mocked by his contemporaries, especially the notion that humans might still have remnants of tails.]

The abbot said to Taliesin, "Sit;" and to his conductor, "Retire, and be silent."

"Will it not be better," said the monk, "that I cross my lips with the sign of secrecy?"

"It is permitted," said the abbot.

Seithenyn held forth the goblet to the monk, who swallowed the contents with much devotion. He then withdrew, and closed the door.

"I bid you most heartily welcome," said Seithenyn to Taliesin. "Drink off this, and I will tell you more. You are admitted to this special sitting at my special instance. I told the abbot I knew you well. Now I will tell you what I know. You have told King Arthur that King Melvas has possession of Queen Gwenyvar, and, in consequence, King Arthur is coming here, to sack and raze the castle and abbey, and cut every throat in the isle of Avallon. I have just brought the abbot this pleasant intelligence, and, as I knew it would take him down a cup or two, I have also brought what I call my little jug, to have the benefit of his judgment on a piece of rare wine which I have broached this morning: there is no better in Caer Lleon. And now we are holding council on the emergency. But I must say you abuse your bardic privilege, to enjoy people's hospitality, worm out their secrets, and carry the news to the enemy. It was partly to give you this candid opinion, that I have prevailed on the abbot to admit you to this special sitting. Therefore drink. GWIN O EUR: Wine from gold."

"King Arthur is not a Saxon, at any rate," sighed the abbot, winding up his fainting spirits with a draught. "Think not, young stranger, that I am transgressing the laws of temperance: my blood runs so cold when I think of the bloodthirsty Saxons, that I take a little wine medicinally, in the hope of warming it; but it is a slow and tedious remedy."

"Take a little more," said Seithenyn. "That is the true quantity. Wine is my medicine; and my quantity is a little more. A little more."

"King Arthur," said Taliesin, "is not a Saxon; but he does not brook injuries lightly. It were better for your abbey that he came not here in arms. The aiders and abettors of Melvas, even though they be spiritual, may not carry off the matter without some share of his punishment, which is infallible."

"That is just what I have been thinking," said Seithenyn.

"God knows," said the abbot, "we are not abettors of Melvas, though we need his temporal power to protect us from the Saxons."

"How can it be otherwise," said Taliesin, "than that these Saxon despoilers should be insolent and triumphant, while the princes of Britain are distracted with domestic broils: and for what?"

"Ay," said Seithenyn, "that is the point. For what? For a woman, or some such rubbish."

"Rubbish, most verily," said the abbot. "Women are the flesh which we renounce with the devil."

"Holy father," said Taliesin, "have you not spiritual influence with Melvas, to persuade him to surrender the queen without bloodshed, and, renewing his allegiance to Arthur, assist him in his most sacred war against the Saxon invaders?"

"A righteous work," said the abbot; "but Melvas is headstrong and difficult."

"Screw yourself up with another goblet," said Seithenyn; "you will find the difficulty smooth itself off wonderfully. Wine from gold has a sort of double light, that illuminates a dark path miraculously."

The abbot sighed deeply, but adopted Seithenyn's method of throwing light on the subject.

"The anger of King Arthur," said Taliesin, "is certain, and its consequences infallible. The anger of King Melvas is doubtful, and its consequences to you cannot be formidable."

"That is nearly true," said the abbot, beginning to look resolute, as the rosebud at his nose-tip deepened into damask.

"A little more," said Seithenyn, "and it will become quite true."

By degrees the proposition ripened into absolute truth. The abbot suddenly inflated his cheeks, started on his legs, and stalked bolt upright out of the apartment, and forthwith out of the abbey, followed by Seithenyn, tossing his goblet in the air, and catching it in his hand, as he went.

The round-faced brother made his appearance almost immediately. "The abbot," he said, "commends you to the hospitality of the brotherhood. They will presently assemble to supper. In the meanwhile, as I am thirsty, and content with whatever falls in my way, I will take a simple and single draught of what happens to be here."

His draught was a model of simplicity and singleness; for, having uplifted the ponderous vase, he held it to his lips, till he had drained it of the very copious remnant which the abrupt departure of the abbot had caused Seithenyn to leave in it.

Taliesin proceeded to enjoy the hospitality of the brethren, who set before him a very comfortable hot supper, at which he quickly perceived, that, however dexterous King Elphin might be at catching fish, the monks of Avallon were very far his masters in the three great arts of cooking it, serving it up, and washing it down; but he had not time to profit by their skill and experience in these matters, for he received a pressing invitation to the castle of Melvas, which he obeyed immediately.

CHAPTER 14

THE RIGHT OF MIGHT.

The three triumphs of the bards of the isle of Britain: the triumph of learning over ignorance; the triumph of reason over error; and the triumph of peace over violence.

TRIADS OF BARDISM.[1]

"FRIEND Seithenyn," said the abbot, when, having passed the castle gates, and solicited an audience, he was proceeding to the presence of Melvas, "this task, to which I have accinged[2] myself, is arduous, and in some degree awful; being, in truth, no less than to persuade a king to surrender a possession, which he

---

1.   [The Triads of Bardism (*Trioedd Barddas* or *Trioedd Barddol*) are collections of three-part sayings attributed to Welsh bards, particularly from the medieval period. They are distinct from the historical and legendary Triads of the Island of Britain (*Trioedd Ynys Prydain*), which recount myths and heroic figures. These bardic triads focus more on poetic philosophy, moral principles and the duties of bards in society.]

2.   [A word derived from Latin: *accingere* (ad- "to" + cingere "to gird, encircle, prepare"). It means to gird oneself for a task, or prepare or equip oneself for an undertaking.]

294

has inclination to keep for ever, and power to keep, at any rate, for an indefinite time."

"Not so very indefinite," said Seithenyn; "for with the first song of the cuckoo (whom I mention on this occasion as a party concerned,) King Arthur will batter his castle about his ears, and, in all likelihood, the abbey about yours."

The abbot sighed heavily.

"If your heart fail you," said Seithenyn, "another cup of wine will set all to rights."

"Nay, nay, friend Seithenyn," said the abbot, "that which I have already taken has just brought me to the point at which the heart is inspirited, and the wit sharpened, without any infraction of the wisdom and gravity which become my character, and best suit my present business."

Seithenyn, however, took an opportunity of making signs to some cupbearers, and, when they entered the apartment of Melvas, they were followed by vessels of wine and goblets of gold.

King Melvas was a man of middle age, with a somewhat round, large, regular-featured face, and an habitual smile of extreme self-satisfaction, which he could occasionally convert into a look of terrific ferocity, the more fearful for being rare. His manners were, for the most part, pleasant. He did much mischief, not for mischief's sake, nor yet for the sake of excitement, but for the sake of something tangible. He had a total and most complacent indifference to every thing but his own will and pleasure. He took what he wanted wherever he could find it, by the most direct process, and without any false pretence. He would have disdained the trick which the chroniclers ascribe to Hengist, of begging as much land as a bull's hide would surround, and then shaving it into threads, which surrounded a goodly space. If he wanted a piece of land, he encamped upon it, saying, "This is mine." If the former possessor could eject him, so; it was not his: if not, so; it remained his. Cattle, wine, furniture, another man's wife, whatever he took a fancy to, he pounced upon and appropriated. He was intolerant of resistance; and, as the shortest way of getting rid of it, and not from any blood-thirstiness of disposition, or, as the phrenologists have it, development of the organ of destructiveness, he always cut through the resisting body, longitudinally, horizontally, or diagonally, as he found most convenient. He was the arch-marauder of West Britain. The abbey of Avallon shared largely in the spoil, and they made up together a most harmonious church and state. He had some respect for King Arthur; wished him success against the Saxons; knew the superiority of his power to his own; but he had heard that Queen Gwenyvar was the most beautiful woman in Britain; was, therefore, satisfied of his own title to her, and, as she was hunting in the forest, while King Arthur was absent from Caer Lleon, he seized her, and carried her off.

"Be seated, holy father," said Melvas; "and you, also, Seithenyn, unless the abbot wishes you away."

But the abbot's heart misgave him, and he assented readily to Seithenyn's stay.

MELVAS. Now, holy father, to your important matter of private conference.

SEITHENYN. He is tongue-tied, and a cup too low.

THE ABBOT. Set the goblet before me, and I will sip in moderation.

MELVAS. Sip, or not sip, tell me your business.

THE ABBOT. My business, of a truth, touches the lady your prisoner, King Arthur's queen.

MELVAS. She is my queen, while I have her, and no prisoner. Drink, man, and be not afraid. Speak your mind: I will listen, and weigh your words.

THE ABBOT. This queen—

SEITHENYN. Obey the king: first drink, then speak.

THE ABBOT. I drink to please the king.

MELVAS. Proceed.

THE ABBOT. This queen, Gwenyvar, is as beautiful as Helen, who caused the fatal war that expelled our forefathers from Troy: and I fear she will be a second Helen, and expel their posterity from Britain.[3] The infidel Saxons, to whom the cowardly and perfidious Vortigern gave footing in Britain, have prospered even more by the disunion of her princes than either by his villany, or their own valour. And now there is no human hope against them but in the arms of Arthur. And how shall his arms prosper against the common enemy, if he be forced to turn them on the children of his own land for the recovery of his own wife?

MELVAS. What do you mean by his own? That which he has, is his own: but that which I have, is mine. I have the wife in question, and some of the land. Therefore they are mine.

---

3. According to the British Chronicles, Brutus, the great grandson of Æneas, having killed his father, Silvius, to fulfil a prophecy, went to Greece, where he found the posterity of Helenus, the son of Priam; collected all of the Trojan race within the limits of Greece; and, after some adventures by land and sea, settled them in Britain, which was before uninhabited, "except by a few giants."

THE ABBOT. Not so. The land is yours under fealty to him.

MELVAS. As much fealty as I please, or he can force me, to give him.

THE ABBOT. His wife, at least, is most lawfully his.

MELVAS. The winner makes the law, and his law is always against the loser. I am so far the winner; and, by my own law, she is lawfully mine.

THE ABBOT. There is a law above all human law, by which she is his.

MELVAS. From that it is for you to absolve me; and I dispense my bounty according to your indulgence.

THE ABBOT. There are limits we must not pass.

MELVAS. You set up your landmark, and I set up mine. They are both moveable.

THE ABBOT. The Church has not been niggardly in its indulgences to King Melvas.

MELVAS. Nor King Melvas in his gifts to the Church.

THE ABBOT. But, setting aside this consideration, I would treat it as a question of policy.

SEITHENYN. Now you talk sense. Right without might is the lees of an old barrel, without a drop of the original liquor.

THE ABBOT. I would appeal to you, King Melvas, by your love to your common country, by your love of the name of Britain, by your hatred of the infidel Saxons, by your respect for the character of Arthur; will you let your passion for a woman, even though she be a second Helen, frustrate, or even impede, the great cause, of driving these spoilers from a land in which they have no right even to breathe?

MELVAS. They have a right to do all they do, and to have all they have. If we can drive them out, they will then have no right here. Have not you and I a right to this good wine, which seems to trip very merrily over your ghostly palate? I got it by seizing a good ship, and throwing the crew overboard, just to remove them out of the way, because they were troublesome. They disputed my right, but I taught them better. I taught them a great moral lesson, though they had not much time to profit by it. If they had had the might to throw me overboard, I should not have troubled myself about their right, any more, or, at any rate, any longer, than they did about mine.

SEITHENYN. The wine was lawful spoil of war.

THE ABBOT. But if King Arthur brings his might to bear upon yours, I fear neither you nor I shall have a right to this wine, nor to any thing else that is here.

SEITHENYN. Then make the most of it while you have it.

THE ABBOT. Now, while you have some months of security before you, you may gain great glory by surrendering the lady; and, if you be so disposed, you may no doubt claim, from the gratitude of King Arthur, the fairest princess of his court to wife, and an ample dower withal.

MELVAS. That offers something tangible.

SEITHENYN. Another ray from the golden goblet will set it in a most luminous view.

THE ABBOT. Though I should advise the not making it a condition, but asking it, as a matter of friendship, after the first victory that you have helped him to gain over the Saxons.

MELVAS. The worst of those Saxons is, that they offer nothing tangible, except hard knocks. They bring nothing with them. They come to take; and lately they have not taken much. But I will muse on your advice; and, as it seems, I may get more by following than rejecting it, I shall very probably take it, provided that you now attend me to the banquet in the hall.

SEITHENYN. Now you talk of the hall and the banquet, I will just intimate that the finest of all youths, and the best of all bards, is a guest in the neighbouring abbey.

MELVAS. If so, I have a clear right to him, as a guest for myself.

The abbot was not disposed to gainsay King Melvas's right. Taliesin was invited accordingly, and seated at the left hand of the king, the abbot being on the right. Taliesin summoned all the energies of his genius to turn the passions of Melvas into the channels of Anti-Saxonism, and succeeded so perfectly, that the king and his whole retinue of magnanimous heroes were inflamed with intense ardour to join the standard of Arthur; and Melvas vowed most solemnly to Taliesin, that another sun should not set, before Queen Gwenyvar should be under the most honourable guidance on her return to Caer Lleon.

CHAPTER 15

THE CIRCLE OF THE BARDS.

The three dignities of poetry: the union of the true and the wonderful; the union of the beautiful and the wise; and the union of art and nature.

TRIADS OF POETRY.[1]

AMONGST the Christmas amusements of Caer Lleon, a grand Bardic Congress was held in the Roman theatre, when the principal bards of Britain contended for the pre-eminence in the art of poetry, and in its appropriate moral and mystical knowledge. The meeting was held by daylight. King Arthur presided, being himself an irregular bard, and admitted, on this public occasion, to all the efficient honours of a Bard of Presidency.

To preside in the Bardic Congress was long a peculiar privilege of the kings of Britain. It was exercised in the seventh century by King Cadwallader. King Arthur was assisted by twelve umpires, chosen by the bards, and confirmed by the king.

____

1. [See note on page 224.]

The Court, of course, occupied the stations of honour, and every other part of the theatre was crowded with a candid and liberal audience.

The bards sate in a circle on that part of the theatre corresponding with the portion which we call the stage.

Silence was proclaimed by the herald; and, after a grand symphony, which was led off in fine style by the king's harper, Geraint, Prince Cei came forward, and made a brief oration, to the effect that any of the profane, who should be irregular and tumultuous, would be forcibly removed from the theatre, to be dealt with at the discretion of the officer of the guard. Silence was then a second time proclaimed by the herald.

Each bard, as he stood forward, was subjected to a number of interrogatories, metrical and mystical, which need not be here reported. Many bards sang many songs. Amongst them, Prince Llywarch sang

GORWYNION Y GAUAV.
THE BRILLIANCIES OF WINTER.

Last of flowers, in tufts around
Shines the gorse's golden bloom:
Milkwhite lichens clothe the ground
'Mid the flowerless heath and broom:
Bright are holly-berries, seen
Red, through leaves of glossy green.

Brightly, as on rocks they leap,
Shine the sea-waves, white with spray;
Brightly, in the dingles deep,
Gleams the river's foaming way;

Brightly through the distance show
Mountain-summits clothed in snow.

Brightly, where the torrents bound,
Shines the frozen colonnade,
Which the black rocks, dripping round,
And the flying spray have made:
Bright the icedrops on the ash
Leaning o'er the cataract's dash.

Bright the hearth, where feast and song
Crown the warrior's hour of peace,
While the snow-storm drives along,
Bidding the war's worse tempest cease;
Bright the hearthflame, flashing clear
On the up-hung shield and spear.

Bright the torchlight of the hall
When the wintry night-winds blow;
Brightest when its splendours fall
On the mead-cup's sparking flow:
While the maiden's smile of light
Makes the brightness trebly bright.

Close the portals; pile the hearth;
Strike the harp; the feast pursue;
Brim the horns: fire, music, mirth,
Mead and love, are winter's due.
Spring to purple conflict calls
Swords that shine on winter's walls.

Llywarch's song was applauded, as presenting a
series of images with which all present were familiar,
and which were all of them agreeable.

Merlin sang some verses of the poem which is called

AVALLENAU MYRDDIN.
MERLIN'S APPLE-TREES.

Fair the gift to Merlin given,
Apple-trees seven score and seven;
Equal all in age and size;
On a green hill-slope, that lies
Basking in the southern sun,
Where bright waters murmuring run.

Just beneath the pure stream flows;
High above the forest grows;
Not again on earth is found
Such a slope of orchard ground:
Song of birds, and hum of bees,
Ever haunt the apple-trees.

Lovely green their leaves in spring;
Lovely bright their blossoming:
Sweet the shelter and the shade
By their summer foliage made:
Sweet the fruit their ripe boughs hold,
Fruit delicious, tinged with gold.

Gloyad, nymph with tresses bright,
Teeth of pearl, and eyes of light,
Guards these gifts of Ceidio's son,
Gwendol, the lamented one,
Him, whose keen-edged sword no more
Flashes 'mid the battle's roar.

War has raged on vale and hill:
That fair grove was peaceful still.
There have chiefs and princes sought
Solitude and tranquil thought:
There have kings, from courts and throngs,
Turned to Merlin's wild-wood songs.

Now from echoing woods I hear
Hostile axes sounding near:
On the sunny slope reclined,
Feverish grief disturbs my mind,
Lest the wasting edge consume
My fair spot of fruit and bloom.

Lovely trees, that long alone
In the sylvan vale have grown,
Bare, your sacred plot around,
Grows the once wood-waving ground:
Fervent valour guards ye still;
Yet my soul presages ill.

Well I know, when years have flown,
Briars shall grow where ye have grown:
Them in turn shall power uproot;
Then again shall flowers and fruit
Flourish in the sunny breeze,
On my new-born apple-trees.

This song was heard with much pleasure, especially by those of the audience who could see, in the
imagery of the apple-trees, a mystical type of the doctrines and fortunes of Druidism, to which Merlin was
suspected of being secretly attached, even under the
very nose of St. David.

Aneurin sang a portion of his poem on the battle of Cattraeth; in which he shadowed out the glory of Vortimer, the weakness of Vortigern, the fascinations of Rowena, the treachery of Hengist, and the vengeance of Emrys.

THE MASSACRE OF THE BRITONS

Sad was the day for Britain's land,
A day of ruin to the free,
When Gorthyn[2] stretched a friendly hand
To the dark dwellers of the sea.[3]

But not in pride the Saxon trod,
Nor force nor fraud oppressed the brave,
Ere the grey stone and flowery sod
Closed o'er the blessed hero's grave.[4]

The twice-raised monarch[5] drank the charm,
The love-draught of the ocean-maid:[6]
Vain then the Briton's heart and arm,
Keen spear, strong shield, and burnished blade.

"Come to the feast of wine and mead,"
Spake the dark dweller of the sea:[7]
"There shall the hours in mirth proceed;
There neither sword nor shield shall be."

2. Gwrtheyrn: Vortigern.
3. Hengist and Horsa.
4. Gwrthevyr: Vortimer: who drove the Saxons out of Britain.
5. Vortigern: who was, on the death of his son Vortimer, restored to the throne from which he had been deposed.
6. Ronwen: Rowena.
7. Hengist.

Hard by the sacred temple's site,
Soon as the shades of evening fall,
Resounds with song and glows with light
The ocean-dweller's rude-built hall.

The sacred ground, where chiefs of yore
The everlasting fire adored,
The solemn pledge of safety bore,
And breathed not of the treacherous sword.

The amber wreath his temples bound;
His vest concealed the murderous blade;
As man to man, the board around,
The guileful chief his host arrayed.

None but the noblest of the land,
The flower of Britain's chiefs, were there:
Unarmed, amid the Saxon band,
They sate, the fatal feast to share.

Three hundred chiefs, three score and three,
Went, where the festal torches burned
Before the dweller of the sea:
They went; and three alone returned.

'Till dawn the pale sweet mead they quaffed:
The ocean-chief unclosed his vest;
His hand was on his dagger's haft,
And daggers glared at every breast.

But him, at Eidiol's[8] breast who aimed,
The mighty Briton's arm laid low:

---

8. Eidiol or Emrys: Emrys Wledig: Ambrosius.

His eyes with righteous anger flamed;
He wrenched the dagger from the foe;

And through the throng he cleft his way,
And raised without his battle cry;
And hundreds hurried to the fray,
From towns, and vales, and mountains high.

But Britain's best blood dyed the floor
Within the treacherous Saxon's hall;
Of all, the golden chain who wore,
Two only answered Eidiol's call.

Then clashed the sword; then pierced the lance;
Then by the axe the shield was riven;
Then did the steed on Cattraeth prance,
And deep in blood his hoofs were driven.

Even as the flame consumes the wood,
So Eidiol rushed along the field;
As sinks the snow-bank in the flood,
So did the ocean-rovers yield.

The spoilers from the fane he drove;
He hurried to the rock-built tower,
Where the base king, in mirth and love,
Sate with his Saxon paramour.[9]

The storm of arms was on the gate,
The blaze of torches in the hall,
So swift, that ere they feared their fate,
The flames had scaled their chamber wall.

---

9. Vortigern and Rowena.

They died: for them no Briton grieves;
No planted flower above them waves;
No hand removes the withered leaves
That strew their solitary graves.

And time the avenging day brought round
That saw the sea-chief vainly sue:
To make his false host bite the ground
Was all the hope our warrior knew.

And evermore the strife he led,
Disdaining peace, with princely might,
Till, on a spear, the spoiler's[10] head
Was reared on Caer-y-Cynan's height.

The Song of Aneurin touched deeply on the sympathies of the audience, and was followed by a grand martial symphony, in the midst of which Taliesin appeared in the Circle of Bards. King Arthur welcomed him with great joy, and sweet smiles were showered upon him from all the beauties of the court.

Taliesin answered the metrical and mystical questions to the astonishment of the most proficient; and, advancing, in his turn, to the front of the circle, he sang a portion of a poem which is now called HANES TALIESIN, the History of Taliesin;[11] but which shall be here entitled

---

10. Hengist.
11. [A legendary biography of Taliesin, a mythical poet and seer whose historical counterpart was a 6th-century bard in the court of British kings. The tale explains his miraculous birth, wisdom and poetic abilities, blending mythology, folklore and bardic tradition.]

THE CAULDRON OF CERIDWEN

The sage Ceridwen was the wife
Of Tegid Voël, of Pemble Mere:
Two children blest their wedded life,
Morvran and Creirwy, fair and dear:
Morvran, a son of peerless worth,
And Creirwy, loveliest nymph of earth:
But one more son Ceridwen bare,
As foul as they before were fair.

She strove to make Avagddu wise;
She knew he never could be fair:
And, studying magic mysteries,
She gathered plants of virtue rare:
She placed the gifted plants to steep
Within the magic cauldron deep,
Where they a year and day must boil,
'Till three drops crown the matron's toil.

Nine damsels raised the mystic flame;
Gwion the Little near it stood:
The while for simples roved the dame
Though tangled dell and pathless wood.
And, when the year and day had past,
The dame within the cauldron cast
The consummating chaplet wild,
While Gwion held the hideous child.

But from the cauldron rose a smoke
That filled with darkness all the air:
When through its folds the torchlight broke,
Nor Gwion, nor the boy, was there.
The fire was dead, the cauldron cold,

And in it lay, in sleep uprolled.
Fair as the morning-star, a child,
That woke, and stretched its arms, and smiled.

What chanced her labours to destroy,
She never knew; and sought in vain
If 'twere her own misshapen boy,
Or little Gwion, born again:
And, vexed with doubt, the babe she rolled
In cloth of purple and of gold,
And in a coracle consigned
Its fortunes to the sea and wind.

The summer night was still and bright,
The summer moon was large and clear,
The frail bark, on the springtide's height,
Was floated into Elphin's weir.
The baby in his arms he raised:
His lovely spouse stood by, and gazed,
And, blessing it with gentle vow,
Cried "TALIESIN!" "Radiant brow!"

And I am he: and well I know
Ceridwen's power protects me still;
And hence o'er hill and vale I go,
And sing, unharmed, whate'er I will.
She has for me Time's veil withdrawn:
The images of things long gone,
The shadows of the coming days,
Are present to my visioned gaze.

And I have heard the words of power,
By Ceirion's solitary lake,
That bid, at midnight's thrilling hour,

Eryri's hundred echoes wake:
I to Diganwy's towers have sped,
And now Caer Lleon's halls I tread,
Demanding justice, now, as then,
From Maelgon, most unjust of men.

The audience shouted with delight at the song of Taliesin, and King Arthur, as President of the Bardic Congress, conferred on him, at once, the highest honours of the sitting.

Where Taliesin picked up the story which he told of himself, why he told it, and what he meant by it, are questions not easily answered. Certain it is, that he told this story to his contemporaries, and that none of them contradicted it. It may, therefore, be presumed that they believed it; as any one who pleases is most heartily welcome to do now.

Besides the single songs, there were songs in dialogue, approaching very nearly to the character of dramatic poetry; and pennillion, or unconnected stanzas, sung in series by different singers, the stanzas being complete in themselves, simple as Greek epigrams, and presenting in succession moral precepts, pictures of natural scenery, images of war or of festival, the lamentations of absence or captivity, and the complaints or triumphs of love. This pennillion-singing long survived among the Welsh peasantry almost every other vestige of bardic customs, and may still be heard among them on the few occasions on which rack-renting, tax-collecting, common-enclosing, methodist-preaching, and similar developments of the light of the age, have left them either the means or inclination of making merry.

CHAPTER 16
THE JUDGMENTS OF ARTHUR.

Three things to which success cannot fail where they shall justly be: discretion, exertion, and hope.

Triads of Wisdom.[1]

King Arthur had not long returned to his hall, when Queen Gwenyvar arrived, escorted by the Abbot of Avallon and Seithenyn ap Seithyn Saidi, who had brought his golden goblet, to gain a new harvest of glory from the cellars of Caer Lleon.

Seithenyn assured King Arthur, in the name of King Melvas, and on the word of a king, backed by that of his butler, which, truth being in wine, is good warranty even for a king, that the queen returned as pure as on the day King Melvas had carried her off.

"None here will doubt that;" said Gwenvach, the wife of Modred. Gwenyvar was not pleased with the compliment, and, almost before she had saluted King Arthur, she turned suddenly round, and slapped Gwenvach on the face, with a force that brought more

____

1.   [See note on page 224.]

crimson into one cheek than blushing had ever done into both. This slap is recorded in the Bardic Triads as one of the Three Fatal Slaps of the Island of Britain. A terrible effect is ascribed to this small cause; for it is said to have been the basis of that enmity between Arthur and Modred, which terminated in the battle of Camlan, wherein all the flower of Britain perished on both sides: a catastrophe more calamitous than any that ever before or since happened in Christendom, not even excepting that of the battle of Roncesvalles;[2] for, in the battle of Camlan, the Britons exhausted their own strength, and could no longer resist the progress of the Saxon supremacy. This, however, was a later result, and comes not within the scope of the present veridicous narrative.

Gwenvach having flounced out of the hall, and the tumult occasioned by this little incident having subsided, Queen Gwenyvar took her ancient seat by the side of King Arthur, who proceeded to inquire into the circumstances of her restoration. The Abbot of Avallon began an oration, in praise of his own eloquence, and its miraculous effects on King Melvas; but he was interrupted by Seithenyn, who said, "The abbot's eloquence was good and well timed; but the chief merit belongs to this young bard, who

---

2. [A legendary battle fought in 778 CE, which became one of the most famous episodes in medieval literature and chivalric legend. The battle took place in the Roncesvalles Pass in the Pyrenees, between France and Spain. Charlemagne, King of the Franks and later Holy Roman Emperor, had invaded Muslim Spain but was forced to retreat. The Basques, who were defending their territory, took advantage of the mountainous terrain to launch a surprise attack on the rear guard of Charlemagne's army as it was returning to France. Among those killed was Roland, one of Charlemagne's commanders.]

prompted him with good counsel, and to me, who inspirited him with good liquor. If he had not opened his mouth pretty widely when I handed him this golden goblet, exclaiming GWIN O EUR, he would never have had the heart to open it to any other good purpose. But the most deserving person is this very promising youth, in whom I can see no fault, but that he has not the same keen perception as my friend the abbot has of the excellent relish of wine from gold. To be sure, he plied me very hard with strong drink in the hall of Dinas Vawr, and thereby wormed out of me the secret of Queen Gwenyvar's captivity; and, afterwards, he pursued us to Avallon, where he persuaded me and the abbot, and the abbot persuaded King Melvas, that it would be better for all parties to restore the queen peaceably: and then he clenched the matter with the very best song I ever heard in my life. And, as my young friend has a boon to ask, I freely give him all my share of the merit, and the abbot's into the bargain."

"Allow me, friend GWIN O EUR," said the abbot, "to dispose of my own share of merit in my own way. But, such as it is, I freely give it to this youth, in whom, as you say, I can see no fault, but that his head is brimfull of Pagan knowledge."

Arthur paid great honour to Taliesin, and placed him on his left hand at the banquet. He then said to him, "I judge, from your song of this morning, that the boon you require from me concerns Maelgon Gwyneth. What is his transgression, and what is the justice you require?"

Taliesin narrated the adventures of Elphin in such a manner as gave Arthur an insight into his affection for Melanghel; and he supplicated King Arthur to command and enforce the liberation of Elphin from the Stone Tower of Diganwy.

Before King Arthur could signify his assent, Maelgon Gwyneth stalked into the hall, followed by a splendid retinue. He had been alarmed by the absence of Rhûn, had sought him in vain on the banks of Mawddach, had endeavoured to get at the secret by pouncing upon Angharad and Melanghel, and had been baffled in his project by the vigilance of Teithrin ap Tathral. He had, therefore, as a last resort, followed Taliesin to Caer Lleon, conceiving that he might have had some share in the mysterious disappearance of Rhûn.

Arthur informed him that he was in possession of all the circumstances, and that Rhûn, who was in safe custody, would be liberated on the restoration of Elphin.

Maelgon boiled with rage and shame, but had no alternative but submission to the will of Arthur.

King Arthur commanded that all the parties should be brought before him. Caradoc was charged with the execution of this order, and, having received the necessary communications and powers from Maelgon and Taliesin, he went first to Diganwy, where he liberated Elphin, and then proceeded to give effect to Teithrin's declaration, that "no hand but Elphin's should raise the stone of Rhûn's captivity." Rhûn, while his pleasant adventure had all the gloss of novelty upon it, and his old renown as a gay deceiver was consequently in such dim eclipse, was very unwilling to present himself before the ladies of Caer Lleon; but Caradoc was peremptory, and carried off the crest-fallen prince, together with his bard of all work, who was always willing to go to any court, with any character, or none.

Accordingly, after a moderate lapse of time, Caradoc reappeared in the hall of Arthur, with the liberated captives, accompanied by Angharad and Melanghel, and Teithrin ap Tathral.

King Arthur welcomed the new comers with a magnificent festival, at which all the beauties of his court were present, and, addressing himself to Elphin, said, "We are all debtors to this young bard: my queen and myself for her restoration to me; you for your liberation from the Stone Tower of Diganwy. Now, if there be, amongst all these ladies, one whom he would choose for his bride, and in whose eyes he may find favour, I will give the bride a dowry worthy of the noblest princess in Britain."

Taliesin, thus encouraged, took the hand of Melanghel, who did not attempt to withdraw it, but turned to her father a blushing face, in which he read her satisfaction and her wishes. Elphin immediately said, "I have nothing to give him but my daughter; but her I most cordially give him."

Taliesin said, "I owe to Elphin more than I can ever repay: life, honour, and happiness."

Arthur said, "You have not paid him ill; but you owe nothing to Maelgon and Rhûn, who are your debtors for a lesson of justice, which I hope they will profit by during the rest of their lives. Therefore Maelgon shall defray the charge of your wedding, which shall be the most splendid that has been seen in Caer Lleon."

Maelgon looked exceedingly grim, and wished himself well back in Diganwy.

There was a very pathetic meeting of recognition

between Seithenyn and his daughter; at the end of which he requested her husband's interest to obtain for him the vacant post of second butler to King Arthur. He obtained this honourable office; and was so zealous in the fulfilment of its duties, that, unless on actual service with a detachment of liquor, he was never a minute absent from the Temple of Diana.

At a subsequent Bardic Congress, Taliesin was unanimously elected Pen Beirdd, or Chief of the Bards of Britain. The kingdom of Caredigion flourished under the protection of Arthur, and, in the ripeness of time, passed into the hands of Avaon, the son of Taliesin and Melanghel.

THE END

FROM P-WAVE CLASSICS

THOMAS LOVE PEACOCK

Headlong Hall & Nightmare Abbey

Maid Marian & The Misfortunes of Elphin

Crotchet Castle & Gryll Grange

P-WAVE PRESS

Thank you for reading!

We hope you enjoyed this book. At P-Wave Press, we're passionate about unique and thought-provoking stories.

Scan the QR code below to:

- Explore all our books
- See upcoming titles
- Share your comments and book reviews
- Order any P-Wave Press book

We'd love to hear from you at p-wavepress.co.uk.